THE ART OF THE BODY

ALEX ALLISON

d dialogue
books

DIALOGUE BOOKS

First published in Great Britain in 2019 by Dialogue Books
This paperback edition published in 2020 by Dialogue Books

10 9 8 7 6 5 4 3 2 1

A CIP catalogue record for this book
is available from the British Library.

ISBN 978-0-349-70076-2

Typeset in Berling by M Rules
Printed and bound in Great Britain by
Clays Ltd, Elcograf S.p.A.

Papers used by Dialogue Books are from well-managed forests
and other responsible sources.

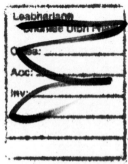

Dialogue Books
An imprint of
Little, Brown Book Group
Carmelite House
50 Victoria Embankment
London EC4Y 0DZ

An Hachette UK Company
www.hachette.co.uk

www.littlebrown.co.uk

Alex Allison was born and raised in London. He holds a BA in Art History from University of York, and an MA in Creative Writing from University of Manchester's Centre for New Writing.

His work has been published by *Civil Coping Mechanisms, The Red Ceilings Press, Popshot, Willow Springs* and *Artifice Magazine* among others. He can be found on Twitter at @alex_j_allison where he mostly posts about AFC Wimbledon and his poor luck at poker.

'This isn't an easy read, but it is raw and powerful ... An uncompromising look at what it means to be "able" in life'
Image

'Beyond describing in vivid detail Sean's disability, Allison uses it to pave new literary ground, making use of unusual figures of speech that allow the reader access to another way of looking at the world ... *The Art of the Body* offers the reader a multi-layered exploration of the able and disabled body. Through the experiences of Janet, who shares with us her enthusiasm and disappointment, love and loss, care for others and self-loathing, we discover the possibilities a disabled body offers, which is far from incomplete or needing to be fixed. Allison's talent transforms it all into a tale worth reading'
Northern Review

'[A] bold, unflinching debut ... Finely written and thoughtfully devised, this is also a disquieting and unsettling read about the balance of power, cruelty and compassion ... Allison writes unobtrusively, setting up illuminating parallels and gently guiding the reader to unexpected understanding'
Guardian

'What a brilliant book! I tore through it. Brutal, tender, philosophical, visceral, complex and so well written. A deft exploration of two entwined lives that is deeply moving without ever being sentimental. The character of Janet is incredible. I have never encountered anyone like her, and yet she was utterly believable. This is one of those books that sneaks under your skin and expands you. Sheer brilliance'
Emma Jane Unsworth

Chapter 1

Maintaining one person's dignity comes nearly always at the expense of someone else's. I have learned this for you.

My morning ritual begins in the bathroom. At the sink, I wet my hands and lather, dancing my fingers through their trained routine: tips to palm, knuckles to palm, lock, lace, relace, clasp, pray, covet, beg and rinse. I fill a plastic tray with warm water and shower gel, testing the heat against the inside of my wrist. From a white cardboard box, I peel out two purple gloves and work the plastic down over my hands. Latex pinches between my fingers, tight against my slightly damp skin. I look medical; feel medical. I flex my fingers and take a deep, steadying breath.

Sean's flat is heavy with the polite, chemical smell of air freshener. Every surface and fixture is perfect white – all human materials, polished to a sheen that's almost wet.

I set down the tray of water on his bedside table and ease open the blinds.

Sean is awake, but yet to respond to my presence. He is in bed, just as I left him, laid foetal and still, rolled into the wall, his arms over the covers and T-Rexed into his chest. It is the posture of poverty. His breaths are shallow, testing only the tops of his lungs.

You wouldn't guess that I am two years older than him. Sean is twenty-two, but there's a greyness to his skin.

Now comes the long groan, the sneer, and an awkward attempt to shield his eyes.

'Good morning, Sean.'

'Uhhhgh. Morning,' he says.

'Radio?'

'Yes, please.'

For our first few months together, we talked through this routine. I'd warn Sean what was coming, where my hands would hold him next. Now, the radio spares us the pleasantries that accompany the maintenance of a person. After eight months with his body, I'm lucky to get a 'lower', a 'softer', a 'finished'. I still always get a 'thank you'.

'Did you sleep well?'

'I always sleep well. I sleep well until you come in and ruin it.'

'It is nice out.'

'Do not tell me that, please. I want to listen to the weather report.'

Sean's top has ridden up his back during the night – the material evidence of a struggle. I ease the rest over his head and examine the rawness.

'Does that hurt at all?' I say, pressing.

'No.'

'And here?'

'A little.'

Sean is Irish, raised in Yorkshire, but cerebral palsy has its own accent. Sean's voice belongs more to his limbs than his mind. It comes from a curled, chafed place. But I'm fluent in Sean. I know his pain from his relief, his 'biscuits' from his 'business'.

I move to the end of Sean's bed to double-check that the wheels are clamped before we begin. Down here, more evidence of a struggle – his feet protrude from the bottom of the covers. Some of his toes are crossed, as though for luck or lying. The soles of Sean's feet are smooth – untested by the weight and pressure of a working body. His knees point at a forty-five-degree angle through the sheets, into the wall. Sean would be tall if he could stand.

'Aren't your feet cold?' I ask.

'No.'

'I wish you'd wear socks.'

'You know that I hate socks.'

'Are we ready to start?'

'Ten more minutes.'

'I asked if we were ready to start.'

Sean grunts and jerks his head in his own approximation of a nod.

'Give me your hand and we'll sit you up, then,' I say.

Sean offers me his arm and I pull him to an awkward seated position. He lolls heavily into the wall and, after a moment, seems to slip back to sleep. He begins to mock-snore.

'Please, Sean. Not this morning.'

He opens his eyes and throws me a toothy, gurning grin. There's a long, thin scratch down the middle of Sean's nose. His face is permanently marked by a series of scratches – each of my attempts to trim his nails is met with vicious protest. Nails allow Sean an added degree of purchase. He can't afford to sacrifice them.

Scratches, rawness. I have to be conscious of it all. I am responsible for fashioning a socially acceptable version of Sean. A version of Sean that raises the fewest questions. The version which attracts fewest lingering stares.

Sean sleeps with his left forearm in a beige cast that sculpts his hand into the shape of a swan's neck. The barbed sound of ripping the cast's Velcro makes my teeth tickle. Without the cast, Sean's hand curls into a shape more like an inelegant question mark, turning his every gesture into something critical and cutting.

'May I have some water, please? Before I lie back down.'

I'm ready with the straw and bottle before he's finished speaking, but Sean finishes his sentence anyway. He speaks one word at a time, completing each with a flourish. Comprehension is a form of achievement.

'Thank you,' he says once satisfied.

I set out a green continence sheet to protect the bedding, lie Sean back down, shuffle off his pyjama bottoms and undo his pad. Sean has no front to lie on. He favours sleeping on his left side, so that's the way we work, both of us faced into the same wall. I turn off my mind, and clean him with the lukewarm water and some baby wipes, disposing of the quarried shit into an airtight medical waste bin that lives disturbingly close to the bed. Cleaning in the morning is much easier than at night, when Sean's waste is caked into his crack and hair – a natural result of sitting down all day.

'Does that feel okay for now?'

'Yeah,' he says, now focused on the radio.

Sean momentarily lifts himself into his own version of the crab, allowing me to remove the soiled continence sheet and slip his blue polyester sling into position. Motorised chairs, hoists and a little cooperation have made it possible for anyone to do this job. I could be anyone.

I pull the sheets up over Sean's exposed body to keep him warm as I change gloves and fetch the hoist. Once in the hoist, Sean closes his eyes, and dangles with the absolute vulnerability of an infant. I wheel him across to the bathroom and set him down onto the plastic shower seat. I work from top to bottom, lathering his sharp black hair, over his chest and back, and down to all the useless bits that cause him such pain. Patches of hair clot under the circular motions of my scrubbing. I allow Sean to clean his own crotch, which he does with a curled stabbing motion that I can't watch. Leaving the shower room, I almost slip. A laugh moves through Sean like a contraction.

'You won't be laughing when I leave you there.'

'You would not do that to me, Janet.'

Once Sean is dry and back in bed, I oil up my naked hands, and we begin our first massage of the day. My fingers track the pain under his skin, the knots and nodes splayed away from any symmetry. He makes a show of not reacting. I remind myself to be gentle.

I think of each massage as a process of feeling through Sean's secrets. These are the only secrets that he can have. Everything else is known, filed in medical records and news articles. Google Sean's name and you'll find 326,000 results, innumerable accounts of his court case and the £800,000

NHS settlement. The articles will tell you just what I was told upon meeting him. They'll tell you he was the first of two premature twins, both assessed as stillborn. They'll tell you he was left aside while the nurses excavated the corpse of his brother. They'll tell you that over three minutes passed before anyone noticed that Sean was breathing. They'll tell you that by then, it was a matter of damage control. They'll even try to tell you that Sean is lucky, lucky to have a mind at all.

I lead his legs through a series of exercises and extensions that wouldn't seem out of place on a football pitch, deep into injury time: left knee to chest, left knee to nose, crab for ten. Right knee to chest, right knee to nose, crab for twenty. Left foot roll, right foot roll. Piraformis stretch, ninety-degree hamstring stretch. Left foot to bum, right foot to bum. Repeat three times.

'I am sweaty again.'

'No you're not. Look, you're fine.'

'I feel like I am hot.'

'You'll be fine once you're in the chair.'

'Okay. If you say so, Janet.'

'You picked out something to wear yet?'

'It sounds like I will need something warm. Jeans and a jumper.'

'Fancy.'

Sean's room is decorated with his favourite art – mostly abstract and Christian, though never a combination of both. There's a plain crucifix high above his bed. I think his mother put it there when he moved in.

When we're set to spend a day in the studio, Sean wears an extra absorbent pad instead of a catheter bag. Sean's preferred brand of pads are devoid of the branding associated with infant equivalent products. They attach with blue adhesive tags bearing a small corporate logo.

On these days, I will only offer Sean a drink when he expressly asks for one. It is significantly more inconvenient to change a pad than to empty a catheter bag.

As I hook a functionless belt through Sean's jeans, I am entirely thoughtless. My mind is empty – empty, but very present, present in the moment. My mind is empty, but there's no coldness between us – there is only trust. I am fully committed to this routine. There is a part of me that enjoys the seemingly endless burdens imposed by disability, because ultimately, they are all eminently solvable problems. Every burden can be lifted through my labour. There is a zen-like peace to this, to applying brute force and persistence to each issue. There is very little intricate logic to maintaining a body.

It is said that the great geniuses worked menial jobs. Work that allowed their minds to breathe. Patent attorney. Librarian. I no longer suspect that I am among the great geniuses.

Once Sean is dressed, I step back and admire my work, catching my breath. We share a smile.

'What?' Sean asks.

'Nothing – you look good. Big day ahead.'

I hoist Sean into his chair and set about strapping him in. His feet sit heavily on the footplates, toes pointed inward like innocence. I am on my knees, applying his shoes – now finding some purchase, I sheath the plimsoll around Sean's heel, and it becomes a foot like any other.

'Do you want a shave today?'

'What do you think?'

'You know I hate shaving you.'

'Then I want a shave,' he says, smiling. 'Please.'

'Of course,' I say. 'Of course.'

The sun is up. Our regular taxi driver acknowledges us with a vacant nod. I load Sean's chair into the car, and we set out for the college. This is our routine on Tuesdays, Wednesdays and Fridays. The rest of Sean's care schedule and medical appointments have to fit around his studio time.

Our driver has a headset on, and speaks in an animated, foreign rush – male and heavy. I try to convince myself he is not speaking about me. About me and Sean.

It's early. Sean will only bloom into his regular, talkative state once he's woken up fully. For now, he's happy to look out the window at the passing city.

It's been eight months, and I still don't know any of London's street names. They blur past, all part of the same whole. On foot, I'm guided by my phone – my absolute faith in Google Maps blinkers all my journeys. I let the arrow in my palm spell out a perfect route, complete with the little nub of me, bobbing up the screen in reassuring progress.

8.35. It's important for Sean to be the first to arrive. Each time we're late, we're liable to be stuck with one of the smaller studios, which are completely unworkable. So some good-natured student is forced to recalibrate around us to accommodate. The studio rooms weren't built with Sean in mind. Of course, everyone will pull dull smiles and insist that they don't mind moving.

'Do you have the tape?' Sean says.

'I've got everything. We'll do meds at lunch.'

'You okay?'

'Fine,' I say.

The driver and I make eye contact via his rear-view mirror. He sees earring holes, no earrings. A grown-out bob cut, no-frills. The same grey coat I've been wearing all winter. I do not look away.

When I interviewed to work with Sean, his mother had made a big deal of my maturity. I was already twenty-four, but still the youngest candidate by the margin of a decade. Brigid wasn't bothered by my lack of experience in care work, she insisted it would be good for Sean to be around someone close to his own age. We spent the first hour of the interview discussing my own background in the arts. Brigid explained how her own casual interest in the visual arts had flourished because of Sean's infectious passion. From the moment Sean was exposed to a different way of expressing himself, he wanted to discuss little else.

Brigid claimed that my two years at art school would offer Sean experience that was far more relevant to him than two years of care work would be. She asked about my techniques, my inspirations, my theory, waiting in turn to tell me about Sean's.

Now eight months in, my contact with Brigid has reduced down to about twice a week, either by phone or by email. At this point, I know my way around his body – I know how to navigate his pain. Sean objects whenever I'm forced into calling his mother, especially when he is in earshot. He says we shouldn't bother her. He knows she will only worry.

Now our routine is settled, I mostly send pictures of how Sean's portfolio is developing. According to Brigid, no other carer could have ever understood Sean in the way I do. She says he is lucky to have me. She says he doesn't realise how lucky he is.

By the time Sean's settlement came through, Brigid had been quagmired in legal fees for over a decade, and it was too late for most things. Too late to stop his father running away. Much too late to save any motor function in his legs. But the money arrived eventually, and led him here – to me.

Brigid chose not to move to London with Sean. Though I am sure they never formally discussed it, it seems clear to me that Brigid wasn't comfortable with the kind of art Sean wanted to create. I am certain that she couldn't bear to put him in any kind of pain. When we discussed his plans during the interview, I insisted that it would be fine with me.

My closest friend in London, Chloe, is a little obsessed with Brigid. Based on the stories and scant information I've shared, Chloe has built her up as a feminist icon – the working single-mother, deeply disillusioned with shitty men, devoted to being the best parent possible in the most challenging circumstances. Devoted even when that means stepping back to let your only living child realise their dreams by moving across the country.

Every time we're out, I indulge Chloe by sharing stories from Sean's upbringing and childhood. I tell the story about the crib Brigid had custom-made for him, the crib that took a week for her to design and four months to pay for. I tell Chloe about the hairdressing course Brigid took, so that Sean wouldn't have to suffer in front of nervous barbers, wary of the spasm that could remove Sean's ear. I fully acknowledge why these stories make their relationship sound incredible. I am aware that Sean's mother has established an impossibly high bar for what it means to care for him.

We are on the third floor of Central Saint Martins in King's Cross. Sean is lying on a yoga mat in the middle of the art studio floor, stripped to just his pad, which is dry for now. Before starting, I slather his limbs with Vaseline. We've learned that this will minimise the chafing and redness, and aid removal of the bindings after the shoot.

'Keith let me try some of his cigarette on Saturday,' Sean says.

'I'm not sure what you want me to say to that,' I reply.

'I asked him if I could try and he let me.'

Keith is one of the weekend staff at the Mills Grand Estate. On the days when I'm not with him, Sean doesn't really leave the flat unless there's a medical emergency.

'I don't recommend that you start smoking, Sean.'

'I only had a bit. It made me cough.'

'Was Keith too cheap to offer you a whole cigarette?'

'I did not want a whole cigarette. I only wanted to see what it is like.'

I fetch the cord and zip-ties from our supply closet in the hallway. The cord is industrial black plastic, weighty and challenging to knot. On previous shoots, I've needed to watch YouTube tutorials on knotting while pausing to catch my breath.

I put on a portable tradesman's radio and make a vague attempt at stretching before we get started. Today, we work bottom to top, starting with cord around his ankles, binding up the mess of his legs. Sean makes a compliant effort to lift his lower half. Once he's bound to the waist, I cut the cord with shears, leaving around six inches of reprieve.

Next, I sit him upright, slumped forward into the weight of his legs, bound into a mermaid tail. I zip-tie his wishbone wrists into a hostaged mass. Sean winces, but doesn't make a sound.

The tape we use to bind his chest and torso is expensive, self-adhesive PVC, intended for bondage. It's supposedly reusable, but we've worked through a dozen rolls in the last month. To our knowledge, the tape is only available in black, red and pink.

'Do you need some water before we continue?' I ask, breaking my own rule on offering drinks.

'No, thank you.'

'Breathing okay?'

'Yes.'

I lie Sean down into an L-shape, his legs as straight as they are capable of being. While my general fitness level has increased dramatically since beginning care work, I am still a sweaty mess within twenty minutes of commencing this set-up. If I try to stand straight to stretch, my shoulders roll forward like a Neanderthal.

Jordan is visiting for the first time this evening. I have made all the necessary preparations. The fridge is stocked. I have cleared my browsing history. New sheets, new underwear.

Not everything in our relationship is done on Jordan's terms. We see the films I want to see, we eat in the restaurants I'm comfortable with. His marital home just happens to be a much nicer space than the basement flat I share with my brother. Until now, it wouldn't have been appropriate to invite him.

Today, Sean is to be the *Agnus Dei*, a la Francisco de Zurbarán. I drag the yoga mat under the overhead camera rig, and clumsily tip the weight of his body onto a black linen sheet. To prop him up, we're using the leather seat cushion from his wheelchair. Sean insists that the contrasting textures won't matter, because the chiaroscuro can be accentuated when he edits the photographs later. He uses the edits to draw out more than the whiteness. He takes great care to show where his skin is troubled with the opal of a new bruise, the reddened swell of bound flesh.

I force his body into a clumsy imitation of the sacrificial lamb, his neck twisted painfully to balance his head upright, his drool-soaked chin taking the strain. He keeps his facing eye sleepily open to the camera. It is a look of pale resignation.

'Ready?'

Sean gives the cue and I take five quick shutter photos, then remove the camera from the rig and bring it over to him for inspection. We repeat this process, making the appropriate adjustments until he is happy.

By the time he's unwrapped and dressed, it's lunch and I'm ready to pass out.

Before starting care work, I never imagined that there could be dignity to sitting on a chair. But for Sean, dignity is in the choice. I've already sweated through the awkward choreography that is necessary to translate him from his wheelchair to a place at the table.

It's lunchtime, and we're in a large, open plan café five minutes away from the Central Saint Martins Granary Building. Lunch works by airline emergency protocol: always take care of oneself before attempting to assist others. I'm eating an overdressed salad while Sean runs me through his thoughts on smoking.

'Now that I have tried it,' he says, 'I think I understand why people do it.'

'We do it because we like it,' I say through a mouthful of couscous. 'Don't overthink it.'

Sean continues. 'I think people do it because it gives them control over their breathing. Usually, you do not have to think about your breathing like I do. Smoking forces you to think about it.'

'If there's a reason, it's to start conversations and to break up the day. Don't pretend to be an expert after one cigarette. You're not suited to being philosophical.'

I finish my salad and unload Sean's meal onto the wobbly metal table. The table seems sad and cheap next to the hulking mass of Sean's chair. Though he could now afford to, Sean justifies not switching over to an electric wheelchair on the basis that they're trickier to get in and out of. It's far more convenient for him to rely on me to push him around London, up every slope, every kerb.

Sean's diet is limited and strict; you can use up a surprising amount of energy just sat in a chair all day. Sean's nutrition plan is designed to prevent dehydration and constipation. He's mainly dependent on baby food, soft bread, mashed potato, jellies and mousses. Soup tends to be too messy. Once I've unpacked the pots and punnets, I tie a bib round Sean's front and prepare his medication (8mg Zanaflex; 150mg Lamictal; 50mg Zoloft; 2 × 300mg aspirin). Aside from the palsy, there is a host of exact conditions Sean needs to be medicated for. Brigid had stressed that no one expects me to know everything, but I take some small pleasure in my new medical vocabulary.

'Do I have to wear the bib?' he says. 'I look stupid.'

'What am I supposed to do?' I ask, popping his pills from their blister packets. 'You only feel stupid because we're in a café. You said you wanted to eat here, so here we are.'

'I wanted to talk to the others,' Sean says in his rusted staccato, gesturing blandly to the rest of the customers, mostly hip-looking students. 'I thought I could chat to them.'

'I don't think lunch is ever a good time to chat,' I say.

Throughout our eight months together, feeding has remained the most testing part of my work. It's a slow, slow process, particularly as Sean insists upon doing things for himself. There's a selection of paraphernalia to enable this: a rubber slip-mat to go under Sean's plate, and a shallow shield ring to surround it. Both are designed to grant Sean some purchase. He eats with the focused intensity of a westerner using chopsticks. Sean holds a spoon like I would a stubbed toe: tight and pained, his knuckles white with the stress of independence. He'll stab or scoop, scrape up the side of the guard, then carefully elevate the spoon in a wide, wide arc to the very edge of his lips, pursed in concentration. I still wince each time his mouth locks down on the metal. Often, he'll miss his lips entirely, and the food will smear his mouth or decorate his lap. Each successful spoonful can seem a triumph.

'I should take my meds first,' Sean says.

'Fuck,' I say, 'I don't think we have any straws. You can't take them dry.'

'Are you sure?' Sean says. 'Check my bag.'

'No, we ran out yesterday. I was supposed to top them up. Hold on, and I'll ask if they have any behind the counter.'

We only use straws because Sean is too stubborn to drink from a beaker. He claims that beakers are for babies, and that he is not a baby. Consequently, I've spent the last eight months wiping up innumerable spilled drinks.

Brigid told me up front that Sean was stubborn. She told me about how he used to kick out at physiotherapists, blaming spasms. How he would lock his jaw in protest at meals he didn't like. She complained about how impossible it is to put a shirt on a person who doesn't approve of the colour. At the time, I nodded and—

A scream – shrill as brakes. I know before I turn. Of course it's him – on the floor, spasming. And for a moment – two – everything is slow motion – buffering around me. A second scream and I'm back beside him.

'It's an epileptic fit,' I say aloud, then louder, repeating myself as I part a small crowd and clumsily shove our flimsy table away from Sean's body.

'Just give him space and clear the chairs,' I command, gesturing the screamer backwards. In one movement, my jumper is off and under Sean's head. His face is slick with drool; there's froth at the edge of his lips.

I'm on my knees, in a posture of prayer. Sean's vibrating in place, arms tight to his chest, his legs a rigid deadweight. His eyes are rolled way back into his head and he's blinking wildly. His body seems to be protesting each taut breath that makes it through his bluing lips.

'Do something!' the screamer demands.

'This is what I'm supposed to do,' I say, mostly to myself.

I close my eyes and steady myself. I attempt to summon Brigid's voice, her training. This is the first time Sean's had a fit while I've been on duty, but I've been warned for what to expect. The protocol is to only call for an ambulance if the fit lasts longer than twenty minutes. Once it's over, I'm supposed to put a suppository up his bum and bring him home to sleep.

In spite of this, I feel lightheaded and nervous, still exhausted from the studio. The smugness of my diagnosis has fizzled away, and most of my attention is now being devoted to willing the fit to stop. I'm peripherally aware of the crowd around us growing larger. Those who can't bear to watch Sean are looking at me, as if I'm somehow responsible – the artist behind this grim performance piece.

'I've called an ambulance,' someone shouts.

'No,' I say, my hand hovering over Sean's head like a blessing. 'Please cancel it. Everything is fine.'

Sean's body continues to riot. It looks like he is boiling. His mouth contorts in a silent scream.

My legs have begun to ache from crouching, but I'm completely engrossed. This is pure spectacle, something barely human. Witnessing this, possession seems completely plausible. Sean is seismic. There's a demon within him, fighting through his skin.

For one moment, it seems to be abating, settling from boil to simmer, but then Sean launches back into himself. I've lost all sense of time. He twitches, jerks and snorts, grinding his teeth like an addict. To someone who didn't know better, this could look like an overdose.

Four paramedics storm into the cafeteria. The moment has the timbre of a season finale. Sean doesn't register their presence. They're speaking at me in rushed imperatives. I insist everything is fine, that I've got it all under control.

'He's not on drugs,' I say. 'He's got cerebral palsy.'

'What's his name?' says a female paramedic from above me.

'It's a tonic-clonic seizure,' I say, almost proudly.

'What's his name?' she repeats, looking at me sternly.

'His name is Sean.'

'Sean,' another paramedic calls, gripping his shoulders. 'Sean, Sean.'

I've been moved to one side. In a slim gap between two uniforms, I can just make out Sean's body, its sharp shiver.

'Really, everything is okay,' I say, smiling. 'I know what I'm doing.'

'You his girlfriend?' asks the female paramedic. She has a northern accent and a wide, blemished face.

'No,' I say in a disgusted voice, 'No – carer. I'm his carer.'

'How long has he been going for?'

'Ten minutes, twenty? I really don't know.'

'This happened before?'

'Yes. I mean, not since I've been with him, but yes.'

'And no drugs?'

'God, no,' I say. 'Just his meds.'

'Right,' she says. 'Well, give yourself a break. Go get some water.'

I make it to my feet, lightheaded. The world moves at three frames a second – lagged and glitchy. I press the palms of my hands into my eyes and breathe deeply, moving to the bar as instructed, but in my head, I keep going. I'm heading out the back exit, hailing a cab. I'm on my way to the airport. I'm on the first flight available. I'm on a beach, in the sun, cocktail in hand. I'm a postcard moment. I'm deactivating Facebook, withdrawing every penny from my savings account, then every penny from Sean's. I'm a new person, in a new life, with no Sean to speak of, and no one left to care for or about.

But no. I'm still here. Here as always. Stood at a distance, dutifully sipping water. Resisting the urge to check my phone.

From the bar, I concentrate on admiring the calm efficiency of the paramedics: their supreme confidence, their deliberate gestures. This is an atmosphere of recovery. These are conditions to soothe a soul. And sure enough, it soon seems to be over: a few gentle twitches, then nothing.

Laid still, Sean looks like a husk, curled and small, all the life force shaken from him. By the time he comes round, the café has mostly emptied, lunchtime long over. In the brief moment between waking and throwing up, Sean says my name across two slow syllables.

'Ja-net—'

The paramedics make way, begin packing up.

'Sorry, Janet,' Sean says. A long string of vomit hangs off his bottom lip.

'Don't be silly,' I say, wiping him with the back of my hand. 'Come on now, let's get you up and away from that sick.' I hold Sean by his slightly reddened wrists and gently help him into a seated position. He moves as though the air were pure friction, grating against him. He has the expression of a child post-tantrum – flushed and embarrassed.

'How long was I out?' he asks.

'About twenty minutes,' I say. 'And you know what that means.' I fish a suppository sachet from my bag and dangle it in front of Sean's face, summoning a light laugh.

With the assistance of two paramedics, I move Sean into his chair, take him to the disabled bathroom, and pop the jelly bullet up his bum.

'Please do not tell Mum,' Sean says in our taxi home. 'She will just worry.'

'Are you sure?' I ask. 'I'm supposed to tell her immediately if you have a fit.'

'I will be fine. By the show, I will be fine. Please do not tell her.'

'If you're sure,' I say. Through the taxi window, London looks scuffed and grainy – low resolution.

'How do I look?' Sean asks sleepily. He has bitten himself – his lip looks fat and beaten.

'Does it matter?'

'It matters to me.'

'You've looked better,' I say.

We sit in silence for a while. I gaze out the window, absently visualising myself alone with a convulsing Sean. Without witnesses.

Sean rests, his eyes closed, head lolled to one side, heavy with valium. He doesn't seem aware that he's still wearing his bib.

My flat is four doors down from a house that Engels lived in. This is the extent of my knowledge of our local area. Alex told me on the day I moved in; he referred to Engels as one of history's greatest sidekicks. I promised myself that I'd study some Marxism, get a basic education in my historical neighbour. In eight months, I haven't come close to achieving this.

We split the rent, but this is very much Alex's space. When he gets home, he immediately gets changed out of his suit, and spends his evenings watching old episodes of *The Simpsons*. Sometimes I watch with him, and we spend the rest of the evening quoting lines at each other, smiling. This is how we avoid knowing each other as adults.

I keep the money I steal from Sean in a shoebox on my bookshelf. Alex rarely comes into my room, but he is not the type to question why a shoebox would be on a bookshelf. It contains all the fivers and tenners I add onto receipts. Taxi fares, lunches. I have no plans for the money, though I have considered fur.

After hard days, I allow myself to pick up the box – test the weight of it. This is much more reassuring than counting. I am very aware of the comic-book melodrama of this habit. I allow myself this indulgence.

Alex wouldn't notice the box, but Jordan might, so for tonight, it has been stashed under my bed.

I get home just before six, and shower – Sean's smell clings like onion. I take pleasure in thoroughly cleansing myself of him.

My handover to the night staff at the Mills Grand Estate tends to take longer after a day in the studio, because Sean is still on a high. He insists on commandeering my iPhone to flick through the photo album of framing shots for our latest creation, while explaining to anyone who will listen how this piece fits in with the broader portfolio.

The staff at the flats are employed by the building, not by

the residents. They're not paid to care. They're paid to be on call for minor emergencies, and to summon ambulances for anything more serious. Part of the Mills Grand Estate's promotional material advertises the fact they're only five minutes by ambulance from University College Hospital.

Sean's made me promise not to tell Brigid about the fit. She is due to come to London at the end of the month, for the end-of-term show. Brigid has emailed me three times over the last week, confirming and reconfirming flight times, seeking my advice and approval on her planned outfit. I am indulging this because she's offered to take care of Sean on Thursday and Friday while she's in town, meaning I can look forward to two days of paid leave in bed.

After our evening massage, I set Sean up in bed with his iPad where he edits our photographs in Photoshop – rather, his photographs. I leave the night staff with instructions on what to do if he has another fit.

'Where's the bathroom?' Jordan says, stepping through the door just after eight. He's in a blazer, shirt and jeans, but moves past me before I can admire.

'There are only five rooms,' I say, pointing down the hall. Still moving, he puts one large, Rodin-esque hand round the back of my head, and kisses me on the forehead. I tell myself there is nothing fatherly about this.

I move to the kitchen, take a gulp of wine and listen to him pee, heavy and stern. I don't think I'm capable of stern peeing. I rearrange my bra and practise my seductive face.

After my first time with Jordan, he told me about his father's cancer diagnosis. How terrible the timing was, with the divorce and the travel and Beatrice moving out. He told me about the nurses and how amazing they'd been with his father. How impossibly noble the job seems. He told me about how his own injuries and recovery felt ridiculous in comparison to the chemotherapy.

Jordan has never expressed any concern that I am a smoker.

'You okay in there?' I say towards the bathroom.

'Yeah,' he shouts back.

That first time, while we were still dressed, he made me watch a video of him from some World Championships in 2010. He talked me through each piece of equipment, sat with his legs straddled around me, his chin on my shoulder, kissing my neck occasionally. Vault, pommel horse, rings, parallel bars. Deceptively simple, he assured me. His voice was low but excited. I remember listening more to his intonations than his words – his assessment was highly technical and full of unfamiliar terms. My attention was on the video – the routine.

I've watched the video a few times since. In it, Jordan is dressed in a Union Jack leotard. His shoulders look like cuts of meat – huge and prime. The way he moves, the fluid grace of him, so sure, so deliberate and measured. Every time I watch, I feel calm. There's no risk to his rolls, his flips and leaps. It is clear that he is in complete control. Gravity seems to work with him, not against him. This is a body operating at its peak. This is how a body is supposed to be. There's no mind to this body. It's all instinct and focus, complete focus – everything about Jordan's movements looks innately programmed into him.

He's mentioned more than once since that he still has the leotard, if I'm interested.

'Is he here?' Jordan says, coming out of the bathroom.

'Is who here?'

'The man – you know, Sean.'

'How would he be here? We're in a basement. You've just come down a flight of stairs.'

'For some reason I always imagined him living with you. Or you living with him.'

'You're an idiot.'

'Well, what does it tell you?' Jordan says, removing his blazer, casually tossing it with perfect accuracy into Alex's couch space.

'It tells me you're an idiot,' I say playfully, reaching for him.

'Well, it tells me,' he says, allowing my hands to explore, 'that you speak far too much about that little fucker, and that you need to take an evening to yourself.'

'Does it count as an evening to myself if I subject myself to you?' I say, presenting my neck to be kissed.

'Do I get a tour?'

'There are only five rooms!' I tell him again. 'And Alex's room is probably locked. I've told him he's not allowed home before ten.'

'Two hours seems ambitious,' says Jordan, checking his watch over my shoulder.

I grab my wine glass and lead him into my room, turning on the bedside lamp, hoping my efforts at tidiness aren't lost on him.

'Do you want to put your stuff on a hanger?' I say, playing the part of host, unsure of where to stand.

'Nah, it'll be fine out there.'

'It was more of a suggestion than an offer.'

Jordan huffs as I leave the room to fetch his jacket from the couch.

'Is this what you were telling me about?' Jordan says as I return, referencing one of my own artworks, hung in the corner of my room. It is a piece from my final term at art college – a high-resolution photograph of an elderly woman's face and neck.

'She was called Nina,' I explain. 'I did her make-up and hair. It was part of a series. I went home to the morgue most weekends to get new pictures. This was back when my parents actually pretended to be supportive of my dreams.'

'It's really creepy,' Jordan says.

'That was sort of the point,' I say, perching on the end of my bed. 'Her jaw is sewn shut and her eyes are glued down. The make-up is supposed to be kind of garish under that light.'

'Did you have to ask the families' permission?' Jordan says, examining the picture closely.

'Yeah, I was supposed to.'

'And you think people would buy these?'

'I wasn't taking the photos to sell them,' I say, trying not to sound insulted. 'They were for my portfolio. The portfolio would have been about thirty pictures if I had finished. We had to take the pictures and then write about our process, using some art-historical context.'

'Right,' Jordan says, now scanning through my bookcase.

'I'm over here, you know?'

'I'll get round to you eventually,' he says playfully. 'Have you read all of these?' He has pulled out my copy of *The Edible Woman* by Margaret Atwood.

'Does it matter?'

'Can I borrow this?'

'Only if you ask nicely.'

'May I borrow this book, please, Janet?'

'I'll consider it if you're very well behaved,' I say, standing and wrapping myself around the back of him as he reads.

'Is this where I'm supposed to say something about being naughty or a bad boy?' Jordan says, still pretending to read as I grope between his legs.

'Finish your wine and stop being so serious,' I say, pulling him by his belt in the direction of the bed.

'So keen,' he says, undoing his top button and facing me as he slides his shirt and vest over his head in one. His body is hairless and firm. My hands feel damp against his skin. When stood, Jordan is a Greek sculpture, carved from flesh and animated for my pleasure.

'Do you want the light on or off?'

'I don't care,' I tell him, hoping he leaves it on.

'I'm keeping my socks on,' he says.

'I don't care,' I say, fumbling to undo his belt.

'This feels so studenty,' Jordan says, turning to my small, frosted window. 'I can hear people walking outside.'

'You're going to need to shut up now,' I say.

As I lie on top of him, Jordan effortlessly removes my top and bra, and I make a crude attempt at going back between his legs, but he swiftly guides my hand away, back up to his sides, his chest, the PG territories.

'So, so keen,' he says, kissing my neck, pressing his chin into me.

I make small encouraging sounds, leaning into his hands as he gropes the map of me, teasing up the insides of my thighs – I shiver into him.

With this, he lifts me and kicks off his trousers and boxers. I take the sight in, then look away to find a condom, which he promptly rolls on with impressive nonchalance. Through the latex, his penis looks huge and medical. The rubbery smell hits my nose and for a second – just a second – I think of gloves, of Sean.

Jordan moves me up the bed and presses his forehead into mine, holds the back of my head, my hair. He moves inside me carefully, peppering my cheek and ear with soft, slight kisses, easing my legs wider, higher. I catch my breath, breathe for him, in time with him as he finds a rhythm. I have no control over my face. I kick out at the air and open my eyes to take him in. He is hulked over me, his mouth is just open, sharp jaw jutting forward. His watch is right by my ear, ticking a distracting, dull thud.

I use one hand to roam his body, searching for flesh, for purchase, but Jordan has no flesh to spare. Taut muscle. Full and beating and heavy and creaking the frame.

In one movement, I'm back on top of him, his face buried in my chest, hands clamped over my shoulders like a pull up, controlling me, blunt and warm, my own mouth slack and panting, wounded sounds bleeding from me. I push down into him and feel a deep groan.

'It's now. I can't,' he says.

'Do it,' I manage, opening my eyes to watch his face as he finishes.

He pulls out, rolls onto his back, breathing heavily, eyes

covered by the inside of his arm. His forehead is damp with sweat. His breathing sounds victorious. This is my doing – this is the effect I've had upon him. He finds my hand and grips it tightly. I commit to letting him speak first.

'I told you two hours was ambitious.'

After, and we're lying on top of the covers. My new sheets – manhandled and storied from their start.

'And this one?' I say to his elbow.

'Keyhole surgery. I was sixteen, maybe seventeen. It didn't hurt.'

'What do you mean it didn't hurt?'

'I don't remember it hurting,' Jordan says slowly and pointedly, rolling onto his front, legs cocked in the air, powerful as weapons.

'But it must have hurt at the time.'

'Pain is nothing once it's passed.'

'Do you know how cheesy that sounds?' I say. 'Did you have that prepared?'

'Do you want me to apologise?' Jordan says.

'Pain can echo,' I say, louder than I intend to. 'People feel phantom pains. I've heard about people feeling pains in limbs they've lost.'

'I don't know about that,' Jordan says. 'I'd never dismiss pain though. There are good pains.'

'Good pains?' I say distractedly, trickling one hand down Jordan's back, flattening over his bum.

'Well, there's the burn. Everyone trains for the burn. That's a good pain.'

'But you were telling me last week that the burn is bullshit because the human isn't a machine, and it's based on a misunderstanding of thermodynamics.'

'Well then,' Jordan says, pausing to think. 'Grief is good pain. You must have grieved.'

'Are you asking me or telling me?' I say, biting my lip, hoping to look seductive.

'Can I do both?' Jordan says, playing along.

'Grief has always been associated with business for me. It was everywhere and I was never part of it.'

'Did you ever get to work with them?'

'My parents?'

'Yeah,' Jordan says, scratching his neck. 'Other than doing the make-up.'

'Sometimes,' I say, deliberately vague. I light up a cigarette and draw deeply, keen to seem mysterious.

'So you had to touch the bodies? Did you have to drain them and stuff?'

'My father did the draining. Our main job was to dress them and shave them and do the make-up. I got pretty good at shaving people. Old women can have a lot of facial hair. Like Nina,' I say, pointing to the corner. 'And the make-up took a lot of focus. We used this really expensive moisturiser all over the face and hands, because those were the places people would touch. I had to paint their fingernails with gloss polish.'

'I would have thought the families would dress them.'

'I don't think anyone ever requested to do that actually. Rigor mortis sets in pretty quickly so sometimes you needed to massage them on the gurney before you could do anything with clothes. You're better off not forcing the bodies.' I lean across Jordan's back and ash into an empty wine glass.

'Sometimes we had to cut out the backs of the clothes and lay them on top. You lay them on top and fit them round the sides. It's illusion. Open caskets are pretty popular. Surprisingly popular with older people. I don't remember anyone in their twenties or thirties having an open casket.'

Jordan's eyes are closed and tensed. He has the look of someone attempting to comprehend a series of large numbers.

'Are you okay?' I ask, stubbing out the cigarette and fanning away the smoke from around him. 'I didn't mean to upset you.'

'No, no,' he says, waving dismissively, eyes still closed. 'It's nothing. Just thinking about things.'

'What things?'

'Just things.' Jordan slips away to lie on his front, ready for sleep. For a while, I sit in silence. Jordan begins to breathe deeply, nose to mouth. I concentrate on gauging the appropriate amount of time to wait before lighting another cigarette.

'I dreamt of beating him again last night,' I say.

'Sean?'

'Always Sean.'

Jordan reaches out his hand and spreads it across my belly, flat and warm, groping gently.

'It's definitely me,' I say, 'in the dream, I mean. But a larger version of me. Not male, but almost. He's always naked in his bed, on his side, and I'm holding his jaw, pressing my nails into his cheeks, twisting his head to look at me. Sometimes I spit in his face – I can't always remember the details. But then I flick his forehead with my free hand, and I'm shouting at him. I'm holding him there, and then I'm punching him in the chest and the side, still shouting. He's just sobbing softly – more like feeling than sound – and he's wincing each time my fist connects. His body feels so tight and bound. It goes on like that. I never break anything. I don't remember there being any blood. There are no marks on him. I think the radio's on sometimes.'

'Mhmm,' Jordan mumbles, squeezing my belly, sliding down.

'I don't ask him any questions. I'm mostly shouting. Non-sense shouting.'

'Mhmm.'

'Then I step back and look at him, and he's still cowered and convulsing, but he's markless, and I know I've got away with it, and it feels great.'

Jordan's hand has come to rest at the top of my thigh, slipped inside my hipbone.

'I never used to dream. When I had insomnia, I never dreamt. The physical exhaustion of this work has cured the insomnia, but the trade-off is that I have to dream.'

Jordan gives no sign of response.

'Am I evil, Jordan?' I say, prodding him.

'Of course you're not evil.'

'It's just – I feel like normal people don't have those kind of dreams. And I don't even dislike him. It's not like he's done anything to me. I would never actually hurt him. But surely it's not normal to imagine harming anyone like that?'

'Okay,' Jordan says tetchily, 'then you're not normal. Fuck normal anyway. Not being normal doesn't mean you're evil, Janet.'

'Okay, so not evil. Not quite. But I think I want to be a good person,' I say, sensing the shoebox of stolen cash under me. 'I want to be a better person.'

'Then start tomorrow.'

Chapter 2

My morning is his morning.

While Sean feeds himself a breakfast of puréed peach, I scroll through my inbox on my phone. My weekly payslip tells me that I've paid off another eight pounds from my student loan.

After completing basic training at the start of the year, the agency automatically subscribed me to four or five medical science and care-based newsletters. The content is a mixture of clickbait research, and some genuinely amazing medical breakthroughs, quoted out of context. Judging by these newsletters, a new body part is discovered around once a week. This week's discovery of the anterolateral ligament is described as causing a paradigm shift in the way the world will assess knee injuries – the Higgs boson of anterior damage. Last week, an optometrist discovered a sixth layer to the cornea. I consider asking Sean how long it will be until some-one discovers the soul.

I'm yet to come across anything in the newsletters address-ing cerebral palsy. There's nothing futuristic or engineered about Sean's disability. No prosthetics or 3D printing. It's awkward and makeshift, made liveable through brute strength and endless labour. To my knowledge, there's no research or investment being pumped into CP. Just lots of families sacrificing themselves for love and guilt, and plenty of companies profiting off them.

'Listen to this,' I say, quoting from an email. 'Vitamin B12 deficiency during pregnancy linked to increased risk of preterm birth.'

'I do not want to hear, thank you,' Sean says, spitting purée.

I continue. 'In countries where vegetarian diets predominate, such as in India, the percentage of pregnant women with B12 deficiency can exceed two thirds.'

'I do not care,' Sean says, focused on the radio.

'I think it's interesting,' I say, scrolling through the rest of the piece, running my hand over his sleek kitchen table, enjoying the invisible grains of salt and grit, sharp against the surface of my fingers.

Sean manages his own email inbox. He keeps it very tidy, deleting as he goes. He gets most excited when he receives correspondence from someone in his online community of disabled artists. There's a painter in Canada called Ashley with phocomelia who he's been speaking to since his teens. She's been very encouraging of his latest work. Sean made me email Ashley the unedited photos from our session last week even before we left the studio. I had bound his head in black fibre, leaving only his open mouth visible, facing the camera, a handful of pills on his protruding tongue.

'I may start smoking,' Sean announces.

'That's not how smoking works,' I say, not bothering to make eye contact.

'I would buy my own.'

'I don't have a problem buying you cigarettes,' I say. 'I just mean that people don't make the decision to start. It just happens. You have one cigarette – you hate it. Then you drink more, have another. Then you stop bumming cigarettes and start buying your own.'

'My father smoked,' Sean says.

'Then I'm sure he still does,' I say, clearing his plate and fetching his medication.

It's 20 November. As of today, Jordan is the longest relationship of my life. I have convinced myself that this is because Jordan is the only boyfriend who has not met a single member of my family.

None of my boyfriends were willing to openly admit that the funeral parlour bothered them. They'd make a point of pretending it was interesting and different, just like me, apparently. I got into the habit of disclosing it early, like a sickness. It seemed the responsible thing to do. They'd pull earnest expressions and ask questions about the practicalities: the electric bill run up by all those freezers in the morgue, the opening hours.

Alex sincerely claims that none of the girls in his life have ever been bothered by the parlour. He points out that our father happily married into the trade. Alex argues that a genuinely good boyfriend might find it appealing to have the option of working in a steady, rewarding business, where the company will sponsor your qualifications and training.

But of course, it is easy for Alex to say that. It wasn't Alex who was earmarked from birth to inherit the parlour. Besides his gender, Alex has always had the excuse of brilliant academic performance and a weak stomach.

Soon after Mum came into his life, our father abandoned his career as an archivist and threw himself into learning the trade of undertaking – both the skills and its history. He still regularly bores the rest of us with the particulars. Dad ran Mum's ancestry back to the 1850s, when the parlour first opened in the centre of Bedford, just around the time that urbanisation was becoming rampant in the Home Counties, and there was greater demand for civic cemeteries. In the UK, funeral parlours are one of the few trades overwhelmingly run as family businesses. In our family, women have been running the parlour for three successive generations. Pride of place in our reception, there's a grainy photograph of my great-grandmother stood outside the front door – very recognisably our front door – celebrating the end of the Great War.

My first camera was technically the parlour's. One of Dad's innovations was a portfolio of added-value services, including commemorative photographs and albums. Generally, people are distracted at bereavement and funeral services – no one ever stopped to question why a teenage girl was taking the photos. Dad let me use the morgue as my dark room.

In their wedding photos, my father is in his work suit. Alex was two, hugging my mum's leg, and I was on the way, a subtle curve under the white of her dress. Neither side of my family were bothered about having children out of wedlock, but my mother's parents had insisted that Dad would never really be a proper part of the family business until there was some paperwork to commit him for life.

At the wedding, Uncle Jeremy ended his best-man speech by encouraging everyone to toast to the Grim Reaper for his good custom.

My parents are yet to accept that I will not be continuing the family business. They think it is a matter of time until I accept my fate and return home. I'm sure my mother is delighted by Alex's miserable weekly reports about my life and work. I'm sure she is thrilled to hear about the life we share in our tiny basement flat.

When it comes to running the parlour, my mother's preference has been to hire people as apprentices. The work is hard and gory. She argues that exposure from a young age decreases sensitivity. For my whole life, we've maintained a staff of six or seven; the older staff have come from nursing homes or abroad. Some adapt quickly, but most struggle. Apprentices are generally more malleable, and there are government subsidies available to cover the costs of their training. Despite being forced through the exact same training, I refused to take the formal qualification.

There are small variations when it comes to processing a corpse post autopsy. These variations mostly depend on whether the family chooses to have an open casket. Dad maintains that everybody is owed the same quality of treatment, no matter which level package he has convinced the family to pay for.

While I was never required to be involved with the heavy lifting, I've shadowed Dad with the transfer crew, collecting the corpses, bagging and tagging them up, completing the required paperwork. I've seen them carry corpses down stairwells, negotiating turns like a removals crew, bumping off walls and corners, fumbling and stumbling their way back to the van.

From the van onwards, the corpse is laid flat, with the head propped up by a pillow or block to prevent purging – an unholy seepage from the nose and mouth.

Back at the morgue, the apprentices and myself would be responsible for stripping and cleaning the corpse while Dad prepared for the embalming and completed the rest of the paperwork, double checking the tags and itemising the corpse's valuables – rings, watches, pacemakers.

There are various grades of embalming, and strictly speaking, none of them are really necessary. It's all just another clever upsell, sold on notions of dignity and peace of mind. Embalming is only really justified if the corpse needs to be transported for a long distance, or if there's a huge delay before the funeral can take place. The whole practice is terrible for the environment – embalming liquids are highly toxic and prone to leaching into graveyard soil.

Temporary preservation requires the body to be drained of blood through two cannulas – one in a major artery, the other in a vein. Blood tends to pool in the organs, so the draining has to be supplemented with a vacuum aspirator, inserted just above the navel and fanned about the guts. Dad loves to claim that these tools are the greatest innovation in over three millennia of human embalmment.

Once the body has been pumped full of embalming fluid, Dad would supervise as the apprentices massaged the liquid through the body with hesitant, gloved hands, relieving as much of the rigor mortis as possible. We would wrap clingfilm around the entry holes for the cannulas, then plug and stuff every orifice with cotton wool, from nose to throat to arse.

Dad would take responsibility for putting in the eye caps – small flesh coloured discs, slotted under the eyelids, lined with tiny spikes to keep the eyes closed. Without caps, the eyes look recessed and sunken.

Once Dad was satisfied, we'd sew up the jaw and apply make-up and moisturiser, softening the parts worthy of touch. We'd dress the corpse in whatever outfit the family had selected. Dressing is a two-person job, involving lots of rolling and force. On a handful of occasions, Dad has had to cut off toes in order to get the corpses' feet to fit in their shoes.

We'd go through this process two or three times a day. More during the winter months. December is peak season for my family business.

I'm pleased to be in London.

Before I lived in London, I only really visited for the galleries. These began with school trips, with the typical forced focus: the Pre-Raphaelites at Guildhall, Turner at the Tate.

Things changed during my teenage weekends – I was free to develop my own tastes. London offers free entry to most of the major galleries, meaning that if a boy was willing to indulge me and see past the parlour, he'd get away with a reasonably cheap date. I'd arrange these dates a week in advance, picking out the gallery and studying the collection online, keen to be my date's guide, focusing on the pieces that interested me.

I knew the National Gallery best. I developed a standard

route, ending at the Seventeenth Century, the Low Countries and Spain. Those rooms were the happiest place in the world for me. Temperature controlled, guarded – spaces in perfect stasis, reassuringly familiar at every visit.

My dates were the ideal captive audience. They'd indulge my pseudo-intellectual ramblings, offering no resistance and even some occasional insight of their own. The important thing for teenage Janet was to demonstrate that she was refined, destined for bigger and better things.

Today, Sean and I are visiting the Tate Modern for the second time this month. Sean's course encourages regular visits to the major galleries.

Sean had visited London only twice before gaining admission to Central Saint Martins. Once to meet a specialist ahead of a surgery, and once in 2009 when he'd convinced Brigid to bring him to see the National Gallery's exhibition *The Sacred Made Real*. The exhibition set works by Velázquez and Zurbarán from the Spanish Golden Age alongside realist, life-size painted polychrome sculptures, created for processions through the streets on religious holidays. Sean has referred to the exhibition multiple times in his method essays.

Sean is remarkably well read on art history and theory. He's been reading art blogs since his teens, chatting in forums and immersing himself among online communities of artists and amateur theorists. I may have been an art geek as a teenager, but Sean is borderline obsessed. He still spends hours on YouTube each evening after I leave him, watching documentaries and talks and exhibition reviews.

Upon enrolment to Central Saint Martins, Sean elected not to apply for any special dispensation. He is eligible for (among other things) extended deadlines, adjusted assessment, free computers and specialist software. Against the collective wisdom of his tutors, Brigid and myself, Sean insisted that he works better within strict limits, and that there were other students who could make better use of the college's limited funding. His tutors made it clear that he could reverse these decisions at any time, should there be any complications which could be thought of as a change in circumstances.

As it stands, Sean is required to attend all the same tutorials, critiques and seminars as his course mates. In group sessions, I am reminded that Sean is not a typical art student. He is both smarter and harder working than everyone in his class. He is the only person I have ever known to read and relish all the prescribed material. From Maggie Nelson, to Hegel, to Merleau-Ponty, Sean immerses himself in the theory and history of his craft. I am sure Sean is aware of the gap in effort and comprehension between himself and his peers, but he has never made any direct comment to me, beyond acknowledging that he is a few years older than his teenage class mates, and that he has a huge amount of time on his hands to apply to his limited range of passions.

In any other body, I am sure the other students would resent him. I am convinced he would be judged as a teacher's pet, or some oddball savant. Instead, people behave with an awkward reverence around Sean. His intelligence is fierce and vibrant, even through my translations. From the first session, his seminar group fell into the habit of allowing Sean the final word on most discussions.

When we are on campus, everyone seems to know Sean's name.

At the Turbine Hall entrance, I open up the backpack on Sean's wheelchair for the security guard to vaguely prod through, and once he's satisfied, we head to the lift.

Spaces like this mean so much to Sean. Even more than they meant to me during my teens. To him, they are holy ground. The promised land. He is somehow both solemn and animated. Waiting for the lift, he strains his neck to look at a series of standing Gormley casts in the lobby. It's an intense look – like a judge at a prize fight, engaged but neutral.

I wheel him into the corner of the lift and crush myself alongside. A family of tourists armed with cameras fills up the rest of the space, the parents staring down at Sean shamelessly. A little girl reaches a free hand to the wheel of Sean's chair, hovering over as if it were an artwork itself. I meet her eye and she snaps her hand away, embarrassed. I suspect children can sense evil in the way dogs sense the weather.

'I like Gormley,' Sean says. I acknowledge him with a nod and look at my reflection in the lift mirror. I look winter flushed, my eyes seem deep set and weary.

Unlike the Gormley casts, alike in their Virtruvian male-ness and uniformity, each of Sean's bindings is unique and unpreserved. They're the entropy of the body, the collapse of design. All tension and strangeness of proportion. Casts would be an inappropriate medium for Sean. A cast of Sean's body would miss the point – it would transform him into some foetal Vesuvian victim, glossing the indexical signs, the scars, the pallor.

Sean's portfolio to gain admission to Central Saint Martins was a series of photos of ballet dancers' bare feet, set in diptychs alongside the feet of people with cerebral palsy, all without context on a white medical surface.

Generally, my memory is quite poor. My theory is that it's a coping mechanism; if I don't set my life in context, the present is made more bearable. But I have a clear memory of my first session in the studio with Sean. I can picture Sean prostrate, tipping slightly on the gym mat, legs cocked for balance, his wrists bound together behind him. The moment is fixed in my mind, as monochrome and precise as an etching.

'You're going to have to check that into the cloakroom,' a guard says to me as we head into the first room, indicating the backpack on Sean's chair, overlooking Sean entirely.

'Since when? It's already been searched.'

'Miss, it's for safety reasons.'

'The safety of who? It's got all his medication in. We've never had to check it in before.'

'It's policy for everyone, miss,' the guard says, her voice practised in confrontation, clipped and terse.

'I am not everyone,' Sean says.

'You'll have to check it into the cloakroom,' she repeats, now pointing and moving herself directly in front of us.

'Are you worried he's going to turn suddenly and bash the bag into a painting? Where's the risk? We were searched at the door, do you need to search it again?'

'I am not everyone,' Sean repeats, slightly louder.

'What's the matter here?' says a different security guard, male and bald, who seems to have crossed over from the adjacent room.

'I've explained that it's policy to check the bag in,' says the female guard.

'Come on now, Sandra,' says the bald guard, waving us through. 'Don't be daft.'

'Yeah, Sandra,' I say, pushing Sean into the room. 'Don't be daft.'

We spend twenty minutes in that first room on Sean's insistence, the guard eyeing us suspiciously, doing the nervous shuffle of the terminally bored.

'Is there anything specific you want to see?' I say quietly, leaning over him.

'No. I just want to look around.'

'Okay then.'

I push Sean from room to room, stopping when something catches his eye. These days are by far the easiest part of my work. I barely think about quitting while we're visiting galleries.

The rest of the time, I think about quitting a lot. These thoughts are a well-worn pair of shoes, and I can walk around in them for hours at a time. I have painted an exquisite image of Sean's shocked and panicked reaction when he finds out I'm leaving. I imagine a slew of opportunities instantly presenting themselves to me. I am the under-appreciated servant, revolting in triumph, realising her nascent potential. I am back to my genius narrative.

Inevitably, reality leaches in, usually prompted by some particularly menial or undignified task – Sean is an alarm clock that never stops ringing. In the dreamy halfway house, I am reminded that my liberation condemns me nearly instantly to working in a coffee shop or Topshop or some other interchangeable customer-service torture. Worse still, I end up back above the morgue.

We've moved through to the South Wing. We're in a room of abstract works from the sixties and seventies. Whilst there is a cross over between my taste and Sean's, I'm far more predisposed to classical works – things placeable in the art-historical canon. Works where the commentary always involves biography. Sean is more drawn to abstract pieces with strong theoretical grounding. He likes modern works, tied to major political and cultural movements. Sean always says his favourite living artist is his online friend in Canada, Ashley, who makes painted grids with her wheelchair, driving over acrylic paint, then straight onto the canvas. Ashley has promised to send him one of the canvases through the post for Christmas.

We are stood in front of a wall-sized Bridget Riley painting. Vertical pastel stripes, a spectrum of harsh, intense colour, warping in and out of focus. The stripes are spaced unevenly to trick the eyes and generate dizziness. I grab Sean's chair for support and try moving my eyes across the canvas.

'Do you feel that?' I say, swaying a little.

'I am squinting,' Sean says, somewhere below me.

'I need to sit down,' I tell him, turning his chair away.

'Riley is great,' he says below me. 'Because she forces you to engage with her art as a body. The sensory flare. It is so clever.'

'What are you talking about?' I feel lightheaded. I begin doing the yoga breathing I learned on YouTube – in through the nose, out through the mouth.

'It is the disloyalty of perception,' Sean says. 'You have to acknowledge the physical impact of the work. You cannot engage with it in some distant way. She blurs the line between consciousness and the body. She reminds us that we are totally physical things.'

'Mhmm,' I manage. I have led us through three rooms. I feel sure I saw seats in one of these on the way through.

'Like, how would you even be able to describe her work? Like that piece. You cannot rely on any figurative words. You are forced to talk about it in terms of physical effect.'

There's a fully occupied bench in the Rothko room. I park Sean and hover at the end of the bench, next to an old lady checking her phone with big mechanical touches.

'I'm having some of your water,' I say, unzipping Sean's bag and rummaging for the bottle.

'Like, compare that piece to the Rothkos. These are almost as hard to articulate, but with the Rothkos, people only speak about their emotive reactions to them. Not their physical reactions.'

'Could you just give it a break,' I say, making a weak pounce for a newly vacated place on the bench at arm's length from him. I lurch forwards dramatically, hanging my head between my knees. I try counting down from ten, then back up. I suck on the bottle, trying to avoid the thought of sharing Sean's spit.

'We need to keep moving,' Sean says.

'This isn't a fucking action film, Sean. We're not under threat here. Give me a minute.'

'But the taxi is back in two hours.'

'He'll wait. He doesn't get paid unless he takes us back.'

'And I want to type up my notes when we get back.'

I raise my head to see a big dumb smile on Sean's face. He's reaching out an arm, offering to help me up. I stand on my own and bend over to take the brakes off his chair.

'You mean that you want me to type up your—'

Saying this, I catch my finger in the swivelling bracket of Sean's wheelchair.

'What happened?' Sean says, seeing me recoil, still on haunches, my fingers bunched and stuffed under my armpit.

'What the fuck do you think happened?' I say sharply, tears swelling, red hot and throbbing.

'Are you okay?'

I think about doing something dramatic. Screaming. Punching the wall. Punching the art. I consider stamping.

'I'll be fine,' I say, shaking out the pain, breathing sharply. 'I'm fine. Let's go.'

I doubt there has ever been an illness named by someone suffering from it. The power to name lies with those who propose to heal. Sean has been diagnosed with a dozen names. Given the power, I imagine he'd call his own condition something dreadfully noble and abstract.

Our evening massage takes place back at his flat. Looking at him, his body crooked across the bed, I can't think of a name that fits. Spastic quadriplegia is far too broad a classification, and far too uncomfortable to say aloud. It'd be a mistake to call him something sickly. Sean is not sick.

'That hurt,' Sean says, muffled under the mounds of pillow and towel surrounding his head.

'That's what your pain-management training was for.'

'Mm,' Sean says as I move from his shoulders to his spine.

'My hand is fine by the way. Thanks for asking.'

'Good. I am glad.'

Sean's massages require me to be very firm. Typically, my hands begin to cramp after two or three minutes of work. This is roughly around the middle of his back. I involve my whole body in the effort, relying on my elbows to attack the misaligned mess of his spine. If I lean too far over, my top gets oily.

To touch someone in this way requires surprisingly little formal training. I have learned through YouTube, where lithe models instruct on beautiful, hairless bodies. Jordan's even introduced me to a whole branch of porn devoted to massage parlour fantasies – though the technique in those videos seems questionable at best.

I remind myself to let the oil do the work, thumbing his shoulder blades, Sean twitching, breathing slowly.

'That pressure better?'

'Mm. Nice.'

I know where to press to make him wince. I allow myself to inflict brief moments of pain, for the sake of contrast, if he asks.

I hold his right foot in both my hands, oiling over the surgical scars, buttering the untested soles of his feet, anointing him in the manner of the beloved.

By the time we finish, I'm sweaty and cramping. Sean needs the oil washed off in the shower.

'Give me a minute,' I tell him, stepping out to the balcony, struggling to use my lighter with greasy thumbs. I smoke and think about using flammable massage oil. I calmly imagine his body engulfed in blue-green flames – a rejected sacrifice to a picky God.

According to my research, professional masseuses charge around a pound a minute. By my calculations, I could be a millionaire in a few short years. Yet another way to be intimate with near strangers.

I return inside to the greased sheen of him – the glaze of temporary ease. In the shower, I wash him back to pain.

'You okay?' I ask, drying him.

'Sore.'

'Sore good or sore bad?'

'I am not sure yet.'

'It will be worth it,' I say. 'It's always worth it. I promise.'

It's just after six and Alex is home early. We're watching the episode where the Simpson family get flown to Australia to apologise for Bart's $900 collect phone call. Alex knows every word and is quoting over a lot of the jokes. It is Alex's turn to make dinner, but I'm hoping he'll get lazy and buy me a takeaway. Alex pops his finger joints with dramatic flourish.

'I wish you wouldn't do that,' I say, wincing away from him.

'You sound so much like Mum.'

'You know that I don't like it, and you're doing it to spite me.'

'You're supposed to be a medical professional,' Alex says, adjusting his crotch and scratching himself. 'It is ridiculous that you get so bothered.'

'You're an arsehole,' I say, putting my feet on the sofa and across his legs.

We keep our TV on a low volume. Alex and I are used to low volumes and speaking in hushed tones. The parlour was open seven days a week, 9 a.m. to 7 p.m. We have been conditioned to be considerate. There were always grieving families downstairs, arguing about which wood for the casket, or what poor old Mildred's favourite flowers were. We got home from school around 4 p.m., and played *Mario Kart* on mute, stifling our wails as we got blue shelled from first place.

During the break, Alex switches between channels, pausing on an advert for frozen turkey.

'Do you want to take responsibility for Christmas decorations?' he says.

'I didn't think you would bother.'

'Yeah,' Alex says indignantly, pushing my feet off. 'Got to make an effort for Christmas. I've got a bag somewhere with stuff from last year. We're not students, Janet.'

'But aren't you going home for a week anyway?'

'I don't know yet. I may not even be in the country; Isabel has invited me to America. And anyway, Christmas isn't just a week. And if you insist on not going home, I don't like the thought of you here on your own, watching *The Muppet Christmas Carol*, drinking a Cup-a-Soup in the dark without at least some fucking tinsel up or something. It's too awful.'

'Are you trying to be sweet?'

'If I don't end up in New York, you could just come home with me,' Alex says, facing away.

'You know that's not going to happen.'

'Okay,' he says. 'I need the toilet. Call me when it's back on. I like the knifey-spoony scene.'

I reclaim Alex's sofa space with my feet and check my phone. Jordan has sent me some flirty messages. Up to this point in our relationship, I have refused to send him any naked pictures of myself.

I took myself off antidepressants in May and started dating Jordan soon after. At the time, I told myself these things were unrelated.

I draft a few responses to the messages but settle on sending a winky emoji.

'You didn't say it was back on!' Alex says, re-entering the room.

'Oh fuck off, Alex. You know every line anyway.'

Jordan is trying to convince me to come over. I remind him that I'm on my period.

Doesn't matter, he sends.

'I'm going over to my boyfriend's place,' I say.

'So he *is* your boyfriend?'

'You know what I mean.'

'Play safe, then. Anything you want me to tell Mum?'

'No.'

'She was asking about you again,' Alex says. 'I don't like playing messenger, Janet.'

'Don't, then,' I say, pulling on my coat.

On my way, I text Jordan.

The lighting in Jordan's en suite bathroom is exponentially better than anything on offer in my basement. I'm topless, brushing my teeth in front of his mirror. Somehow, without noticing it, I have become physically fit. Eight months of moving and maintaining Sean's body have developed my muscles to be actually visible. I pull a gun-show pose with my left arm and spit confidently into the sink.

'Do you think I'm fit?' I ask, standing in the bathroom doorway.

'What's that?' Jordan says from his bed, removing one earphone and looking up from his laptop.

'Do you think I'm fit?' I repeat, pulling a gun-show with both arms.

'Is that a trick question?' he says, more annoyed than suspicious.

'Not at all,' I say, pulling on a T-shirt and sitting beside him on the bed.

'Fit like attractive, or fit physically?'

'Physically, obviously.' I take his hand and press it against my tensed stomach muscles.

'I think I have skewed standards about what it means to be physically fit,' Jordan says, squeezing at my belly.

I slap his hand away. 'You can be such a dick.'

'I knew it was a trick.'

'Girls like a little flattery now and again,' I prompt.

'I've seen those old photos of you,' Jordan says, 'the ones with the pre-Orthodontic smile. You've come a long way, Janet from Bedford.'

'Please don't put me in a narrative,' I say, closing his laptop and moving it onto the floor, moving my body atop his, straddling him. 'Tough provincial girl moves to the city to become a truer version of herself through discovering her vulnerability.'

'Have we uncovered yet another sore point?' Jordan says playfully, reaching one hand under the T-shirt I've just put on.

'I'll show you a fucking sore point,' I say, doubling forward to bite softly on his neck. He slips one hand around the back of my head and squeezes my butt with the other.

'When did you stop straightening your hair?' Jordan says, still accommodating my biting.

'I never straightened my hair,' I say, close to his ear, one hand already semi-consciously moving to my fringe. 'Only for nights out.'

'I was just wondering. It looks straight in a lot of those old photos.'

'Does Beatrice straighten her hair?'

'Come on, Janet,' Jordan says, scoffing. 'You're better than that.'

'It just seems like a question you only ask with an agenda. It would be like me asking you—' I pause, yawning to mask the struggle for a good comparison – 'it would be like me asking you when you stopped wearing a suit.'

'I don't get your point.'

'Oh fuck off, you know what I mean.'

'Let's not discuss my wife,' Jordan says, shifting out from under me and grabbing his laptop from the floor.

'Let's not refer to her as your wife, then,' I say.

'If you're serious about getting fit, we can try the boxing routine again?'

'You're changing the subject.'

'I am,' he says, bounding to his feet.

'I've just showered, Jordan.'

But he's already pulling me off the bed, holding me upright from behind, using my hips to position me.

'Bend your knees a little,' he says. 'Pick your hands up by your jaw, chin down.'

'Like this?'

'A little lower. That's it. So you're going to push off your back foot, and you don't want to over-extend. You're going to jab the air, and snap back quickly. We're getting your knuckles to do all the work here. Let's go in slow motion first.'

Jordan helps my arm through a straight, shoulder-level line, twisting my hips slightly into the throw.

'When am I supposed to need this?'

'When I'm not around.'

'So pretty much always.'

I allow him to lead me through a series of punches. We duck and dip as one joint body, my feet positioned inside his, anchoring me, making every angle possible.

'So now we're going to combine them together. Jab, cross, jab, then into a hook right, uppercut.'

Jordan releases me and I flail through an effort at the routine.

'Try visualising,' Jordan says. 'Picture someone you want to hit. Direct your energy into one spot.'

Immediately, I'm imagining Sean. It's a clear picture – his face in a ring, smiling, teeth bared, ready to be knocked out like carnival targets.

'Can't you just get the pads out?'

'This way is better. I thought you wanted to get fit?'

'I think I'm done for the day. I'm too tired now. I'm going to need to shower again if we keep going.'

'Whatever you like.'

'I should check my email,' I say. 'Is it okay if I use your computer? My phone is nearly dead.'

Jordan pauses before answering. His expression looks pained.

'If you really have to, I guess.'

'I promise I won't look at your porn.'

'There's much worse than porn on there.'

'I can wait if you don't want me to.'

'No. I guess you can use it. I need the bathroom.'

My inbox shows twenty-two new messages. Brigid has written to say she's not been able to reach me by phone, but that she's sure everything is fine, and that she sends her love. She's provided a link to Ocado, for a new organic baby food that Sean may enjoy. She's also provided a link to a YouTube video of someone reviewing the lamb tagine flavour. I send a quick reply promising to run it by him.

Half way down the inbox there's an email titled, *FAO Janet Lamb, ref. Miss Florence Pew.* There's a dull familiarity to this name. It feels like something repeatedly learned and then forgotten, like kilometres to a mile, or books in the Bible. I open the email.

Dear Janet Lamb,

My name is Florence Pew, but you never called me that anyway. You knew me in school as Miss Piggy. That was your name for me. It was yours first, then later, everyone used it.

I'm contacting you under the advice and supervision of my psychiatrist. If you have any questions after reading this message, you are encouraged to contact her via email or phone. She would be very interested in talking with you.

I'm writing to explain the impact that you have had on my life. I want you to recall the ways you made my life unendurable from the ages of 13–16. I want you to understand how I was made to suffer. Among all the bullies I've had throughout my life, you were the most spiteful. Your words were the most precise and cutting and wearing. You were prepared to bully me even when we were alone. I don't think you can appreciate how rare this behaviour is among bullies. Bullies are usually cowards who operate in packs. But you were different. You didn't need any encouragement to be cruel.

'Fucking hell, Janet!' Jordan shouts from the bathroom. 'I've just slipped on the floor – you've left the floor soaked from your fucking shower. Have you forgotten how normal people live? Do you have any idea how easily my knee could just go again? Is that something you want to happen?'

'Sorry,' I say, still looking at the screen, scrolling through the rest of the message.

'Sorry is right,' he says, his tone softening. 'What's this?' he asks, returning to the bed and resting his chin on my shoulder.

I feel like I'm on a comedown. I'm sweating and my head feels light.

'It's fucked,' I say flatly. Before I can react, Jordan's taken the laptop out of my hands.

'What the fuck,' he says, just above a whisper, now stood at a distance from me, the laptop lighting up his face like a horror-story.

'Do you think it's real?' I say. 'Do you think she's serious?'

'It says that you convinced this girl her dad left home because he was ashamed of her.'

'Maybe,' I say, hands locked behind my head, posed for the firing squad. 'I don't remember. I can't even picture her.'

Jordan looks up at me, pulling a shocked face. The corners of his mouth are turned up in a smile.

'You mean you can't remember Florence Pew? *The* Florence Pew? Miss Piggy herself?'

'It's not funny, Jordan. You shouldn't be finding this funny.'

'It's quite funny though,' he says, bobbing from foot to foot like an excited toddler. I'd slap him if he was within reach.

'This should be scaring you,' I say. 'You should be judging me. You should be ordering me to get out of your home or something.'

'It says that you sniffed each time she walked past,' he says, almost laughing. 'That's genius, Janet. Oh, God. She's such a loser. This is tragic.'

In a high, nasal voice, he reads the letter aloud, performing Florence's suffering. Performing for me. He's made her pain camp and comic. I can hardly listen. I feel hysterical. I'm laughing, shaking slightly. Is this relief? I certainly feel relieved; relieved that he's not immediately revolted by me. I'm sure that he's behaving quite awfully. He's perfectly awful and I could love him for it.

When he's finished, Jordan gently places the laptop on the floor and pounces on me, pinning me to the bed.

'I really needed that. That was so good,' he says giddily, kissing me. 'Did you really throw Percy Pigs at her?'

'Did it say that? Maybe? I don't know. But this really isn't funny, you know. You shouldn't treat it like a joke.'

He doesn't reply. He just looms and stares and smiles. Wide and crazed. The way he's looking at me – I know he's waiting for me to deliver, to live up to the promise of the email. He's looking for the cruelty in my eyes.

'It's not who I am,' I say, trying to sound assertive. 'I'm not that girl any more. I don't even remember being like that.'

'I wouldn't have expected you to,' he says, beaming down.

'I'm not evil. I'm not an evil person.'

'I believe you.'

'Don't do that,' I say, attempting to push him away.

'Do what?' he says, clearly amused.

'Don't just brush it off. I might be evil for all you know. Don't just believe it because I say so.'

'You're a good person, Janet Lamb.'

'You don't even know me.'

'I know you,' he says, rubbing his nose on mine.

Now is the time to correct him. Now is the time to reveal myself.

'Is this what you want?' I say, feeling ridiculous.

'I want you,' he says softly.

It'll be later that I question his judgement. Much later, when his hands are gone and off me. But later is a space in my head.

'Please, Janet, you have to call this psychiatrist.' Jordan moves off me to fetch the computer. 'You have to call her tomorrow.' I scroll to the end of the email.

I don't know what you've been doing with your life and I have no interest in finding out. I would not be shocked if you were to receive this email in jail.

Please know that I have forgiven you. I forgive you and I pity you. I hope you can learn to forgive yourself.

Sincerely,

Florence Pew

If you have any questions, contact Dr Melissa Ye on (+44)7792965101 or at m.ye@nhs.org.uk.

*

When they caught me, I returned home. There was a conversation about what we'd tell people. Dad insisted on saying that I was too good for a shitty regional art school anyway, no matter what had happened. Mum wanted to tell everyone the truth.

I convinced them to tell everyone I had just changed my mind – that after two years, I had decided art school wasn't for me after all, that I was going to take some time to explore my options.

At that point, we didn't know if they were going to prosecute. I was in limbo, sleeping in my childhood bedroom, helping in the morgue, training the seventeen-year-old apprentices in how to shave the dead, how to apply blusher between wrinkles, how to stuff their throats with cotton wool and sew mouths firmly shut.

Mum brought me to the doctor's. She sat with me whilst our family GP asked whether I was sexually active, whether I was on drugs, and how often I thought about harming myself. The doctor diagnosed depression, recommending SSRIs and exercise.

In spite of Mum, Dad was fixated on getting me back involved with the art world as soon as possible. He claimed that I was at risk of losing touch with my talent. He brought home local newspapers, circling adverts and leaving them unsubtly on the kitchen table. He printed off job listings from the internet, emphasising that they were just suggestions, just options for when I was ready.

I agreed to go forwards with one post – an art tutor at the local young offenders institute. I did it to make Dad happy, not because I wanted the post. The vacancy was being managed by an agency, who called to explain that I would require a basic disclosure Criminal Records Bureau check. The consultant said they could process it for me, but that it would cost thirty pounds. The consultant explained that the check would last for two years before requiring renewal.

Dad insisted I go ahead with the role anyway. He offered to pay the fee – the fastest processing turnaround available. He thought it was best to act immediately, before anything could show up on my record, in the event that the college decided to prosecute. For Dad's sake, I agreed to go ahead with the job and the interview. I wore my smartest dress and brought along my incomplete portfolio: two dozen high-resolution photographs of dead faces. I rehearsed answers about my favourite artists, my favourite theorists. But at the interview, it was clear the prison governor had no interest in art.

She asked me questions about how I handled conflict. She asked me for examples on how I had dealt with discrimination. She asked me why I thought rehabilitation was important. She asked me if I was ready and able to handle lewd comments.

After thirty minutes, she said she'd be in touch.

The agency confirmed I'd been unsuccessful later that afternoon, but suggested that with my experience in the parlour, and my newly completed Criminal Records check, I'd be a perfect candidate for care work. They mentioned a vacancy available in London, working as a 'Personal Assistant', for a man due to start at art college. The man was from Ireland. His name was Sean.

*

It's Friday night. Chloe's picked a bar in Soho, just off Wardour Street. We're stood in the smoking area outside, dressed for fun, not for the weather. These are my only pair of heels, and I'm convinced that Chloe has seen them at least three times already. Chloe tells me we're close to the fashion magazine she works for, and that her colleagues may join us later. For now, we're drinking 2-4-1 cocktails. I drink significantly faster than Chloe, and I'm trying to determine an acceptable amount of time to wait before starting work on my second Mojito.

I've known Chloe since we were both in school, back in Bedford. She is a reliable option when Alex insists on needing the flat to himself. These sessions have become more regular recently, as there's a girl in America he has been Skyping most evenings. He's assured me that he isn't paying for her time.

Chloe's been living in London since university and always suggests meeting in the West End. She's out most evenings, so it's more a case of inviting myself along, rather than relying on her plans. I know most of Chloe's life through social media, but she's alarmingly keen to catch up on mine. Chloe's social media presence is overwhelmingly feminist. Articles about empowerment and statistics. She has promised me that she won't share anything about Brigid without my permission. It occurs to me that Chloe is too chubby to work for a fashion magazine.

'Is it still just Sean, then?' Chloe asks, lighting another menthol.

'Yeah, just him. There was supposed to be a guy with dementia, but it was too tricky to make the timings work. I would have needed a bike.'

'Yeah, and the roads are a death trap for cyclists,' Chloe says, interrupting.

'The good thing is that Brigid basically loves me now, and she's going to probably hire me directly after Christmas. So I won't have to deal with the agency any more.'

'Oh my God, I love her so much. I will never get bored of hearing about that woman.'

'Please don't write about her, Chloe.'

'Okay, but you are denying the world an actual legend.'

'That is a very generous thing to say about someone you haven't met. I am sure there are plenty of nasty stories about her too.'

'Yeah, of course, but who cares? I'm not interested in writing some balanced think piece. And I didn't expect to hear so much about her. I didn't really realise that all this care work would be such a big part of your life – I thought it was meant to be a short-term thing? Like, just for your initial move to London. You sound so committed now.'

I'm not sure how to respond, so I reach for my glass of ice and suck cold air through the straw.

'I suppose you did do all of that training stuff. How long did the training take? To get qualified, to do this type of work.'

'Not long,' I say. 'A few weeks. There were group classes. I got an NVQ certificate. Most of the other people at the class were older. There was one Bangladeshi lady from Birmingham who didn't really speak any English. They usually partnered us.'

'But how did you get matched with Sean?'

'Please don't make me tell you the full story, Chloe. I

needed to move and Sean was the only option. I did an inter-view and we spoke about art.'

'Right,' Chloe says. 'Don't stress. I'm just showing an inter-est! Like, are you still making any art for yourself?'

'Not really. Not on my own anyway. Working with him, I do. It has spoiled art a bit. Overexposure, maybe. I go to gal-leries a lot, but never on my own. I don't feel like I'm making the most of being in London.'

'Yeah, it's crazy how quickly you take things for granted. I went home like a month ago, and it was like a twenty-minute wait for an Uber.'

'Right, yeah,' I laugh.

'So is his stuff any good?'

I take my phone back out and show her a few pictures of our recent work.

'He hasn't photoshopped these yet,' I say, slightly defensive.

Chloe takes the phone out of my hands and zooms in to examine the poses.

'I didn't expect it to be so fucked up,' she says, showing me a bound Sean, his ass pointed up in a presenting pose. 'Is this like, his kink?'

'He's making a point about our expectations of disabled behaviour and suffering. There's something called *The Theatre of Cruelty*. He explains it pretty well. There's this show coming up, if you want to come see his work?'

'Yeah, sure. Definitely,' Chloe says.

'Brigid is coming because of the show, so I get a few days off, but I still need to go to the show. It'd be really good if someone could join me.'

'I would love to meet that legend. Does your man not want to?'

'I don't want him there.'

'Probably a good choice. Are you going home while you've got time off, then?' Chloe says. 'How are your parents?'

'Let's go inside,' I say, putting out my cigarette on the wall.

Balancing in an uneven corner of the bar, I start on my second Mojito and show Chloe Jordan's Facebook profile: the pictures of him at his peak, smiles and pecs and medals. She makes impressed vowel sounds. I hold her shoulder for balance in the heels.

'So what's it like being with a married man?' she asks, with an impressive lack of judgment in her voice.

'I thought about it a lot at first,' I say in a serious tone, 'but now it seems ordinary. They are separated, so almost none of her stuff is at his flat. What do you think? Am I a bad person?'

'If you're a bad person, then so am I. And for that matter, so is he,' Chloe says, raising her glass in a cheers gesture.

'So, something pretty crazy happened,' I say. 'Do you remember a girl called Florence Pew?'

'You've got an amazing memory, Janet. Do you remember literally everyone from school? Did you know Susie McDermott died?'

'But Florence,' I say. 'There was a girl called Florence Pew. I'm pretty sure she was in our Maths class. You know, Miss Piggy?'

'Oh shit!' Chloe says. 'Did she finally kill herself?'

'No, no. She wrote me a letter.'

'What? Like an actual fucking paper and pen letter, through the mailbox letter?'

'No, an email. She wrote me this long email, and sent it via her therapist. She wrote all about how I was this terrible person but she's forgiven me.'

'Makes sense that she would get a therapist.'

'It's an NHS therapist,' I say. 'Well, it was from an NHS email address. So I'm guessing it was.'

'So your tax dollars are going towards people writing reprisal letters to you?'

'I'm not paid in dollars. Are you paid in dollars?'

'You know what I mean,' Chloe says. 'Are you ready for another drink?'

'I just don't know what to feel about it. I feel like I may be a terrible person.'

'So?'

'So what should I do?'

Chloe's expression is bemused. She gestures to the barman for four more cocktails. 'You don't have to do anything. Why would you do anything? You need to shut up about this bad person thing. It's boring.'

'Do you think I was a bully?'

'Yeah, probably. But so what? This is her problem. She's clearly writing for closure.'

'Then why would they say that they wanted to hear from me?'

'Forget about it, Janet. That girl will just keep creating problems and excuses. I bet she's sent out that same letter to like ten people. Yes, you're probably a terrible person. We're all fucking terrible people. Every time you buy a Nestlé product you're a terrible person. Every time you ignore a beggar you're a terrible person. The whole of society is set up to make us selfish, horrible people. Now let's go poison ourselves.'

Chloe's colleagues arrive and I play civil, knowing the opportunity to discuss Florence is gone. The email will be a blip on the radar. This isn't a confirmation of everything I've been quietly suspecting for years. This is just another thing to obsess over, until I stop caring. Until the next time I need to confront myself and refuse to change.

Chapter 3

There's a history of twins in Sean's family. Brigid has twin brothers, one now working for the Church, the other missing. She says that her paternal grandfather had been also been a twin. He was Mayor of Galway just before the First World War – just before being a mayor stopped meaning anything.

They named Sean's brother David. There was some debate at the hospital about baptisms. The parish priest explained to a distraught Brigid that he could baptise Sean, but insisted that a stillborn child went straight to heaven. He explained that he could arrange for a full Catholic burial, but that he could not baptise the deceased.

Sean was still in the neonatal intensive-care unit during David's funeral. They knew Sean's funeral was likely next. Likely any day. They bought a double plot at the cemetery – the smallest plot available.

David didn't receive a birth certificate. Beyond what was reported in newspapers, and Brigid's precious ultrasound scans of two healthy boys, there's no paper trail of his existence. There are no photographs of David.

But there are plenty of Sean.

It's the day of the end-of-term show. Brigid is due to touch down in four hours. It's 10 a.m. and Brigid's been in contact three times today already. I know that she's made it to the airport and the flight is on time. I know that she's planned for the risk of rain. I know that she's going to eat lunch before she arrives, so I shouldn't worry about preparing her anything. Brigid has suggested an outfit for Sean that he hasn't picked for himself in the whole time I've been caring for him.

The end-of-term show is being held at the Lethaby Gallery, by King's Cross. Aside from the students and their families, the show is supposedly attended by graduates, art world insiders, collectors and journalists. All the work at the show has already been examined and will be up for sale. Sean has been uncomfortable about pricing his work. Our work. In seminars, conversations about the art market are the only dialogues that Sean visibly withdraws from. Sean has a very naive sense of finance and debt and economics. He never really had the chance to learn how to navigate money. He has a wallet and a contactless card, but he never handles cash – he certainly doesn't check his bank account. For Sean's whole life, Brigid controlled whatever little money they had. She shielded him from the reality of finance entirely.

I suggest we price each piece at £5,000, but he ultimately settles on £800 for each of the photos on display, arguing that people will want to buy the full set.

Sean is fresh out the shower, naked on his bed. I've been telling him about an article from one of my weekly news-letters, arguing the importance of human touch. The article describes how cuddling releases oxytocin and how massages create serotonin surges and all sorts of other therapeutic endorphins. He's focusing on the radio.

I hold his penis firmly between my thumb and forefinger, and apply a toothpaste pea of lubricant with my other hand in a precise, medical movement.

'We're going to need to trim down here again,' I say.

'Yeah,' Sean says, his head turned firmly away.

The condom catheter has an adhesive at the base that can make removal painful for Sean, who is hairy across the map of his body. Once the condom is on, I have to pinch at the base for ten seconds while it dries, which we pass in the silence of radio chatter.

I tab his pad in place, carefully running the catheter cord towards his left leg. I thread Velcro straps through the catheter bag and strap it to his thigh.

'Too tight?' I say, gently shaking his leg to test slippage.

'It is fine.'

Through the course of the day, I will need to empty the bag at least twice. Because Sean prefers the bag to be strapped to his thigh rather than his shin, I will need to take him to a disabled toilet and bunch up his trouser leg until I get access to the small plastic toggle that releases the urine. I'll press the swollen bag through the fabric of his trouser leg, forcing the urine to flow into a sperm-shaped screw-top bottle that travels with us everywhere, typically pressed up against my lunch inside Sean's backpack. The liquid is then poured down the disabled bathroom toilet, before I wash out the bottle and clean my hands twice.

During my training with Brigid, she provided a colour

chart for Sean's pee and what the respective gradients of yellow could mean for his overall health and medication. I promptly disposed of the chart.

Spots are another symptom of Sean's medications. In spite of everything, Sean is very vain and the spots bother him more than nearly anything else. They affect his face and shoulders. They affect the gaps in his beard. The spots form a constellation across the map of his skin, guiding me, helping me navigate a safe route over his body.

I'm hunched forwards over the bed, my nails digging into a particularly ripe spot in his eyebrow. I'm aware that he can see down my shirt.

'Ow, ow, ow.'

'Nearly got it all. One more bit.'

I squeeze firmly, until the oil runs clear, replaced by a spec of red.

'Next one,' I say, moving to the Big Dipper of spots along his jaw.

'Be careful,' Sean says, turning his cheek compliantly.

My nails are painted a light medical blue. I have filed them to points. I am not supposed to wear any jewellery – rings are particularly unsanitary. Necklaces catch in sensitive places. A watch would be asking for trouble.

'How did the editing go last night?' I ask, pinching firmly on his jaw.

'Fine,' he says through pursed lips.

'Just fine?'

'It is nearly done.'

'Are you happy with the way they came out?'

'I sent them to Ashley. She likes them.'

'But do you like them?' I say, tearing off a piece of toilet paper to dab the pus.

'I think they are fine.'

'We can try something different, if you like. We could use that fancy exposure you were talking about. Or we could order those bits of rope?'

'I will decide,' Sean says, pausing to wince in pain. 'I will decide if we need to do something different.'

I bite my tongue and squeeze more firmly, twisting my nails, his skin blooming, from white to red to purple. I move my face close to his, close enough to feel his heat, his pain – he is in widescreen, filling my vision. He is my canvas, twitching and clenching.

Other side effects of Sean's medication include constipation, increased body odour, greying of the skin and sudden irritability. There are other medicines available to counterbalance these side effects, but it could quickly become an infinite regress.

Last week, I read Sean an article about a new form of toxin injection that is supposed to prevent drooling for a few months. There's even surgery available now to redirect the saliva glands straight down the throat. I shared the article with Brigid, but she replied saying that Sean's had enough surgery for one lifetime.

'What about this outfit, then? Your mum has specifically requested it.'

'I do not like wearing shirts.'

'I know, but it will make her happy.'

Sean makes a sound like he's being impaled – guttural and anguished.

'Don't be such a cry baby. It won't be that bad. Wait until you see what I'm going to be wearing.'

'You will look good,' Sean says, rolling to help me remove the sling from under him.

'Are you sure you don't want to let her know about the fit?'

'Please do not tell her. There is nothing to worry about. I am fine.' Sean smiles convincingly, still just in a nappy, totally at ease.

'I don't know where I'm going to get changed. I'll have to hide in some bathroom at the college.'

'Just get changed in the studio,' Sean says.

'I'm not getting changed in front of you.'

'I will not look,' Sean says, smiling even more broadly.

'Now where's that horrid shirt,' I say teasingly, prompting Sean to make the same anguished, guttural sound.

Chloe had agreed to join me at the exhibition when she finished work. I can see on WhatsApp that she's online right now, seemingly ignoring my messages. I make a mental note of the time, turn off Mobile Data and promise myself not to check my phone again for another twenty minutes.

I'm dressed like mourning. I ended up ordering a simple black dress online. I have no desire to draw attention to myself, particularly while I'm technically off-duty. *Duty* – the word feels totally appropriate and yet ridiculous.

The exhibition flyers promise a drinks reception that is nowhere to be found. I can't be the only one who has noticed the lack of drinks. Standing at the far wall of the gallery, I'm picking out the people most in need of a drink, imagining how differently they'd behave with wine glasses in their hands.

In my own hands, I'm semi-consciously making small tears around the edges of the exhibition pamphlet. Prices in the pamphlet range from £500 to £3,000, meaning Sean has sensibly priced his own works on the more affordable end of the spectrum. One of Sean's pieces is printed on the cover of the pamphlet, along with three others in a two-by-two grid.

Sean's two canvases have the best position in the room, a direct sight line from the entrance. They're among the largest pieces in the exhibition, and seem to be receiving a reasonable amount of attention. It's strange to see them blown up to full size. I'm not sure whether I'm proud, but I'm definitely feeling something. For a moment, I feel at peace with the idea that these collaborations with Sean may end up being the extent of my artistic output as a human on this planet.

Supposedly, dealers and would-be collectors attend the show, examining the next generation of talented prospects, gauging the works and their human creators for their nascent investment potential.

I wander over to the most expensive piece in the exhibition: a portrait of a woman choking. It's been painted in tar and crimson wax. Viewed up close, the work has an incredibly tactile appeal. I have to clench my bum to resist reaching up and touching the canvas. The surface is tumour-like. The woman's face is an outline, framed by a pool of black hair. Wax make-up runs from her hollowed eyes. She claws at her neck with wiry, smeared fingers, arms cut off just below the wrist. The piece is titled *Breathe*.

The canvas looms over me, large and curious. I try hard to tune in and imagine myself as the woman. I try to focus, adjusting my mental frequency, dulling the noise around me.

I squint, trying to isolate parts of the canvas, reading it left to right, then top to bottom. I stare long enough to feel inadequate. I feel like a boring date with nothing interesting to say. I have absolutely no interest in meeting the creator of *Breathe*.

I check my phone. It has been six minutes.

In the corner, a cherubic blonde toddler sits quietly, playing with an iPad beneath a large, photorealistic painting of a lung transplant. I allow myself to imagine the painting slipping off the wall, falling and crushing the child.

Sean is with his mother. Brigid is pushing him along the gallery wall, maintaining an attentive expression as he speaks below her. They pause at each artwork, read the description and discuss for a while, allowing Sean to strain out an interpretation and summarise his connection to this particular classmate. Sean is keen to prove that he's okay, coping well without her.

Brigid looks ghostly. Her wrinkles are deep and earned. This is not how I visualise the woman who emails me, the woman who liberally uses exclamation marks, and emphasises how much I'm appreciated, what a blessing I've been. This woman looks wounded. Her movement is a prolonged wince.

Within ten minutes of arriving at Sean's flat earlier in the afternoon, Brigid was dusting. She stressed that the mess wasn't my fault, that I couldn't be blamed, but that she would be having words with the property managers. She treated the flat like a crime scene, taking photos on her iPhone, running her finger over the top of doorframes, inspecting with a detective level of focus, complaining loudly about what they were paying all that money for if they couldn't be bothered to dust the place properly.

Sean wasn't fazed. He occupied himself with the art magazines she'd brought him – Brigid changed the address for Sean's subscriptions to her new home in Galway, rather than getting them sent to London. I suspect that she still thinks there's a possibility that Sean will get sick of London and drop out, not that she'd ever admit to it.

When Sean came to London, Brigid left Yorkshire behind to live closer to the rest of their family. During my first two months with Sean, she would email every day to justify herself, to explain how she'd made the right choice, why she needed to step away from her son, to give him a life of his own. She emphasised how she was getting too weak to manage him on her own anyway. She'd list all the activities she was getting up to, things she'd never have been able to do otherwise: pottery classes, nights at the theatre, dinner with her sister, Mass at her brother's church, yoga classes.

Even for Brigid, it's hard to have a conversation over the phone with Sean. Without seeing his face and his attempts at body language, it is even more difficult to decode Sean's words, to reach an understanding. Their chats tend to be formal and brief, Sean awkwardly pressing the phone to his ear with the heel of his wrist, responding in yeahs and okays, always finishing with an 'I love you too'.

'Isn't it wonderful?' Brigid says, now stood beside me. 'Everyone here is so nice. Sean's very lucky. Aren't you now?'

'Yeah,' Sean says, his smile as wide as Christmas.

'They're all so talented. Don't you think so?'

'I do,' I say. 'I really do. I'm going to head out for a smoke. If you'll excuse me.'

'Go on ahead, girl,' Brigid says, her hand on Sean's shoulder, rubbing in a nervous circle.

I turn on my data. Chloe's messaged saying that she can't make it, but that she hopes the show goes well, and that Brigid has a lovely time in London.

The smoking area is a fenced rectangle on the pavement outside. Cool air sings into my lungs. My hand shakes slightly as I light my cigarette. I look deep into my phone, hoping to be left alone. I write a reminder into my phone to shave my legs tonight, knowing I will not bother.

An elderly man approaches to tell me that he's here to support his niece, the artist behind the photographic triptych of birds with human genitals. He tells me that he's very proud. When I mention that I care for the man in the wheelchair he says he's sorry. I ask him what he's sorry for and he turns back inside.

After the show, there's a reception scheduled for the students close by. Alcohol will be involved. Narcotics will almost certainly be involved. Sean has been invited and is keen to be involved. Sean knows I won't be joining him for the after party, meaning Brigid will have to.

Back inside, Sean and Brigid are positioned under one of our pieces – a photograph of Sean nude, bound to his own wheelchair, a black bag over his head. Sean is speaking to a sizeable group of people around him, with Brigid acting as interpreter. Making eye contact from across the room, she beckons me over. I pretend not to notice her.

'Great show,' I say to a man beside me, turning my back on Brigid. The man is not dressed for winter. His oversized T-shirt says POETRY IS DEAD in block capitals. He has horn-rimmed glasses and a neat beard.

'Third this week,' the man says, chewing gum, smiling politely.

'Do you work for the college?'

'No, for *Frieze*. The magazine.' He raises one hand to show a glossy magazine. 'I'm Owen.'

'I'm Janet,' I say, not sure if I'm supposed to try to shake hands.

'Did you see there's a *Suggested Donation*?' Owen says. 'Doesn't that seem super passive-aggressive?'

'Is that not normal?'

'Not at anything where the work is on sale. I've never seen it at a student event before.'

'Well, the theme of the show is *Innovation*,' I say, opening my ripped pamphlet to the curatorial notes on the first page. 'Maybe that's the innovation. Maybe this is what they mean.'

Owen opens up his own pamphlet and scans over the introductory paragraphs.

'What the fuck do they mean? Since when does innovation have anything to do with art? Doesn't innovation only apply when something is practical – when you use it? Do you think it's some kind of play on *Make It New*?'

'I really don't know,' I say, wary of wading out of my depth.

'Well, there was supposed to be a free bar.'

'I'm so glad you said that. I thought I was the only one to notice,' I say, attempting a flirtatious voice.

'What do you do?'

'I help take care of that man,' I say, pointing in the direction of Sean with a vague gesture that could only mean him.

'Oh cool – he created those pieces, right?' Owen says, picking out Sean's work. 'Everybody's talking about them.'

'I take the photos,' I say. 'I mean, I set him up, get him in position and then I take the exposure.'

'They're incredible,' Owen says, yet to turn his attention back to me, still looking at the pieces on the other side of the room. 'I'd love to talk to him.'

It seems clear that Owen is expecting me to volunteer an introduction. Now I'm turned back in their direction, Brigid has caught my eye again and is beckoning me over more fiercely.

'I have to go help,' I say. 'You can come, if you like.'

'Thanks for permission,' Owen says.

I squeeze between the huddle of bodies crowded around Sean's chair, and slide in behind him, my thigh pressed against his wheel. Brigid is leaning against the wall, looking sweaty.

'Would you take over, Janet? I could do with some air.'

Without waiting for an answer, Brigid excuses herself and heads for the door, moving as though she's in the final mile of a marathon.

Conversation amongst the group is being conducted by Suzanna, Sean's main tutor. In theory, Sean and Suzanna are supposed to meet twice a month to discuss his progress and process. In reality, it's physically impossible to fit Sean's chair into Suzanna's faculty office, so they've staged a handful of impromptu meetings in his studio, where he mumbles, constricted or bound in awful poses, I translate, before Suzanna recommends some books and leaves.

Suzanna is about a foot taller than me. She looks too young to have grey hair, but it suits her. She pronounces her name with a sigh in the middle.

'I'm no expert,' Suzanna announces in a firm, academic

voice, 'but there's a rich vein of important photography focused on torture. And let's be clear – this—' she motions vaguely to Sean's work – 'is torture. Our friend Janet here is the torturer in chief.' I feel myself blushing lightly. The wings of my mouth are kicking up a smile.

'My personal assistant helps with all my work,' Sean says. 'She is the most beautiful, patient person I know.'

I feel dumbstruck. Suzanna puts her arm around my shoulder and squeezes gently. I feel like a dog being coddled and told she's a good girl.

'Sean just mentioned that I help out with getting him set up,' I translate.

'I'd be happy to lend a hand, if you ever need any more assistance,' says a girl from Sean's studio group.

'We'll be fine,' I say.

Owen is stood in the centre of the crowd, typing notes into his phone, looking over the top of his glasses from his phone to Sean, Sean to his phone.

'Think of Abu Ghraib,' Suzanna says. 'Am I pronouncing that right? Think of Abu Gh-raib. These are the few, few occasions in modern culture when we even begin to question the morality of an image – whether we have a right to produce and preserve a visual history of violence. Think of Goya. Think of Susan Sontag on Sarajevo – she anticipated the clichés about the banality of images of war, but she bypassed the need for a call to action. She knew we couldn't ration horror or control the image culture, she refused to defend our desires to transform suffering into spectacle. She only highlighted the incompatibility of comparing one type of suffering with another.'

I spot Brigid re-enter the room, moving gingerly towards

the corner, now standing over the toddler, staring over his shoulder at the iPad screen, the rest of the room oblivious to them both.

'This work,' Suzanna says, gesturing again, smiling broadly at a dormant Sean. 'It avoids being medical – it taps into archetype and sacrifice. Catholic notions of the body as materiality. Ash to ash, dust to dust. How the body lurches between the realms of health and illness.'

I'm biting my cheek to suppress a smile. The rest of the group are loving it. My leg's nearly gone dead from the pressure of Sean's chair.

'Do you find,' Suzanna says, addressing me directly, 'that there's an emotional toll to producing these images?'

'What do you mean, sorry?' I say, intensely aware of the group's shift in focus onto me.

'Are you affected emotionally in the process of aiding Sean in his art?' she rephrases without hesitation.

I make eye contact with Owen. His phone is poised, waiting for my answer.

'I've never thought of myself as a torturer,' I lie, feigning a note of indignation. Suzanna looks disappointed in the answer, so I continue. 'I guess it is so physically demanding that I don't think about the meaning or purpose too often. I do have to check with him constantly if the position is putting him in any unmanageable pain, but we mostly just toe the threshold of what he's capable of putting his body through.'

I look to Sean for some back-up. He nods a vague assent, with the pained, open-mouth expression of someone trying to catch their breath.

'The really interesting thing,' Suzanna says, 'is how these

works disrupt the narrative of how the disabled state should always desire to move towards ableness or a cure.'

The group murmurs with concurrence.

'Instead, Sean is compounding and exacerbating the limitations of his physical state, both in method and depiction. So much so, that he literally removes himself from being the author of the piece,' she says, gesturing to me.

'There is no value in suffering,' Sean says breathlessly below us.

'Sean says there is no value in suffering.'

'Suffering is not brave,' Sean continues, as I translate to the group, a few words at a time. 'My body is a political site. I like art that you experience as a body in space. I want to use my body to provoke reactions in you. I am interested in your reaction to my body as the other. I am interested in the difficulty of confronting suffering. I am interested in the beauty of vulnerability.'

'The idea of the adult as an infant is very unexplored,' says the girl from his seminar group.

'What do you think of the show's theme?' says Owen from the back, directed at Sean. 'What do you think about innovation in art?'

'I think innovation means identifying a demand for something that does not exist yet,' Sean says. 'I think that art should confront the places where we are uncomfortable to look. I think innovative art helps us to see a future that we may never be part of.'

Owen looks a little stunned as I finish repeating. Sean looks up and gives me a grateful smile, aware of the impression he has made.

'And what does the future look like for you? For Sean?' Owen says.

'We are going for drinks after the show,' Sean says, eliciting a laugh from the group that goes on slightly too long to be natural.

After a while, the group disperses, leaving Suzanna and Owen with us, talking familiarly, as though they've known each other for years.

'Where's Mum?' Sean says to me softly, over his shoulder.

'Over there,' I say, pointing to the corner of the gallery, where Brigid is now leant up against the wall, her eyes closed, posed like a grim installation.

'Is she okay? I cannot see her.'

'She's fine,' I say. 'I think.'

'Excuse me,' Owen says nervously, standing like a schoolboy. 'I work for *Frieze* and I'd love to meet up with you to do an interview, if you like? We could run it with some of your work. I could get you a free subscription.'

'That would be amazing,' Sean says loudly, wild with excitement.

'He says he'd like that.'

'I got that,' Owen says, a slight tone of condescension. 'Will you be around to help out?' he says to me.

'Until he gets sick of me,' I say.

Owen offers his phone and I type in my number.

'What should I save it as?'

'Whatever you like.'

'You've forgotten my name, haven't you?'

'Sorry,' Owen says.

Sean's been interviewed before, but only by the local

papers in Yorkshire and only about his body, and his thoughts on the results of the trial. There was no media interest in Sean before the verdict and the cash settlement. No local papers reported the abject failure of the maternity ward. Brigid didn't approach anyone outside her immediate reach to address the lack of support or acknowledgement from those culpable.

Back then, right at the start, Brigid mourned while she weaned, taking Sean for tests and further tests, waiting on a confirmation of the damage to his brain and a guess at his life expectancy. She left her administrative position at the local Catholic school, sparing only a few unpaid hours to train her replacement.

The pictures I've seen of the infant Sean are predictably dull. The same dark hair, but a soft body, yet to calcify into its adult husk.

There was hope for his brain reasonably early on. He reacted to sounds, to lights in an ordinary, albeit twitchy way. He smiled for Brigid, and she loved him for it. Sean's motor development was slower – cerebral palsy was all but confirmed by the sixth month, when he still couldn't roll on to his back, or stay upright without support. He would fidget constantly, his legs jerking with a mind of their own. This made an MRI highly complicated – and the radiologists suggested results would be compromised if they did a scan while he slept.

'It was nice to meet you,' Owen says, reaching down and making a clumsy attempt at shaking Sean's hand, grabbing two fingers and leading the movement. 'I'll be in touch soon.'

'Bye, Owen!' Sean says, nearly shouting as Owen backs

away from us, moving briskly towards the exit, his long T-shirt swaying.

'We should speak to your mother,' I say, taking the brakes off Sean's chair and wheeling him over to Brigid, who is still in the corner, now gazing deep into her purse.

'Guess what?' Sean says.

'Is the show over?' Brigid says, looking up wearily.

'I am going to be interviewed for *Frieze*!'

'Sean!' Brigid says with a parent's love and sudden energy, lowering herself to his eye level, leaning in for a sloppy kiss. 'That's grand! I'm so proud of you. What a wonderful end to the evening. Have you had a lovely time?'

'We are going to the drinks party – remember?'

'Oh,' Brigid says, looking to me hopefully.

'I think it's next door,' I say. 'It will be over by midnight.'

Brigid takes an unsubtle look at her watch and manages a smile.

'Well, I guess it's a celebration. Where's your reporter man, then?'

'I think he is just leaving,' Sean says. 'You can still catch him, if you want.'

'No,' I interrupt. 'I think he was in a rush.'

'Ah well,' Brigid says. 'You'll have to make do with us for now, won't you?' She nudges me, slightly too hard. 'Your two favourite girls.'

'I have to go in a bit,' I say, thumbing the lighter in my purse.

'Oh,' Brigid says, wounded. 'Are you sure now? Won't you stay for the drinks?' Her eyes are pleading, weary and deep.

'I really have to go in a minute.'

'Of course,' she says, shaking her head, as though to clear

the thought. 'You go when you need to. Enjoy your time off. We'll be fine, won't we? It's just like we were never apart, isn't it? My own little Caravaggio. My little Michelangelo.'

'Yeah,' Sean says, not correcting her pronunciation of the Italian names.

'I am feeling a wee bit tired from the journey,' Brigid says, all her weight leant into Sean's chair. 'I may go ahead and find a seat next door, then, if they're open already.'

'That sounds sensible,' I say, moving round the chair to hug her, to send her away.

'Bless you, Janet,' Brigid says. The smell of her is strong, almost fermented. 'Bless you for what you do for him. He'd never be here without you. I hope you have a lovely long weekend.'

'Okay, thank you,' I say, trying not to breathe in.

'See you in a minute,' Sean says, all joy.

I don't envy Brigid's task tomorrow morning. Waking up a hungover Sean is a level of hell that should be reserved for only the most wicked. Sean's sleep is prescription grade even without the influence of alcohol. Sleep is supposedly vital to maintaining his health. But then everything is supposedly vital to maintaining his version of health.

It takes very little alcohol for Sean to become intolerable. Drunk Sean is even more indecipherable and a lot more boisterous. To his credit, Sean is usually very selective about making his voice heard, but drunk Sean has no such qualms.

It's rare for Sean to drink on a weeknight, meaning that in our time together so far, I've only had to deal with hungover Sean twice. I don't envy the weekend and night staff at the Mills Grand Estate. Hungover Sean can only be described as a beached mammal – born from the sea, under-evolved and unfit for land.

But tomorrow is a problem for Brigid.

'Why did you say that stuff about me being beautiful?' I say once Brigid has left the room.

Sean makes a shrugging movement and looks away, embarrassed.

'Do you think I'm beautiful?'

'Please,' Sean says into his chest, his voice monotone and clear. 'Please, do not.'

'Fine,' I say. 'I need a cigarette.'

'Can I have one?' Sean says, still bashful.

'Are you serious? So suddenly you're this cool in-demand artist who smokes?'

'I just want one. I will join you. Outside.'

'No – absolutely not. Brigid would smell it on you immediately. She'd know that I gave it to you.'

'It is fine. She will not know. I will not tell her.'

'You won't have to tell her. She'll smell it. She's feeling ill, not completely stupid.'

'I had one before, with Keith, remember?'

'Keith is a fucking idiot. Please never compare me to Keith again.'

'Please, Janet. I will buy one off you.'

'Are you doing this to wind me up?' I say, thumbing my lighter.

'I will pay you for one.'

'How much?'

'I have ten pounds in my wallet.'

'You're willing to pay me ten pounds for one cigarette?'

'Yes.'

'Okay fine,' I say. 'Who cares? Is your wallet in your blazer pocket?'

'Yes.'

'I'm not actually going to take it, you know.'

It's late. Outside, clouds are banked up in the distance, over the BT Tower, the City. There's a static in the air – a low hum from streetlights just out of view. The wind is cold and sharp. I huddle over, light up two cigarettes and hold one to Sean's lips. He drags deeply, almost suckling on the bud. It feels intimate. My fingers come away damp. His spit chilling on my skin. Sean is coughing.

'Do you need some water?' I ask.

'No. I am fine. Let me try again, please.'

The clouds are rolling in and a light rain begins to fall. Across the road, people stare at us from a bus stop, haloed under the scuffed fluorescent glow. I tell myself not to care. Sean stops coughing after his third drag. He continues to smoke in a shallow rhythm. It still takes him twice as long as me to finish the cigarette. But he does finish.

Of all his smells, shit lingers longest. I convince myself that others can smell it on me. I scrub under my nails, try to blow it out my nose. I imagine myself as a cartoon, wavy stink lines reeling from my head, defining me as poor or villainous.

It's my first day off in four months. Before leaving the exhibition, I drained his catheter bag and gave him his medication. I texted Brigid to warn that he would need changing, that he was starting to smell. I signed off by writing that I hoped she felt better soon.

I'm at home, in our basement. Alex is sprawled on the sofa, watching TV with his hands down his pants, scratching absent-mindedly.

'Seriously?' I say.

'Fuck off, Janet. Read your book.'

'Is this what a typical Friday working from home looks like?'

'I'm taking a break.'

'A break from scratching your arse instead?'

Alex uses his free hand to throw a pillow at me, missing wide to the right.

'I just think you've got a cheek, always telling me to grow up,' I say. 'Always saying that I need to make better choices.'

'How does me taking a break excuse you from taking responsibility for your future?'

'I'm trying to read,' I say, turning my attention back to the Ayn Rand novel that Jordan has lent me. So far, it could only be described as fucking terrible, but I'm seeing Jordan this evening, and it's been three weeks since I swapped him for my copy of Margaret Atwood's *The Edible Woman*. I had planned to use my days off to do some early Christmas shopping, but it's already past lunchtime and I've convinced myself that the West End is a level of suffering that not even I deserve.

I need to buy presents for Alex and Jordan, and probably Sean and Brigid. For my birthday, Brigid got me a candle, two bath bombs and a twenty-five-pound gift voucher for John Lewis. At the time, Sean had insisted these were joint gifts.

Brigid and Sean are scheduled to spend a long weekend catching up over his body, avoiding public transport, and generally spending time quietly indoors at the Mills Grand

Estate. I check my phone to see that Brigid has emailed to say she is feeling much, much better, and that she apologises for making me worried.

Sean's Twitter feed is a stream of retweeted pictures from the exhibition. Among these pictures, he's tweeted that an anonymous collector bought both his pieces. The tweet has forty-five likes and six replies, all sending their congratulations.

Among these notes of congratulations is a message from Sean's father. Sean's only regular contact with his father comes through Twitter. His dad seems to have an account exclusively for the purpose of following Sean and Galway United. He reliably likes all of Sean's posts, but rarely makes a comment. I doubt that Brigid is aware of this channel of contact between them.

Because Sean struggles with keyboards, he does most of his computing on a 12.9-inch iPad Pro using the Apple Pencil.

'How's the book?' Alex says, changing channels with an absent expression.

'Fine.'

'She was mental, though,' he says, not bothering to turn. 'Rand.'

'You shouldn't say mental.'

'She was evil, then. She's the one who all the neoliberals idolise. Paul Ryan justifies Social Darwinism because of her – it's called Objectivism, I think. Something about selfishness being a virtue. Putting yourself first in every situation. That's how the Republicans are getting away with denying health care to most of their country.'

'Have you read it?' I say, holding up the book.

'No. I'm just aware of it. They made a film of it a few years ago and it absolutely tanked.'

'So you're saying that you're not selfish?' I say, putting the book down to check my phone again.

'No, I'm definitely selfish, but not in the way Rand thinks of it. She thinks that people are totally incapable of doing an unselfish act. According to her, you buy and give presents at Christmas just to feel good about yourself. You donate blood for the kick of being a hero, within a socially acceptable framework. She doesn't believe in a sincere form of altruism. She'd argue that you're working as a carer, just because you're being paid to do it.'

'But that's true,' I say, scrolling through my inbox.

'Yeah, but—' Alex starts.

'There's no but,' I interrupt. 'I only care for him because I'm being paid to do it.'

'So you're saying you don't care about him. You don't have any emotional involvement.'

'I'm saying that if they stopped paying me, I wouldn't go back.'

'Sure,' Alex says, turning up the TV volume.

I'm very tempted to message Sean asking about my percentage of the art sales. I draft a message ending with a winking emoji, so he would know I'm only partly serious. I feel like if I took it to court, they'd award me at least fifty per cent of the money. They'd insist that all future listings of the work would name me as a co-creator. They'd recognise the fact that I'm the one who actually takes the photos, and isn't that where the real art happens? Isn't that where the value is created? Isn't that really what's on sale?

It occurs to me that I'm in possession of the memory card

containing most of our unedited work, and that I could easily delete every photo in moments, all the evidence of my labour, the evidence of my compliance. In a few minutes, I could write off months of our shared history. I roll the thought round my mouth like a sour candy, enjoying the sweet sting.

I can't think of an obvious candidate for Sean's anonymous buyer. I can't think of a good reason they'd want to remain anonymous. I can only think that they must have been encouraged by Suzanna.

Suzanna spent the whole evening treating Sean like her disabled prodigy. She spoke as though she'd been integral to the development of his portfolio, like she'd suffered alongside us in creating each composition. She pitched herself as the seamstress behind the complex tapestry of theory behind Sean's work, helping to tie all the frayed bits of pain and theory into a kinky, disturbing whole.

I feel hungry and bored and a little horny.

'You ready for lunch?' I say to Alex, now lying with a cushion over his eyes.

'You offering to make food?'

'If I make you lunch, can that count as your Christmas present?'

'No deal,' says Alex, removing the cushion. 'You're not getting away with giving me Super Noodles as a Christmas gift.'

'Foiled again.'

He's bound to a bed – grand, four-poster, mahogany. I'm standing over him, ashing my cigarette onto his face. He writhes, his skin almost translucent, veins perilously close to the surface, his moans muffled by a cloth gag. I put out the cigarette on his forehead, twisting the bud, only to find another in my hand immediately. I put out cigarettes all over his body, drawing a pattern of welts. He screams silently into the gag. I smell the sharp burn of singed hair.

When I wake up, it's dark in the flat. Alex is gone, and I'm alone.

Based on my Googling, Sean should be brain damaged. He should have learning disabilities and require strong prescription glasses. He should have no conception of post-structuralism or Roland Barthes. He shouldn't be able to fuss about how well ironed his T-shirt is. He should not be able to complain about eating pea purée for lunch twice in the same week.

I can clearly imagine a future for myself as Sean's biographer, telling the story beyond the art, following his long and accomplished career. I will be the expert called on to BBC News after he dies suddenly aged forty-six. I will quote from my well-received but average-selling book, much of which is focused on Brigid: what it must have been like for her to care for one tiny, struggling life while mourning the loss of another. I'll write about how touch-and-go those first few weeks were for Sean – the rush to get him baptised; the expense and spatial demands of all that medical equipment, flooding their tiny Yorkshire flat; the question of whether to bother inoculating. I'll write about the dangerous narratives that permeate through our culture, pinning the blame for a child's disabilities exclusively on mothers – I'll note how fathers are never part of that particular conversation. I will ask the reader to imagine Brigid's anxiety in tracking the markers of her child's development, the spectre of unfore-castable disability looming. I'll include colour plates at page eighty and page 180, captioning myself, stood meekly behind him as he receives another award, another grant, a suited white man with a hand on Sean's shoulder, taking credit. I'll be a consultant on the Hollywood adaptation of my book, his story. I'll help cast my own part, rejecting actresses on grounds of their lack of potential for malice, their accent, their too-perfect hair.

It's Friday night and I'm at Jordan's.

Jordan is preening in front of the bathroom mirror, shirtless and flexed. He's leaning in close, examining his pores.

'It's so much nicer in here without all the make-up,' he says. 'I like that you don't wear too much make-up.'

'Mhm,' I say, toothbrush in mouth, scrubbing away the taste of cigarettes for him. I lean round him to spit, holding my hair with one hand, the other clutching the brush, pressed against the small of his back.

'She had so much fucking make-up,' he says, almost to himself, probing at a small spot under his nose.

'I didn't know you got spots.'

'What do you mean? Everyone gets spots.'

'Here,' I say, reaching up to his face. 'Let me have a go.'

He leans into my hands, mistaking it for affection before realising what I am attempting to do. 'What the fuck are you doing?' he says, swatting me away as I pinch.

'Let me get it,' I say, eyeing him hungrily.

'That's disgusting, Janet. What's wrong with you?'

'I don't mind. I really don't. I do it all the time.'

'I said no,' Jordan says firmly, turning to look me in the eye, his expression stern. I can't help but smile. I tiptoe and give him a quick, precise kiss before he can pull away.

'Have you heard from them today, then?' Jordan says, pushing me backwards into the bedroom. 'Everything going okay?'

'She's been taking care of him for over two decades, Jordan. I think she can manage four days.'

'Okay then,' he says. 'I just know how precious you get when they do things wrong at that place. I thought his mum might be just as bad.'

'I'm not precious,' I say, more defensive than I intend to be. 'They're just not thorough enough, and I'm the one who has to tidy up behind them.'

'Sounds pretty precious to me.'

'You don't get it,' I say, my tone sharp enough to draw blood. I move round to my side of the bed, grabbing and opening *Atlas Shrugged* to cover my face.

'Just trying to take an interest,' Jordan says, moving next to me, softly squeezing one boob through my T-shirt. 'Did you get to the sexy bits in there yet?' he says, referring to the book.

'I can't imagine this book having sexy bits.'

'Oh, they're coming.'

'So far it's only railroads and a long speech.'

'What about your guy? Do you think he gets horny?' Jordan says, still fondling me. 'You know. The man.'

'Sean? Of course he gets horny. He's hard every other morning.'

'What!' Jordan says, high pitched, with a gossipy smile, 'You'd never mentioned that before!'

'Why would I?'

'Well, it's far more interesting than the artsy bullshit.'

'Fuck off, Jordan,' I say, pushing him gently.

'Do you ever touch it?' he says.

'I said *fuck off.*'

'Show me how you touch it,' he says, taking my wrist, steering me towards his crotch.

'Go get undressed,' I say, pointing towards the bathroom.

Once Jordan is out the room, I set aside the book, get onto the floor and force myself through three sets of sit-ups. I focus on counting the reps, suppressing the image of Sean's hard dick. I crunch the image tighter and tighter, straining up, tightening, like a knot, tightening with each push. I'm back in bed before Jordan has finished brushing his teeth.

Jordan emerges from the bathroom in just his socks. They seem to affirm his nakedness.

'You're ridiculous,' I say.

'Do you need to pee?'

'Why would I need to pee?'

'Well, last week you had to stop halfway through to pee.'

'Oh,' I say, remembering my lie. 'No, I'm fine today.'

For that glorious honeymoon period in the summer, fucking Jordan felt like I'd won the lottery. Every time was fresh. It was as though we were inventing something new. We were fucking in unprecedented, unimaginable ways. I was totally at peace with being his rebound. I didn't imagine that come December, we'd still be seeing each other.

'So do you like my T-shirt?' I say, pushing out my chest hopefully.

'I like what's under the T-shirt.'

'Is there any point in me making an effort for you?'

'Whatever makes you feel good about yourself, Janet.'

'You only ever call me Janet. I feel like I should have earned a pet name or something. It feels odd to hear you call me Janet all the time.'

'Are you serious right now?' Jordan says, joining me in his bed, my legs yielding as he runs a hand up the inside of my thigh.

'It just feels very formal.'

'Does this feel formal?' he says, pulling aside my underwear and slipping one finger inside me.

'Feels stupid and medical,' I say, twisting myself away from his hand.

'Come back here,' he says playfully, wrestling me onto my knees, facing the wall.

'Call me "Baby" or something. Even "Bitch".'

'Okay Bitch Baby,' Jordan says, rolling on a condom. 'Be quiet now, Bitch Baby.'

'I don't like you,' I say as he pushes into me.

'I like you a lot,' he says, quickly picking up rhythm, reaching to pull off my T-shirt.

Facing the wall, I close my eyes and think of those videos of him. Jordan at twenty-two and twenty-three, in peak physical condition, the precision of his movements, the effortlessness of his tumbles and leaps. I play a montage of his body, comfortable with the dissonance between that idealised form and the man behind me.

Jordan thrusts with athletic determination. He breathes so heavily – I feel his breath, warm and humid on my back. It's as though he's pushing through the wall, pushing through a sprint. *Gentle*, I say inside my head, willing it to him through brainwaves and wincing. I brace my hands on the wall above the bed, the wet of my palms marking the paint. I feel crampy and a little cold.

'Just like that,' he says, changing speed, leaning over me, holding me by the hips, clutching me like a prize catch, a fish, sprawling for water.

'Careful,' I say as he slips out, reaching back to direct him to the correct place.

'No, get on top,' he says. 'I'm nearly there.'

I refrain from comment and readjust. Straddling him, I lean forward, my hair drags over his face. He spits out the strands that catch in his mouth. He is an animal in pain, gnawing the air with wild little cries, a pitch I only hear when he's inside me. He bucks as I push down into him, now finding a comfortable rhythm.

His eyes are closed, his chin straining up and away, to whatever image he's focusing on. He finishes in me with a juddering, flinching thrust, squeezing my ass so hard I'm sure it will be bruised tomorrow.

'Think you can finish?' he asks.

'Not sure,' I say, not even close.

'I'll go clean up,' he says.

On the wall, my handprints have faded to just the tips. I clean myself and put my underwear back on and plug in my phone to charge. My abs are a little tender.

'That was good,' Jordan says, climbing back in bed.

'Mhmm.'

'Not in the mood to talk?'

'Just sleepy.'

'Okay. I just don't want you to think of me as the guy who you fuck, but never speak to.'

'I don't feel like that.'

'Okay. Good. I just wanted you to know that you can ask me things.'

'What was it like to get married?' I say, noting his expression shift immediately. 'You just said I could ask things!'

'I don't know,' Jordan says, already a little petulant, in spite of his build-up. 'Do you mean the day, or the marriage itself?'

'The day, I guess.'

'The day didn't feel much like it was about us.'

'What?'

'Well, I didn't really contribute too much to the planning, so I didn't really feel any ownership over it. My input was asking a question a year before. Everything just seemed to play itself out from there. But it certainly never felt like it was the happiest day of my life or anything.'

'Did you ever suspect she was gay?'

'What's that got to do with the wedding?'

'Never mind,' I say, shifting away from him.

'I just can't believe you'd ask me that. Of course I didn't suspect she was gay.'

'I need to sleep now,' I say.

'Typical,' Jordan mutters, fanning out his legs like a rooting plant.

'Excuse me?'

'Didn't you just say that you needed to sleep?'

I ball myself to the edge of the bed, away from the damp sex patch, away from his sighing. I think about Brigid. I think about summer. I think about sandy beaches, bonfires, broken limbs.

*

It is Sunday morning under my own duvet. So far, I've found Florence's Facebook and LinkedIn profiles. She's still dumpy – thick-rimmed glasses and a stodgy Home Counties haircut. There's a lack of variety to her publicly viewable profile pictures – all front facing, pursed lips, sections of her head cropped out of frame. I examine the visible parts of her arms for evidence of self-harm. The only cover photo I have access to is of a sad-looking whippet, lying on what must be a pub floor.

LinkedIn says she's been working as a sales support administrator for the past three years at a small party supplies company. I have no recollection of seeing Florence at any parties.

I am restraining myself from messaging Jordan links to my findings. He's spending the next five days working as a judge at a County level gymnastics competition. Apparently, these events are held around six times a year. Jordan's mentioned something about being a Level 5 judge, meaning he's obliged to attend a certain number of regional and national competitions before they will extend his licence to work with older age groups. He says that there's more prestige to working with kids in the sixteen-plus category, and you can earn marginally more, but the largest volume of work will always be tied to the under-twelves, before the kids hit puberty, develop self-awareness and realise they're graceless lumps.

Shortly before his knee injury, Jordan signed some pretty lucrative sponsorship and endorsement contracts. They had no option but to keep paying him through the recovery, while he tested out his new body. Jordan is nine years older than me. His home is the product of those deals, long since expired. He knows he'll never earn close to the same money again. Aside from an occasional bit of TV and web commentary, he's now a full-time coach.

I consider calling up Florence's company. I could make an anonymous complaint about the terrible sales support I received when ordering my very important party supplies. Or I could put in an actual order – I want custom-made bunting, spelling out FLORENCE IS A FAT BITCH.

Over dinner last night, Alex brushed off my concern about where she got my email address. He claimed I was just obsessing over the email to avoid dealing with what she said and its implications. Alex mentioned all the contact information he has access to from his work database of CVs.

Soon after Jordan and I matched and started dating, I conducted a comprehensive stalking of his wife. I had a notebook full of tidbits and a desktop folder full of tagged photos – Beatrice's full biography. I probably learned enough about her to commit credit-card fraud – her maiden name, her birthday, her first pet. With a wig and the right angle, I could build a life as her double.

Though Beatrice is the same age as Jordan, in my mind, she seems so much older. In nearly all the publicly accessible photos of her, she's professional, presentable. She wears heels and lipstick. Somehow, she's found a way of appearing friendly without smiling.

It's difficult to imagine an older Jordan. As an athlete, he may be past his peak, but it seems impossible that Jordan could ever lose his body. He's Olympian – white marble, carved to last. In my mind, Jordan at forty still has perfect posture and perfect abs and a perfect dick. I can clearly

picture him wearing a duffel jacket, waiting on a train plat-
form, impatiently tapping one foot, towering over the other
commuters, a broadsheet newspaper creasing in his massive
hand. I imagine myself waiting for him to come home, baking
something moderately healthy, fussing over the timings. We
do not have children in this future. Instead, we have art on
every wall, and staircases to prevent the possibility of visits
from Sean.

The more time I spend in this fantasy, the more deeply
conflicted I feel about how quotidian it is. This fantasy is only
six years in the future. Six years in the past, teenage Janet
was fully committed to her genius narrative. She was going to
save the world. She was never going to settle down. She was
going to fight for the little guy, make the art that no one else
dared to, fuck the guys that her parents warned her about.

I consider actually stalking Florence. I could wait outside her office, follow her home, learn her routine, get a
proper gauge on how badly I've damaged her. Or I could
just stand across the street, wait for her to spot me, wait for
her to freak out and panic and run into oncoming traffic.
Google Maps suggests that it would take me two and a half
hours on public transport to get to her office. This doesn't
seem worth it.

I reread her email. I consider deleting it. I consider printing
and framing it. I shut my laptop and lie back down, pulling
the duvet over and around me until everything is safe and
still. Despite my four days off work, I feel incredibly drained.
It occurs to me that all the evil in the world is probably in
part caused by fatigue. All the worst parts of me are born of
exhaustion.

'Alex,' I half-shout, banging my fist on our shared bedroom wall.

'What?' he shouts, muffled.

'Could you make me tea?'

'I'm watching *The Simpsons*. And it's your turn,' he says, annoyed.

'Please?' I say. 'Pretty, pretty please, Alex? Just one time for your little sister? For your evil little sister?'

'Oh my God, fuck you so much,' he says. I hear him moving about, the shuffle of slippers, his door slamming.

'Thank yooooou,' I shout over the sound of the kettle being filled.

On Sundays, Sean is usually chaperoned to mass by Keith from the Mills Grand Estate. There's a church just a few streets away, so they don't bother with a cab. Today Brigid is taking him. It will be her first time in his new parish. I am invited, of course, should I feel in the mood for a sudden conversion. I have been to the church once before, one Sunday when Keith was sick, and Sean insisted. Say 'church', and I'll think of tall marble columns and golden frescoes. I'll think of flying buttresses and stained glass, reliquaries and organs. St John's has none of that. St John's has fraying carpets and a crackly speaker system. It has a police station next door, sirens blaring on and off at regular intervals.

I explained my relationship with Catholicism and cere- mony in general at my first interview with Brigid and Sean. After we finished discussing art, Brigid asked some generic questions about my faith and growing up above a morgue, but she hasn't challenged me on anything religious since. I'm sure that she'd prefer me to be Catholic, but she does a reasonably good job of pretending not to be bothered.

Tomorrow, Brigid will be gone, and we'll be back in the studio. Nothing will have changed. My alarm is already set for 6 a.m.

'Which episode?' I say, as Alex enters the room, putting a mug down on my bedside table.

'I think you mean, "Thank you, wonderful brother."'

'Thank you,' I say, grabbing the mug, blowing a cooling ripple over the surface, spinning the hard-water scum to the edge.

'Itchy and Scratchy Land,' Alex says, placing his laptop between us on my bed.

'*Where nothing could possib-lie go wrong,*' I say with a smile.

'*That's the first thing that's ever gone wrong,*' he says, doing a good impression.

'Could you help me write a reply to the therapist lady today?'

'I thought you decided to ignore it.'

'I keep changing my mind,' I say, sipping the tea. 'I don't know what to do.'

'Maybe just call her instead. I don't have time to help you today.'

'Because you're *so* busy.'

'Yeah, what are your fucking plans? You've spent your whole time off just bumming about the house or at your boyfriend's. You haven't even cleaned. You promised you'd clean.'

'I was thinking of going to the National Gallery, actually,' I say. 'You can come if you want.'

'I don't know,' Alex says, picking his laptop back up. 'All of those Renaissance artists just sound like Premier League

Footballers to me. And I told you, I'm busy. I have to be on Skype later with Isabel. New York has a five-hour time difference.'

'We never hang out any more,' I say as he leaves the room.

'We never did. That would be creepy. You owe me two teas. And it stinks like cigarettes in your room again. Open the fucking window if you're going to smoke.'

'It's freezing outside,' I shout, grabbing my laptop back off the floor, opening the screen up to Florence's profile, her big stupid face staring at me.

I finish the tea and draft a few attempts at a reply. I want to sound neutral. I want to acknowledge the hurt, without accepting the blame. I want to make it absolutely clear that I wish to receive no further communication from them. I feel like that must be something they are supposed to respect.

I can hear Alex in the shower, singing to himself.

I pace the room, my laptop in hand, outstretched like a decree. I'm reading my reply aloud, feeling out the words on my tongue, my mouth moving through the shapes of an apology. It feels unnatural. Ridiculous.

I open the window and light a cigarette. The moss on the sill is frosted over and the air is sharp on my lips. Within a few drags, I've convinced myself that it's much too cold to consider leaving the flat. The responsible thing to do is to stay indoors and make it through the day.

'Shower's free,' calls Alex.

'Is that your idea of a subtle hint?'

'You stink, Janet.'

'Thanks,' I say.

*

In my biography, Sean's father will be a footnote.

Peter Keily abandoned his family when Sean was ten months old. Brigid heard rumours he had moved to Spain. She heard he had found someone else, that he was doing well.

Peter was Brigid's first and her only. She'd known him since she knew herself. He was the best friend of her brother, the brother who went on to save himself through God, the brother who married them and took Peter's side in arguments for years after, who begged her to find forgiveness, who begged on Sean's behalf.

Peter drank, but back then she did too. Drinking was a part of their love. He accused her of being a martyr, both before and after their son. There was no affection in this name. Peter thought that his wife was too ready to fall on her sword, too ready to suffer needlessly. When it became clear that Sean would live, he knew that Brigid would sacrifice herself to make sure that he lived well. He saw that Sean would live better than them both.

Brigid stopped drinking and Peter didn't. Brigid went to the doctor's and Peter didn't. Brigid fought when he wouldn't and stayed when he left.

Brigid brokered Peter's contact with her son. She kept him informed of the essentials: medical updates, major surgeries. She permitted short phone calls once Sean could speak. She accepted presents and some cash for birthdays and Christmas.

Peter's parents made an effort. They said no one was to blame, that it was hard on everyone. They mentioned to Brigid how Peter carried a photo of Sean with him everywhere, though they didn't mention which version of Sean, or who had provided the photo.

After the trial, once the money was awarded, Brigid knew to expect Peter. She warned me that he would be looking for a way back into Sean's life. She just didn't know when, or how.

It's a week since the exhibition and we're back in routine.

Once a month, I take Sean to a private gym in Kensington for hydrotherapy. In the morning, I clean him thoroughly, dress him in a disposable swim pad and toggled shorts. The supposed benefits of Aqua Therapy are mostly cardiovascular. In warm water, Sean will experience improved flexibility, improved circulation and muscle relaxation. It's Sean's main opportunity to ambulate freely, to extend himself, to experience how legs work. Movement in water provides ten times the amount of resistance as on land, but at ten per cent of the body weight. All the operations Sean suffered through as a child and in his teens were to make this level of movement possible.

In order to support him, I was required to do a proper qualification in Aquatic Therapy. The full training course took fifteen hours. I did the first session back in May without Sean. That took three hours, which frankly seemed plenty. I had not built up my current levels of fitness, so after the first thirty minutes, it was an ordeal. We worked with dummies similar to the ones used for CPR training. Every session after that involved variations on the same theme, but with our human partners. There's not a lot of nuance to helping Sean move in water, just a lot of effort. Despite the smoking, my lung capacity has always been reasonably good, but even now, an hour in the pool is still pretty wearing.

I undress Sean in a large, private disabled changing room and leave for the women's with my own bag.

'You going to be okay on your own for a second?'

'Go. I am fine,' he says, topless in his chair.

'I will leave the door unlocked.'

'Just go,' Sean says, petulant, self-conscious.

I change into a dismally plain one-piece with a matching swim cap. My boobs are flat and still. I'm wearing no make-up and I feel like the most boring girl in London.

I'm reasonably convinced that once a month is not regular enough for Sean to gain any real benefit from this form of therapy. I'm reasonably convinced that the taxi to and from the spa offsets nearly all the positive relaxation Sean is supposed to experience.

The pool is small and kidney shaped, deep at one end, rising in a slope. There's a Jacuzzi bubbling beside us. This is someone's idea of luxury. New Age music plays through hidden speakers, swooping and ambient, more dignified than we deserve.

Facing him, I lift Sean out of his chair, heavy as penance, shuffling backwards, straining not to drop him as I lower him onto the edge of the pool, his curled feet already dipping into the water.

We pay to rent the spa for an hour, just to ourselves. The Mills Grand Estate have brokered some kind of special discount. I suspect that the gym would prefer their other customers not to see us. I imagine we would contaminate their relaxation. A lifeguard watches me with a weak smile, a Silver Medal look, all soft-eyed pity and kindness. She doesn't look even remotely strong enough to drag a lifeless Sean out the water.

Sean raises his arms like surrender and I pull armbands

down to his biceps, then a travel cushion round his neck.

'Do not let my head go under this time,' he says, moving his head uncomfortably.

'Okay,' I say.

'I am serious.'

'I get it. You ready?'

'Yes,' Sean says, tipping forwards as I release him to slide into the water.

'Ready?' I say, taking his hands. He squeezes his eyes closed and breathes in dramatically, puffing out his cheeks. I pull him into the water with one hard tug – he falls into me heavily, beating his arms against the surface, splashing wildly, his body upright, matching my own height, his feet clambering for purchase, for the floor.

'Easy, easy,' I say. 'I've got you.'

'My head went under,' he says, spitting, spraying me with his words.

'No it didn't.'

'It felt like it went under.'

'I promise you it didn't.'

'It is warm today,' he says, starting to relax. 'It is nice.'

I move behind him, lock my forearms under his pits and puppet him through the water in a graceless stumble, his legs dragging behind us like an anchor, his toes skimming the floor. This is our own stuttered waltz, slowly shifting and sliding, skirting the shallow end, his body pressed into mine, intimate before God. I feel the irregular thump of his heart, swollen by the hydrostatic pressure. I suppress the thought of Sean peeing on me, though it will definitely happen. Is definitely happening.

Sean has deliberately chosen not to consult any of his doctors about his art, about the impact of the bindings on his body. He fears the limits they would almost certainly impose on what he can or should do. Most of the medical professionals in Sean's life have no interaction with each other, all giving independent, disparate and occasionally conflicting advice that we've assimilated into a programme of care and medication. Moving to London took Brigid a year of planning and research. She wanted the best for him. Instead, she got me.

There are large bruises on Sean's thighs and arms from our last session in the studio. They look like something spilled, something toxic. I am sure the lifeguard has noticed.

'Those hurt?' I say from behind him, motioning with my chin.

'A bit. During the massage. I am okay now,' he says, struggling against me.

'We don't need to go so tight next time. If it hurts that much, you need to tell me.'

'Mm,' he says, focusing on moving.

As part of his fitness regime, Jordan still swims twice a week. Tuesday and Thursday evenings, six until eight. There are old pictures of him on Facebook doing one-arm handstands by the side of a pool, toes pointed like habit. Jordan has never invited me to join him in any of his workouts.

Moving to the deep end, I hold Sean's head in my palm and ease him upwards, off the floor, balancing him on his back, the water lapping his hair like a baptism. I stretch round to slide two more strategically positioned child-size armbands over his ankles, raising his legs up to the surface.

I hold him by the shoulders and move him back and forth like a windscreen wiper, his head pressed against my chest, his legs dragging a wake through the surface, arms winged out, wrists curled just above the water. His eyes are softly closed, his breathing slow and nasal. I guide him through eight sets of exercises, counting down from ten in my most reassuring voice as he jerks his legs and knees in his own interpretation of kicking.

'It is in my eyes,' Sean says, flailing.

'I keep saying you need goggles.'

'I do not like them.'

'Then stop complaining.'

To wind down, we repeat our morning stretches, twisting and extending his body in an imitation of health and mobility. Under the surface, both our bodies look distorted – swollen and long.

Getting him out is by far the biggest challenge. The lifeguard watches on as I ease him to the shallow end, until he's sitting, leaning back against the rim, still submerged from the waist down. I move his chair to the edge of the pool and drape a towel over his seat cushion, locking the brakes. I stand in the water, bending my knees, lock my arms back under his, and on the count of three, we strain upright, stepping over the lip of the pool, his legs dragging under me, the weight of gravity all too real again.

'How was that?' I say, breathless, Sean back in his chair.

'Fine,' he says. 'Thank you.'

'We've earned our lunch today,' I say, bunching and squeezing my hair, turning away to hide my nipples, now visible through the costume.

When we are home, I will have to shower him. I will have to feed him, and medicate him, and type up his essay. I'll have to do this again next month, and then the month after. Beneath all the abusive dreams and abstract fantasies about quitting, I am at peace with this future.

Owen from *Frieze* started following Sean on Twitter shortly after the exhibition. They've been exchanging direct messages. Today, without my input, they've arranged for Owen to come by the studio to do the interview while he watches us at work.

Owen's bio on Twitter describes him as a 'writer, finder and keeper'. His profile picture is of him with his arms tight by his sides, stood in front of *Las Meninas* by Velázquez with a neutral expression.

'I don't want him in the way,' I say, pulling a T-shirt over Sean's head. 'I need to get you home by five. I'm not letting you miss dinner again.'

'He is just going to watch and ask me questions.'

'Just this one time? Or is this going to be a regular thing now?'

'I do not know.'

'So what do we need today? What have you got planned?'

'I want to do that pose we discussed. The banana position. The one from the interrogations.'

Sean is referring to a popular torture technique in Israel, where the victim is laid over the length of a stool on their back, with their wrists and ankles bound together under the seat. When the victim can no longer keep their back straight, their head will drop and they curl their body into a painful bow, stretching their internal organs. In actual torture, water is poured on the victim's face to keep them alert. The technique is used in conjunction with sleep deprivation and beatings.

'Do you want handcuffs or zip-ties or rope or what?'

'Cuffs, I think. And the cloth, for a blindfold.'

'Travelling light is fine with me,' I say, working his shoe onto his foot. 'Don't you think we should be doing something more impressive for him?'

'He is already impressed. He said so.'

'You know what I mean. I would have thought this was the perfect chance to do those big bindings.'

'I think he just wants to talk. I think he is going to use some of the finished pictures.'

'Whatever you like,' I say, packing the yoga mat and Vaseline. 'As long as he's not getting in the way.'

'We need to go,' Sean says. 'We do not need the mat for this one.'

'I'll bring it just in case. If you rush me, I'm going to forget something. Is that what you want? Owen can wait five minutes. He's a big boy. He'll understand.'

'Suzanna is coming too.'

'And when were you going to tell me?'

'I forgot.'

'How well do they know each other?' I say.

'I do not know.'

'You don't know much today, do you?'

I take ten minutes to tidy up the flat and pack our kit. The bin in Sean's flat needs taking out almost daily. It's nearly impossible to be environmentally responsible with cerebral palsy. Sean's body creates an inordinate amount of waste, none of which is recyclable. A lifetime of nappies and pads and straws and blister packs, all going to landfill.

I help myself to a crisp twenty-pound note from the supply, knowing the cab will only cost ten. An increasingly agitated Sean scrolls through his iPad, waiting for me to finish, sighing aggressively.

We're running twenty minutes late by the time we leave his flat. The lift arrives with a self-congratulatory ping.

'Do you think Owen is gay?' I say, wheeling him into the lift.

'Please do not ask him that,' Sean says.

'He didn't message me. I gave him my number.'

In the mirrored wall, I see Sean pull an annoyed expression. 'We need to go,' he says, jabbing at the button himself.

My hair looks windswept, angled in ten directions. I brush with my hands, unsure whether I've washed them since changing him.

Outside, there's a woman being sick, one hand holding the railing, the other in her hair. She is hunched slightly, gagging delicately into her feet. You could mistake it for cowering. She is trying to be discreet. There's no one around to help. I load Sean into the taxi, telling myself that she's probably just pregnant. Nothing more sinister. As I close the taxi door, she looks up with the expression of a startled animal and begins to move away.

When we arrive at the college, Owen is waiting for us in the lobby, wearing what looks to be a woman's raincoat, an SLR camera hung round his neck like oversized jewellery. This could be his natural habitat. He looks perfectly at home among the students.

'Hi, Owen!' Sean says, almost shouting.

'Good to see you, dude,' Owen says, keeping his distance. 'How have you been?'

'Sorry we're late,' I say, touching my hair.

'Oh, no problem. That's totally cool. Thanks for having me. This should be great. Congratulations again on selling those pieces. That's a huge deal, dude. That kind of thing gets noticed.'

'Do you know who bought them?' I say, trying to make eye contact as we move as a group towards the lifts.

'No idea. It kind of doesn't matter. From what I was told, it was just Sean's work and two others that got sold.'

'We haven't received the money yet,' I say. 'I mean, he hasn't been paid for them.'

'Yeah, I don't know about that. They can be a little funny about it. I'm sure you'll get it eventually.'

Our usual studio space is already occupied, forcing us into a slightly smaller room.

'Where do you want me?' Owen says, pressed up to the wall, preparing his camera.

'Anywhere,' Sean says.

'Anywhere,' I translate.

I unpack our bags, borrowing a broom to dust the floor. I set up the stool and position the lights and reflector and flash heads. While I work, Owen takes pictures of me and speaks to Sean in a slow, calm voice that could easily be mistaken for the tone of a patronising twat.

'Janet, could you let Suzanna know where we are?' Sean says.

'I don't have her number. Do you have Suzanna's number, Owen?'

'Um, I think so,' he says, getting out his phone.

'You didn't text me to arrange this,' I say.

'Yeah, I think I lost your number or saved it wrong or something,' Owen says, looking away.

'I saved it for you.'

'Oh right,' Owen says, laughing nervously. 'I'll call Suzanna, then.'

Owen steps out of the room while I unstrap Sean from his chair, removing his T-shirt and shoes and socks.

'Ready?'

'Bit cold.'

'You'll warm up under the lights.'

'Should we wait for him?' Sean says, looking to the door.

'We're so far behind. We need to get started.'

Loud drum and bass music thumps from the studio next door. Some students pass our open door, popping their heads in curiously, then quickly looking away.

By the time Owen returns with Suzanna, I have Sean hung over the stool, his head propped up for now by his seat cushion, his Adam's apple protruding sharply.

'We got a bit lost,' Owen laughs, not apologising.

'Hi, Suzanna,' Sean says, spit careering from his mouth, pooling on the studio floor.

'Sean, my love, you look wonderful. This all looks wonderful,' she says, making a royal sweeping gesture. 'This is for you. My own little congratulations.'

Suzanna approaches with a bottle of champagne, initially extending the bottle towards Sean, before thinking better of it, and handing it to me.

'Thank you,' Sean says, his feet twitching.

'Aren't you just terribly uncomfortable on that horrid little thing?'

'Yes,' Sean says. 'It is my method.'

'He says it's his method,' I say, adjusting his feet, rubbing Vaseline into his ankles, up his calves.

'Of course,' Suzanna says, nodding at me, purring. 'You're so strong, Sean. I must find you that Sontag book we were discussing. I know you'll find it useful.'

'Okay,' says Sean, shifting his weight, nearly tipping off the stool.

Owen has his notebook out; he looks down over the top of his glasses with a productive expression, moving his pen over the page, eyes scanning back and forth between Sean and his pad.

'And how are you?' Suzanna says to me, pausing to remember my name. 'Janet – how are you? Our torturer in chief. What a lot of work it is for you.'

'I'm fine, thanks. Nothing too complicated today. Just a bit of light interrogation.'

'Is there anything you'll need?' Suzanna says, clearly looking to excuse herself.

'Actually, we could do with some rim lighting if you could get your hands on some,' I say, ballasting the stool from behind with a big speaker.

'I wouldn't know where to begin with that!' Suzanna laughs haughtily, backing towards the door. 'I'm sure someone will be able to help you though. We're a lovely bunch here. You can quote me on that, Owen.'

'Sure,' I say.

'Bye, Suzanna!' Sean says, raising one arm in a stiff wave.

I check my phone – it's already half past three. I can't forget to do his medication at four.

'He's been really looking forward to this,' I say to Owen. 'If you want to ask your questions, I'll help out with what he's saying.'

'Yeah,' Sean says, smiling toothily, trying to raise his head from the cushion.

'Right – yeah,' Owen says, flicking back through pages in his pad.

'How long have you known Suzanna?' I say, fetching the handcuffs from our bag.

'God, maybe six, seven years? It feels like she's been around forever. She seems to know everyone in the scene. And everyone in London knows her.'

'Right,' I say, locking Sean's left wrist to his right foot under the stool, fastening the clasp to the second tightest notch. 'And how long have you been working for *Frieze*?'

'I think it's been two years now,' he says, taking a photo of Sean from the front as I strap his other limbs together.

'Sorry,' I say. 'My brother's a recruiter, I hear him interviewing people all the time when he works from home. I'll stop asking things and let you get started.'

'No problem. Do you mind if I record?' he says, holding up his phone to show an app that seems to already be running.

'That is okay,' Sean says.

'Ready for me to remove this?' I say to Sean, gripping the cushion under his head.

'Can I have some water first?'

'Owen,' I say, holding Sean in position by the hip. 'Would

you mind helping Sean just drink some water? The straws are in his bag, over there, on his chair.'

'Would that be okay with you?' Owen says in the direction of Sean.

'It's fine with him,' I answer, gesturing him over to the chair.

'You were right,' Sean says to me. 'I am hot now.'

'Told you,' I say, as Owen crouches down beside Sean, bottle in hand, guiding the straw into his mouth, being careful not to touch his lips with his own fingers.

'Thank you,' Sean says once satisfied.

'No problem, dude.'

I tie the blindfold tight around Sean's eyes. Owen props his phone up against the studio wall and stands behind me with his notepad.

'So, you're going to be in our *Questionnaire* series,' he says. 'We ask everyone the same questions. Kind of like *Inside the Actor's Studio*, you know? It's a format. We find that shorter answers work well, so don't worry too much about the detail. Just give me the first answer you think of.'

'Great,' Sean says.

'Hold on,' I say. 'Wouldn't it make sense to ask Sean some questions that are specific to him? About his life and his situation? Surely it's not every day that you get to meet an artist like Sean?'

'Well,' Owen says, nervously.

'He's got a unique perspective. He's going through the world as both prominent and invisible. He's creating art that would be impossible for nearly anyone else to suffer through. Why would you want to stick with a list of generic questions?'

'Janet, please,' Sean says from under the blindfold.

'The answers can be pretty revealing,' Owen says. 'It's a matter of interpreting the question.'

'Whatever,' I say.

I pull the cushion from under Sean's head and his body bends taut over the stool. A small sound leaks from him, sending a shiver through me.

'What was the first piece of art that really mattered to you?' Owen says, oblivious.

'I think it was the Venus De Milo,' Sean replies, his voice hoarse and strained. 'She is this ideal of classical beauty, but we only know her as this disfigured object. I do not think anyone would know her if she had her arms.'

'I'd never considered that,' Owen says as I finish interpreting. He is scribbling fiercely, avoiding my eye.

'There is this version Magritte did,' Sean says. 'Where he painted red onto her stumps – he made her look amputated.'

I prepare the camera and take a dozen exposures, translating at the same time. I've captured Sean mid-sentence, his mouth hung open in a wide gasp. I bring the pictures over to Sean for consultation, squat beside him and pull up the blindfold, holding the camera screen straight above his face. He squints in the light, bunching his eyes into slits.

'Different angle,' he says to me as I scroll through, gesturing with his nose towards the far side of the studio.

'If you could live with only one piece of art, what would it be?' Owen says.

'My friend Ashley is sending me one of her pieces. She is from Canada. She makes grids with her wheelchair.'

'Want me to explain?' I say, aiming the camera.

'No, I can send him the photos of her work later.'

'What have I missed?' Owen says, his pen poised in midair.

'Sean's going to send you work by his friend Ashley. He says she's his favourite living artist.'

'Oh, right.' He flips back to his list of questions. 'What do you wish you knew?' he asks in a profound voice.

Sean takes a while to think, adjusting himself a little. 'What jumping feels like,' he eventually replies.

I take another dozen photos and skip back to his side, slightly knocking the lighting.

'Careful,' Sean says, tensing up. The drum and bass music has switched to London grime, still equally loud.

'Should I go ask them to turn that down?' I say to Sean.

'Leave it. Do not make an issue.'

'What should change?' Owen says from a distance, raising his own camera again to capture our discussion.

'More ramps,' Sean says loudly.

My phone alarm is going off – it's time for Sean's medication.

'He said more ramps.'

'I got that one,' Owen says proudly. 'Is something wrong?'

'It's just my alarm. He needs to take his meds. Four times a day, every single day.'

'What are they for?'

'For keeping him alive,' I say, crouched by Sean's wheelchair, popping tablets out of blister packs.

'Oh, no, I meant what are each of them for.'

'We probably don't have time today to go through all of them. Unless you want to stick it in your interview?'

'Right,' Owen says.

I'm sure I'd have bullied Owen in school. I'd have started simple and trained him up. Being a victim is a learned behaviour. Once formed, habits are hard to break. I'd find his weak point, something other than his stupid glasses, his stupid notepad. Everyone has a weak point.

I feed Sean the pills, holding up his head like a blessing. We adjust his pose a few times, easing the weight on his back, taking another thirty or forty photos – plenty to work with. Owen continues to stumble through his questions.

'Last one,' Owen says. 'What is art for?'

'Making the ugly palatable.'

Before he leaves, Owen tells us the article will probably be published on the *Frieze* website before Christmas. He explains that he doesn't get final say about what makes it into the actual magazine. He mentions that Sean will need to write himself a one-paragraph biography to go under the article.

'Just a little something about you and anything you've got coming up,' he says.

'Everything is coming up,' Sean says. 'This is just the beginning.'

It's nearly eight by the time I get home. Alex has messaged to say he's got news. I've stopped off at Tesco to buy us frozen pizzas and ice cream, expecting a reason to celebrate.

I find Alex spread across the couch, legs up, laptop balanced on his chest. I can see the top of his head over the screen.

'What's the news?' I say, shedding clothes. 'Did you get someone to look at the drip in the bathroom?'

'No, nothing like that. I'm just going to be moving out before Christmas.'

He says it casually, without breaking gaze from his laptop.

'What?' I say.

'I just said I'm going to be moving before Christmas.'

'Just?'

'Yeah, just.'

'We're leaving the flat?'

'Well, I am,' he says, now stood, heading to the kitchen. 'I'm going to New York to be with Isabel. I'm working my notice and sorting the visa. We're going to spend Christmas with her family.'

'Fuck, Alex,' I say.

'I know, right,' he calls happily from the kitchen.

'No, I mean fuck you. Why am I only learning about this now? Who even is this girl?'

I find him taking a beer out the fridge. The knives are annoyingly out of reach from where I'm standing. I'm breathing very deliberately to stop myself from crying.

'What do you mean? I've been speaking about her for literally months. You've heard us Skyping every evening.'

'Yeah, but I didn't realise it was this fucking serious!'

'Well, then it's your fault for not listening.'

'But this isn't something you can just do. People don't just leave for another country. Especially not at Christmas – you're supposed to spend Christmas with your own fucking family.'

'I spoke to Mum and we thought that this would be good timing. You finally seem stable in London. You were only meant to be living with me for six months anyway, Janet. It's been nine.'

'Eight,' I say, biting my lip.

'Right,' he says, 'eight, nine, whatever. I can probably cover another two months' rent for you after I go.'

'So what am I supposed to do now?'

'You don't have to do anything yet! Jesus. Aren't you going to at least ask me about her? I keep mentioning this girl, but you've never once bothered asking about her. I think you'd really get on.'

'I don't give a fuck if we'd get on, Alex,' I say, rushing to my room. I try slamming my door, but it bounces softly back off the frame. I'm still holding the pizzas and ice cream, now thawing, dripping onto the carpet.

I'm stood with my back to the door, waiting for Alex to apologise, surveying the room I'm going to have to leave behind. Aside from the obvious hassle of moving, I can't afford London rent without Alex's support. There's no one I want to live with. Chloe would never have me anyway. I'm not even sure I'd want to live here on my own.

It's been three minutes. I'm now pretty sure I'm not going to receive an apology. I dump the food in the kitchen and rush to the bathroom, splash water on my face, and try to look like I've been crying.

'Well?' I say to him. He's now back on the couch, sipping his beer.

'You want some?' he says, holding up the beer.

'You're supposed to be apologising. Can't you see I'm upset?'

'You're not upset, Janet.'

'So now you know how I feel?'

'You're not upset, you're annoyed. You're thinking about yourself again. If you actually do want a beer, get me one too,' he says, shaking his nearly empty bottle at me without making eye contact.

I put the food away, grab us both beers and move his legs off the couch.

'I got us pizza and ice cream.'

'Nice.'

'You may as well tell me who she is, then, if she's about to ruin my life.'

'Why are you being so melodramatic?' Alex says, initiating a cheers that I reciprocate by instinct. 'Can't you be happy for me?'

'So you quit?'

'Well, I handed in my notice last week.'

'For fuck's sake, Alex. Why are you only telling me now?'

'It wasn't confirmed until yesterday. I didn't want to put up with all this,' he gestures at me with his beer, 'until I was absolutely sure I had to.'

'So you're not offering me the chance to move with you?'

'I'm not going to stop you. But Isabel and I are going to be living together, so you'd be just as fucked in New York as in London.'

'So you admit I'm fucked?'

'You're fucked if you choose to be.'

'That's such a recruiter thing to say,' I say, punching his leg.

'Wanna see her?' Alex says, fishing his phone out from his pocket.

'If I have to. Is she American, then?'

'Half American, half Portuguese. She doesn't need a visa to live there. Here she is.'

Alex passes me his phone – she's a petite blonde, tanned,

with a gentle face. I forget her the moment I hand the phone back.

'What do you think?' he says, smiling.

'She looks kind, I guess. Have you met her?'

'Of course I've met her. Remember when I was in Portugal?'

'Alex, you're always off somewhere. That's why I love living here.'

'I wish you'd tell Mum that you love living here. She thinks you're miserable.'

'So how long has Mum known?'

'For months. Since Isabel and I first met. She thinks the move is a great idea. Mum actually asks about my relationships,' he says, still smiling, now playfully returning the punch.

'Of course she thinks it's a great idea,' I say. 'She can't wait for me to come home and take over the parlour. To fulfil my destiny.'

'I wish you'd stop using that as an excuse.'

'I don't know what I'm going to do,' I say.

'You'll figure it out,' he says, switching the TV to *University Challenge*.

Alex beats me with eight answers to five, reminds me that I now owe him a beer, excuses himself to go to Skype Isabel, and wishes me goodnight.

Chapter 4

Brigid died today. Or maybe yesterday, I don't know.

It's Sunday lunchtime. About an hour ago, I received a call from Keith at the Mills Grand Estate. They said her brother found her in her home, already gone. She hadn't turned up for Mass. That's all they knew. That's all Sean knew.

Keith explained that Sean was asking for me. That he wouldn't speak to any of them. That he was refusing to take his medication. Keith asked if I was prepared to be his new emergency contact. He said there would be some paperwork to sign.

Ten minutes after taking the call, I'm on the bus, trying to think of anything meaningful to say. I consider joking that my weekend has been ruined. I consider mentioning how sick she looked at the exhibition. I practise moving my face in the correct way, thinking of all the grieving families I've had to witness, the performance of their hurt, black and sombre, draped with platitudes.

I imagine how they broke it to him. I imagine the twist of his face, the slow drop of his jaw. I imagine a noise leaking from him, animal and wounded.

The last email in my inbox from Brigid was sent on Friday, just after nine: a summary of her zumba session; a link to a petition to prevent cuts to the NHS; a suggestion for a new spa to try for our hydrotherapy sessions – five-star reviews and a new member's discount.

I look at my reflection in the plastic of the bus window. I had been in bed, watching YouTube. My fringe is pasted to my forehead, rushed and unwashed. I'm in the same clothes I wore with him on Friday.

Off the bus, I take a moment to smoke, to ready myself. I stand across the street and watch other people enter the building, rushing through the automatic doors, busy and cold. I imagine them coming to pay their respects to Sean, the news already spread far and wide, moving in the way that only tragedy can. I imagine his visitors being equally unsure of what to say, what to bring, how best to console a man who struggles to eat solids.

Alex is calling me.

'Where are you? I just got in. I have Chinese takeaway for us.'

'Sean's mum has died. I've just arrived at his flat. They said he's in a state.'

'So do you want me to save some food for you?'

'Did you hear what I just said?'

'Yeah, very sad. I'll save you some Crispy Shredded Beef, but I'm going to eat all the Duck Pancakes.'

'Aren't you going to ask me if I'm okay?'

'Are you okay, Janet?' Alex says, flatly.

'I don't even know. I'm not sure it's registered yet. I'm not really feeling anything. Just cold and a little dizzy. Is there something wrong with me, Alex?'

'There's plenty wrong with you. Gotta eat,' Alex says, ending the call.

Inside, the staff greet me gratefully, pulling serious expressions. They explain that Sean's uncle is already on his way. The plan is for Sean to return to Ireland with him, at least until the funeral. The arrangements are already in motion, I'm assured.

I knock on his bedroom door and let myself in. The blinds are drawn. I see him in the low light, sat up in bed, propped up by pillows, gazing into the middle distance. His face is red and quiet. He's still in his pyjamas; the ones she bought for his birthday. I can smell him from across the room.

'Sean,' I say, all speech crumbling from my mind. He turns his head to acknowledge me and raises his arm, still in its Velcro cast. He moves his arm slowly, in a heavy arc, extending and flexing the claw of his hand, indicating that he needs water. I move beside him and help the straw to his lips.

'You have to take your medication,' I say, the air corrugated and rough in my throat.

'I know,' he says croakily, speaking around the straw. His face is unshaven and blotchy, red with tears.

When he's done drinking, I fetch the medication from his cabinet and head into the bathroom in order to see what I'm doing. I pull on the light switch, and for a moment, I'm blind. It's like a torch is being shone straight in my eyes. I press my palms to my face and stare into the warm darkness. I take a few deep, steadying breaths. When I pull my hands away, I watch the bathroom fade in from an alarming white, developing like a photograph.

I grip the sink with both hands and look into the mirror,

feeling like a cliché, stood in a Hollywood posture of despair. I try to spot the emotion in my face, the feelings I'm supposed to be experiencing. But there's just Janet – pale and heartless.

I take off my coat and tie up my hair. I wash my hands thoroughly, right to the elbow. In the mirror, with Sean's pills in my palm, I look ready to overdose.

Sean allows me to feed him the medication, one pip at a time, swallowing painfully, his eyes closed.

'Should I put on the radio?'

'Okay,' he says, hacking the word out of his mouth.

'We don't have to speak yet if you don't want to. It's okay to cry. You can trust me.'

I open the blinds and we drift into our usual routine. I fetch a bowl of warm, soapy water and pull on some gloves, lowering the guardrails and locking the bed wheels in place. I undress him and remove his pad, cleaning away the waste without comment. He's facing away, breathing in jolts, shallow and tense.

'Did she do it?' he says through sobs, more to the room than directly to me.

'What do you mean?' I say, wiping delicately.

'You know.'

'I really can't answer that, Sean.'

I choose to focus on the task at hand, taking refuge in the mundanity of maintaining his body. I change gloves and begin applying nappy cream.

'Ja-net,' Sean says, stretching me over two dumb syllables, his breathing quickening. 'Did she finally do it?'

'I know what you're saying, but I don't know the answer,' I say, daubing another glob of cream to his skin.

'Never mind,' Sean manages to say.

I fetch his sling and work it under him, more forceful than I'm supposed to be. He puts up no resistance as I hoist him into the bathroom. I lower him onto the shower seat and turn on the water at full blast.

'Cry,' I say. 'As loud as you like.'

It's as though he was waiting for permission. Sean grips onto the shower rail and cries in a long, hiccupping wail, his voice cracking, his breathing serrated, his chin hard against his chest, shoulders twitching up with each sob. He cries and makes the universal noises of anguish. These are the same noises that anyone would make, no matter the body.

Once he is dry and calm, I change his bed sheets and help him into a new pad. I lead his body through a gentle massage. After a while, he falls asleep under my hands. I pull the blinds, raise the guardrails and cover him with a single sheet, quietly leaving the room, updating the weekend staff that he has been medicated, but that he'll need to be fed.

I sign my name to some forms, struggling to stay alert, to read and process the information in front of me. I'm vaguely aware of committing to make medical decisions on his behalf, of being one of his emergency contacts.

After what seems like an hour of paperwork, one of the staff brings over a handset, explaining Sean's uncle is on the phone. He introduces himself as Father John O'Healy, but insists that I should call him John. He says some Catholic things about death and suffering and an infinite plan, about Brigid being at rest and taken from us far too soon. He claims he'd heard a lot about me from her.

Father John says that he'll be in London by midnight, that he's already past security, waiting to board. He asks me to contact the college, but emphasises that he will handle everything else. He will handle getting Sean back to Ireland. He will handle the funeral arrangements. He'll handle everything, but he will need my help in the morning. We arrange to meet at the Mills Grand Estate around nine. He requests that I pray for her, for him, for Sean.

Before leaving, I pop back into Sean's flat to grab my coat and bag.

'Ja-net?' he says, rousing.

'Shhh,' I say. 'You're okay. Just rest.' I stand by his side and place my hand on his forehead, shielding his eyes, posed like affection. 'I'll be back in the morning. I'm here for you.'

Chloe's picked a pub with heaters in the smoking area. We're standing close to each other, huddled for warmth.

'So what the fuck happened?' she says. 'I'm honestly so sad. That shit doesn't just happen, right? People don't just drop dead. Have they done an autopsy yet?'

'I don't know, Chloe,' I say, dragging deep on the cigarette. 'I'm really in the mood to get stoned. Do you know anyone we could get weed from?'

'I know plenty, but I don't think you should. Don't they drug test you or something? Don't you use heavy machinery?'

'Are you serious?' I say, finishing my drink. 'Do you know how many times I've gone to work drunk or hungover?'

'I don't want to know,' she says, covering her ears, her cigarette pointed elegantly away. 'But I do know that I don't want responsibility for a high Janet Lamb.'

'You used to be fun,' I say, poking under her coat, feeling her body give way to my finger.

'I'm still fun,' Chloe says defiantly. 'But shouldn't you be more upset or mourning or something? Shouldn't you be with Sean, comforting him? He must be so upset. She was like, his whole world.'

'His uncle is coming here. He's a priest, would you believe it. He's taking Sean back to Ireland.'

'I thought they were from Yorkshire?'

'Oh, please don't make me fucking explain. I just want to get fucked up. Can't we just have some fun and get fucked up?'

'Okay, we don't have to talk about it, but I want you to know how sad I am. I am sad enough for both of us.'

'Mhmm,' I say, lighting another cigarette.

'Did you see that thing on *Panorama* about the nursing home where they were beating the patients and stealing from them?'

'I think you may be the only person in the world who watches *Panorama*.'

'It was horrible. They were leaving them in their own filth for hours. They were shouting at them for soiling themselves, right up in their faces.'

'The bar is set pretty low for care work,' I say, putting the box of cigarettes back in my bag. I started the evening with a fresh pack – there are now eleven left.

'So, did Brigid own anything?' Chloe says. 'Do you think she's left anything for you in her will?'

'There's no chance. They didn't have any money for ninety per cent of Sean's life. I doubt she even had a will. It was Sean who got awarded all that money – it's in his name. I think he offered it to her and she refused it. She wouldn't even let him pay for her flights when she visited. She knew that that money has to last him for the rest of his life.'

'But wasn't she the one paying you? Didn't she organise all of his money and his affairs? Who's going to do that now?'

'Leave me alone,' I whimper. 'You just said a second ago that we don't have to talk about it. Why aren't we at least drunk yet? Can you hurry up and finish your drink? We're supposed to be talking about places for me to move into. I don't want to go on some website for weirdos.'

'You could always move back home?' Chloe says with absolute sincerity.

'That's not an option.'

'But isn't this like the perfect timing? Your work was always meant to be a short-term thing. You're dating a married guy who can't make you come. What's keeping you here?'

'I need another drink,' I say, grinding the end of my cigarette into the ashtray. 'You stay here, keep our space.'

Waiting at the bar, I check my phone. Sean hasn't posted on Twitter since Sunday. I imagine this is the longest he's gone without tweeting since he moved here. Certainly since I've been working with him.

On Gumtree, there are 490 care assistant jobs available. I filter by highest paying – a live-in position for £735 per week. Must be female, must speak fluent English, must drive. I pay ten pounds for two pints and head back outside.

Chloe is on the phone where I left her. 'Stop it,' she says flirtily. 'I have to go, I'm with my girlfriend. You're awful. I'll speak to you later.'

'Cheers,' I say, handing over the pint.

'On the pints now, are we?' Chloe says, tapping glasses with me.

'Pints until we can't stand.'

'You're so lucky with your figure,' Chloe says. 'This is going to make me so bloated.'

'Will you shut up,' I say. 'The only thing keeping away the beer belly is all the manual labour. I may as well be working in a warehouse.'

'They're talking about standing desks in my office,' Chloe says. 'That's the big new thing. It's the solution to all our problems.'

'Death is the solution to all my problems,' I say, taking a big swig of lager.

'Don't be so melodramatic, Janet. Honestly.' She rolls her eyes like a cartoon. 'You just need to be practical. Start planning ahead. Like, where do you think you're going to move to when Alex leaves?'

'Wherever I can afford, I suppose. There's no way I can stay in Islington. I'm probably going to end up living above some takeaway in Croydon. How did you find your place?'

'I moved into this one when Lottie got sacked,' Chloe says smugly, reaching into my purse and taking a cigarette from my pack. 'I saw it coming, so I got to know her flat mates. I made sure that she always brought them along with us. I went home with them a few times and made a big deal of how lovely their home was. It's all about staking a claim.' Chloe lights up with a villainous grin. 'But when I first moved, I got a place in Dalston through SpareRoom. It wasn't too bad. The whole fuss of doing the viewings is exhausting, but that's the price you pay for all of this.' She gestures with her cigarette, trailing smoke rising into the evening air.

In the sky, planes make up for the stars, twinkling red and white, on and off, into the distance and beyond.

On Monday morning, I help them pack. Father John introduces himself with a sad, tired look, and explains that unless we act quickly, the funeral will have to wait until after Christmas. He says that he's much too busy around the festive period to find the time, so we really have to pull together and get things moving. It seems unclear whether I'm supposed to volunteer to join them in Ireland. They're waiting for confirmation that they can go ahead with the funeral on Friday, so Sean will require at least a week's worth of clothes and pads and medication.

While we pack provisions, Sean takes refuge in his iPad, editing our latest work. He sits at the dining table, earphones in, choosing to remain oblivious to the rush around him. I had arrived by eight to get him washed and dressed. He's being very quiet and oddly compliant. When his uncle arrived, Sean asked him to bless his room. They said a short prayer together, while I left the room to locate his passport.

Fortunately, Father John seems able to understand most of what Sean says. The only full sentence Sean has spoken to me today was to instruct me to inform Suzanna that he wouldn't be able to attend Thursday's seminar.

'I can't believe he's still stuck eating these things,' Father John says, passing me pots of apple sauce.

'Brigid always said to stick to what works.'

'My sister had a lot of strong opinions based on very little,'

Father John says, the frustration barbed in his voice. 'She was stubborn as a mule, right until the end of her. Did you know, when she moved home, she didn't want to give us a key? Can you imagine if she hadn't, now?'

'Right,' I say, imagining a squad of Irish police battering down Brigid's cottage door, finding her body, sprawled on the carpet, arm clutched at her chest.

'She could have done with seeking more help for him sooner. If she'd brought him home, to his family, she wouldn't have needed to suffer like she did. The woman loved to suffer.'

'She was very nice to everyone here,' I say, wary of an argument. 'She was always very good to me.'

'Do you know that she was turning away money from Peter? From the boy's own father? Money she could have used to feed him better than this?' He holds up a pot of rhubarb purée, pinching the pot like evidence at a trial.

The Mills Grand Estate has agreed to let Father John use one of their vans, meaning Sean's set to be strapped in for an eleven-hour drive and a ferry crossing. I imagine the smell in the van and feel my throat clot.

I find Suzanna's number in Sean's phone. She answers after the second ring and makes shocked vowel sounds, swearing a few times. She stresses that Sean shouldn't worry about anything to do with his work or his essays, and that she will ensure that he returns to a safe space. She will make sure it is a loving, welcoming environment, whenever he's ready. She recommends some books on loss and grieving, promising to have them to hand for when he's back.

'Sean,' I say, by his side, using my softest voice. He tugs out an earphone and meets my eyes with a tired look.

'Everything is sorted with college, Sean. There's nothing to worry about there.'

'Okay,' Sean says, looking back to his iPad. 'Thank you, Janet.'

I move hair off his ear and ease the earphone back in.

Wherever possible, Sean's not supposed to go for more than a few hours without moving. Once we're done packing, Sean allows himself to be disturbed, so that I can teach Father John how to get Sean into his chair, and guide him through some basic physiotherapy. I don't correct him when he is too forceful, but neither does Sean. Sean endures the simplified stretching routine with a stoic expression – shutting his eyes, offering no input.

It's nearly lunchtime already. Father John advises that they'll need to leave in the next thirty minutes if they're going to catch the right ferry.

'Have you decided where you're going to bury her?' I ask him, measuring out a week's worth of medication into Sean's extra-large pill case.

'No burial,' Father John says wearily, biting into an apple. 'She wanted to be cremated. That's the one thing we do know. That's the one thing she had written down.'

'I didn't realise that Catholics did cremations,' I say. 'My family runs a fu—'

'It's a grey area,' Father John says, interrupting, throwing half the apple away. 'Cremations are fine, but doctrine says you're supposed to maintain the integrity of the body by burying the vessel in sacred ground. Problem is, she wanted her ashes taken to Lourdes in France, and that'll cause all sorts of trouble. There would be a lot of hassle to bury her.

It'd be easier to scatter. You're best to scatter her – to take her there and scatter her.'

'Oh, right,' I say. 'Well, if you like, I could—'

'Oh, Janet,' Father John says, the warmest I've heard him. 'Would you do that for us? Would you take our Sean out to Lourdes once he's back?'

'I mean, does Sean—'

'Ah, he really should now. That's what she wanted. She would have wanted it to be him taking her. Now that's a wonderful thing you've offered, Janet. That's news for the family. Did you hear that, Sean?' he says, moving beside his nephew, sharply pulling out one of Sean's earphones. 'Janet's going to take you and your mammy's ashes to Lourdes. She's going to get what she always wanted.'

Sean looks up at me, his eyes bloodshot and sunken. I attempt a small smile, but he looks back to his screen, one headphone now dangling helplessly by his side.

It's Friday afternoon and I'm at Jordan's for the third time this week. I'm learning more about his routine, about the endless cycle of exercise and food, food and exercise. I'm making a conscious effort to avoid imposing myself on his schedule and space, to be as undisruptive as possible. My dirty clothes are all stuffed into my backpack, tucked away, out of sight. He's conceded that I may watch him exercise, on the condition that I stay quiet and don't make comments. As he moves through each exercise, I observe him in an academic way, from a safe distance, as though he were a rare creature on a nature documentary, the finest specimen of his species. I watch as he switches from pull-ups to press-ups, from sit-ups to squats. I imagine myself tracking the amount of time he spends preparing meals, eating meals, washing up, all the stupendous effort required to preserve his body.

Brigid's funeral would have finished around an hour ago. I feel anxious about messaging to check in on how it went. Since they left in the van, I've sent a few messages each day to check in. By this point, I've begun to repeat myself. There are only so many ways you can say, 'I hope you're okay. I am here if you need me.' Sean has only replied twice: once to remind me to cancel our hydrotherapy session, and once while they were on the ferry, to say that we'd forgotten to pack straws.

Sean has been completely inactive on Twitter since Brigid died. It seems likely that I am the only person who noticed this.

I've booked return flights to Lourdes, departing next Wednesday and returning on Saturday morning. It took me an hour just to fill out the airline's 'Disability Assistance Form'. I had to call the Mills Grand Estate to get Sean's passport information, which they gave me without any attempt at verifying who I was. I've had to sign a waiver on Sean's behalf, indemnifying the airline against responsibility should Sean receive a serious injury (or death) while travelling. Fortunately, Brigid's credit card details are still working for the time being. I book us the most comprehensive travel insurance available.

The hotel is proving trickier to arrange. Google tells me that Lourdes is much like a skiing resort – there's one main season of activity through the summer, when the whole town is primed to accommodate guests. Then unsurprisingly,

Easter and Christmas are the only other times when anyone visits. We will be travelling just as the Christmas rush gets underway.

According to TripAdvisor, the population of Lourdes is just over fifteen thousand, but there are 185 hotels to choose from. Only a handful of these hotels are equipped to host severely disabled guests. It seems to be more common for people to visit in groups, with arrangements for disabled pilgrims to be put into hospital-style accommodation, with specialist equipment and on-call medical staff.

The only relevant filter available on the search engine is 'Wheelchair Friendly', leaving me seven pages of options to read through.

'When was the last time you went on holiday?' Jordan says, sat opposite me, topless and sweating from his workout.

'I'd hardly call this a holiday,' I say, scrolling through hotel reviews. 'I haven't had more than four days off since I started with him.'

'That's mad,' Jordan says blandly.

'It would be nice to go on a trip together, if that's what you're thinking. You and me.'

'Yeah, maybe,' Jordan says, eyes fixed on his own laptop.

'We could go visit Alex in New York, once he's settled. Sean says the Met is meant to be the best collection of modern art in the world. Or anything really. I always wanted to go to Iceland. Chloe says it's expensive, but amazing.'

'Are you even allowed to take holidays?' Jordan says.

'Of course I'm allowed,' I say, stressing the silliness of his question. 'I'm not a slave. I just have to arrange for someone to cover me. I have to plan a few weeks in advance.'

'Can you afford a holiday, then?'

'I've got some cash tucked away,' I say, the shame rising through me.

'We can talk about it when you get back,' Jordan says, scratching his chest. 'Hey, I nearly forgot. I got you something.'

He jumps off the bed in one movement, bounds out the room and down the stairs, impossibly light on his feet. When he returns, his arms are behind his back and he's smiling broadly.

'Not more Ayn Rand,' I say, sitting up.

'Not quite that good. Just an advent calendar.' He reveals a Simpsons-themed cardboard box, handing it to me nervously. 'Do you like it?'

'I love it,' I say, getting up to kiss him. 'Just what I wanted.'

'Because you're going to be away for a week, you can eat a load of chocolates in advance,' he says, hanging his index finger over the box like a navigator, picking out the flimsy numbered doors, some already slightly open along their perforations.

'Did you get one for yourself?'

'No way – I can't eat chocolate before the junior championships.'

'It's not like you're competing. And didn't you have a beer yesterday? Surely that's worse.'

'I'm setting an example for the kids. They need to look at me and understand what they're capable of. I know my body, Janet,' he says, slapping at his exposed abs with a drumming rhythm. 'I know what I can get away with. Everyone's body is different when it comes to this stuff.'

'What about my body, then?' I say, fiddling with the box to

remove the first lump of chocolate, moulded in the shape of Bart's head. It smells stale. 'What should I be doing to inspire future generations?'

'I don't comment on what women should do with their bodies,' Jordan says playfully. 'I'm far too much of a gentleman. Maybe you should ask your new priest friend.'

'He seems like a bit of a dick. He was best friends with Sean's dad, so I guess it makes sense.'

'I can't tell you how little I care,' Jordan says, now back in position on the bed, his own laptop balanced on his chest.

Sean's sent a message to approve of my travel insurance choice. He's sent me a picture on WhatsApp of his mother's coffin, covered with flowers, and another of her funeral programme, Brigid's face on the front, smiling kindly.

I reply with a heart emoji.

'Thank you for my present,' I say to Jordan.

'Merry Christmas,' he says.

I wake up cold and stiff from one of those wonderful dreams – the dreams he's not part of. From the plane window, the clouds are a cauliflower weave, rolling on, off to the high peaks of the near and nearer Alps. The plane is named after a saint and the mean passenger age must be in the high fifties.

I don't suppose death counts as either business or pleasure. When we learned there was a £650 surcharge to transport ashes internationally, we decided to bring Brigid in a suitcase, bubble-wrapped amongst the medical supplies.

When we land, the whole plane claps gallantly, and a hymn plays through the fuzzy intercom. We wait for everyone else to leave, then I haul Sean from his aisle seat, onto a gurney and down the cabin. The stewardess smiles at me as I struggle with our hand luggage. Sean smiles back with the joy of a newly freed prisoner.

'God bless you,' the stewardess says, sincere and French.

Off the plane, I'm hit by the marinated smell of him – sweat and indignity.

'We're going to have to change you here,' I tell him. Sean says nothing, his smile gone, his head drooped, arms crossed over his chest like a prepared corpse.

I remember Dad telling me that the dead have their arms crossed in caskets because it's the posture that would most easily enable escape, were the corpse somehow reanimated.

Since returning from Ireland, Sean's moods have been erratic. A lot of the time, he seems silent and contemplative, unresponsive to conversation. But on a few occasions, he's seemed full of a manic energy, speaking in urgent terms about his plans for the next pieces in our series, about how amazing the New Year will be.

Ahead of the flight, I took Sean to his usual doctor for a check-up and to seek advice on how best to prepare for the journey. The doctor's version of sympathy looked more like confusion. She consulted her computer and recommended bringing some laxatives.

I wonder how many Catholics sincerely believe that they are going to be resurrected from the dead upon Jesus' return. I wonder if they visualise themselves breaking out of coffins – the body they died in, made glorious by the apocalypse.

I wonder how many pilgrims realise how recently Lourdes became significant – how in the same year as Bernadette Soubirous's visions of the Virgin Mary, the washing machine was patented. Wikipedia said that the town has attracted over two hundred million pilgrims since 1860, with sixty-nine healings officially being recognised as miraculous. That's one miracle in every 2.9 million pilgrimages. When I mentioned this statistic to Alex, he said that you're ten times more likely to be struck by lightning. I told him not many people pray to be struck by lightning.

I'm trying to be as efficient as possible, but moving Sean and the trolley loaded with our suitcases and his medical equipment through customs feels like a logic puzzle.

A tanned, furrow-browed customs clerk tuts at me as I fumble through my pockets and bags for our passports. By the time I've found them, buried under Sean's soiled clothes, the clerk is chatting quite happily in pattered French to a security guard – I am aware he is deliberately keeping me waiting. I imagine myself with my foot on his neck and a gun in his mouth, tapping on his grisly French teeth.

Once we are through security, we wait forty-five minutes for Sean's chair to come off the plane. Through the waiting-room windows, I watch a team of three men expertly assembling wheelchairs of all varieties. They're dressed in cadet-like uniforms, with beauty-show sashes, labelled HOSPITALIER.

I'm not looking forward to pushing a non-motorised chair around the town. TripAdvisor has warned me to wear comfortable shoes and multiple layers.

Once Sean's chair is assembled and he's strapped in, we join a queue for what seems to be the only disabled bathroom in the airport. The whole building smells like mildew and cheap perfume. A self-righteous-looking security guard walks back and forth along the queue. I feel confident that if I were to leave the luggage trolley outside the cubicle, he would remove it immediately, arranging for our stuff to be detonated in a controlled explosion.

Sean has said nothing since we left the plane.

'Are you okay?' I say, gently shoving his shoulder.

'It hurts,' he says.

'What hurts?'

'Everything.'

During our meeting, Sean's doctor pulled me aside, and told me to be alert to suicidal behaviour. She told me that depression is the number one killer of young men. It's been days now, and I still can't imagine a reasonable way for Sean to go about killing himself.

I promised the doctor that I'd stay alert, but I'm not sure what I'm supposed to be looking for. Maybe it's the same as being vigilant for suspicious packages in the airport.

'Do you think there's ever been a disabled suicide bomber?' I ask Sean.

'You should not say that word here,' he says, turning to the patrolling guard.

'It'd be so clever though. Nobody's going to want to do a strip search on you. And no one's going to get suspicious when you set off a metal detector.'

'Not now, Janet.'

Outside, we queue for the special assistance buses, which are more like transit vans. I've bought five hundred euros on Brigid's card to cover our costs for the trip. I plan to keep whatever we don't spend. The bus costs ten euros for both of us, which seems like a promising start. At the front of the queue, the driver tells me in broken English that the town is around twenty kilometres away.

I feel grubby and nasty. It's the dirtiness unique to plane travel. It may only be midday, local time, but I'm ready to shower and sleep.

'So did your mum ever actually come here?'

'I think she came when she was young. At least once. There was a pilgrimage – I think the parish covered the costs. Mum could not afford to go abroad very often. She always said I would love it in Lourdes. She said it was very beautiful.'

Somehow, we've ended up sharing the van with a decrepit-looking old man, and a rather fat, mole-pocked woman. It's unclear to me whether they are together. Regardless, they make no attempt to acknowledge our presence as I load Sean into the van in his chair, and I'm happy to return the favour.

Once we're moving, I look over our itinerary. The whole trip is mapped out. Sean's body is not equipped for spontaneity. Life has to be planned around his body, and that's doubly true when away from home.

I'm wary about spending every waking hour with him. I know that my sanity is anchored in the daily guarantee of an exit. I've always been able to rely on the fact that I'm only hours away from relative freedom. Out here, I'm both alone and committed.

The mole-pocked woman is reading a leaflet with a crude photograph of St Bernadette on the front. I recognise her from my Google research on Lourdes, which only threw up a few variants of the same image.

According to Wikipedia, Bernadette was a miller's

daughter with cholera and severe asthma, who had a vision of the Virgin Mary while collecting firewood from a dump by the river. Her claims drew attention from senior members of the church because the vision used the phrasing, 'I am the Immaculate Conception,' which was not yet part of the Church's nomenclature outside Rome.

Bernadette resented the attention that her reputation drew, and retired from public life to join a hospice. She died aged thirty-five from ongoing health complications, and has been exhumed three times, as posthumous justification for canonisation – her body is supposedly miraculously preserved.

'Did you know this city is built on a dump?' I say to Sean, wiping the drool from his chin. He makes no reply and looks dramatically out of the window towards the Alps. In this light, I can see his cheek is already flecked with fine stubble. I see the scar tissue left by spots. I see the thin red scratches along the ridge of his nose, the zits in the crevices of his nostrils. I see the flaking of the skin around his mouth, roughened by a near constant stream of drool. I see a man in need of healing.

'But we have a reservation,' I say, brandishing a creased email. 'Two rooms.'

The receptionist shrugs in the most stereotypically French way imaginable. He turns his hand to a wall of empty key hooks behind him.

'One room,' he says, holding up a tanned, chipolata finger.

'He is severely disabled,' I stress. Sean does not react. 'He needs a bed with guard rails – like the one we've paid for.'

'The bed, she is good. He will sleep.'

'And what about me?' I say, but he is already turning to answer the phone. A queue has formed behind us.

'I am thirsty,' Sean says. His voice sounds charred and hoarse.

'He needs a room with a bath. He needs to be cleaned.'

'One room,' the receptionist says again, handing me a key with a tumour-sized lump of plastic on the end.

'How is anyone supposed to fit that in their pocket?' I say quietly, showing Sean the key under the counter.

'You are not supposed to bring it with you,' Sean says. 'You hand it back in before you go.'

'I don't trust these people with our key,' I say.

'They are Christian,' Sean says.

'That's not reassuring to me.'

In our room, the curtains are already pulled. There's a bare, monastic feel to the space. A bed, a seat and a table, furnished with a Bible and corded phone.

'Art,' I say, pointing to a waxy still life above the bed.

'Not art,' Sean says, moving only his eyes.

The concierge is back with a mattress before I can get Sean's shoes off. He allows it to fall out of his hands to the floor, hands me sheets, and wishes us *bonne nuit*, touching the feet of a wall-mounted crucifix as he leaves.

The standing shower means I will have to bed-bath Sean. I run downstairs to borrow an ice bucket from the hotel bar and fill it with warm water. Without the reassurance of a radio to fill the silence, the process feels awkwardly intimate. Half-way through, I need to rush downstairs, still in purple latex gloves and a plastic apron, communicating that I need a bag for his waste. When we're finished, I tie up the bag and throw it into the corridor for someone else to deal with. I open the window to air out the smell and immediately a couple of midges fly into the room.

Once Sean is fully clean and in bed, I build a fortress of towels and pillows around him to keep his body in place.

I step out the room, holding the key and my cigarettes, careful not to trip on the bag of waste. I call Jordan.

'How is it?' he says.

'I knew you'd ask that. I knew that would be the first thing you asked.'

'That bad, eh?'

'It's fine. My ear hasn't popped properly since the flight. I feel like a vacuum.'

'I could make a sucking joke,' Jordan says.

'The other kind of vacuum, obviously.'

'You don't seem in the mood for jokes.'

'I'm going to have to sleep on a mattress on the floor. The floor is dusty and I'm exhausted and I just want you to say something comforting.'

'What do you want me to say?' says Jordan in a distracted tone.

'Are you watching football?' I say, changing ears.

'How did you know?'

'It can't even be live – can you please just pause it while we're speaking?'

'I'm tired, Janet,' Jordan says.

'You don't get to tell me you're tired,' I say. 'You don't even know what tired is, Jordan. You have no idea how much I'm aching – the labour I do.'

'I'm pretty sure I know what aching feels like,' he says, now defensive.

'You're aching like a man – like an athlete. I'm doing the work of a man without the body to back it up. I'm just one body working for another. It's thankless, and it's exhausting. So you don't get to tell me you're tired, while you're in bed, watching *Match of the Day*.'

'I thought he always said thank you.'

'That's not the point.'

'I don't need to hear this, Janet,' Jordan says wearily.

'I'm sorry,' I force myself to say.

'I like you a lot, Janet, but I prefer when you're nice.'

'Nice?' I say, baulking, now pacing the hotel corridor.

'What's wrong with being nice?' Jordan says, his mouth clearly full. 'Why are you so afraid of people thinking you're nice?'

'Because what is "nice", really? What does it actually mean?'

'I mean that you can be very gentle and sweet. I mean that you do work that improves people's lives.'

'So my job makes me nice?' I am thumbing the wheel of my lighter, craving a cigarette.

'No, but you're nice because it's not just about the money. It means you care.'

'But I don't – and it is! I'm working to survive here! How is that not clear to you?'

'That's bollocks, Janet,' he says, mouth full again. 'We both know you care about Sean. You wouldn't have volunteered to be out there unless you cared.'

'Don't tell me how I feel,' I say, more sharply than intended.

'You're a good person. Even if you refuse to admit it.'

'Good and nice both make me seem pathetic. I don't want

to be anyone's bitch. I don't want to serve. I do this for myself. If I care – if I admit I care, then this becomes the rest of my life. Do you get that?'

Jordan pauses. 'I get that,' he says, not getting it. I hold the phone away from my face so he can't tell how heavily I'm breathing. I feel a bit dizzy.

'What's your mattress like?' he asks.

'I don't know yet. But the floor seems dusty.'

Jordan makes a high-pitched yelping sound.

'Who scored?' I say.

'West Ham. Payet free kick. Sorry.'

'Thank you. I'm sorry too. I'll go now.'

I head downstairs to smoke. It's much warmer here than in London. It feels strange to only see my breath when smoking. I watch a middle-aged woman struggle with a vending machine, feeding the same euro coin in over and over, increasingly frustrated, cursing in a harsh foreign tongue.

Back inside, Sean's already asleep. His snoring sounds irregular and pained. I make my bed and lie down, my head facing the door. The mattress feels lumpy, and the room's fan unit is a metre away from my head. I watch the midges bump into the intermittent flash of the fire alarm. At ground level there's a faint draught coming from under the door, hitting the bud of my unpopped ear.

And yet, sleep comes quickly, like a blessing.

It's 7 a.m. and I'm naked, only four feet away from Sean. In spite of the bathroom wall between us, I can picture him perfectly, the bracketed curl of his body occupying the bed I'd booked for myself.

The first time I saw Sean hard was our third morning together. Brigid was shadowing, otherwise I would have reacted in a more extreme way. I think I managed not to wince visibly. Because of his night pad, it's impossible to tell whether he is hard or not until your hands are right next to it. The customary waft of faeces that accompanies the big reveal doesn't add to the experience.

On that first occasion, Brigid didn't acknowledge it, and neither did Sean. This established our precedent on the matter. When I got home that evening, I told Alex, and he threatened to post it on Facebook.

Apparently, mourning doesn't stop Sean from getting hard. He has been hard every morning I've cared for him since she died.

'Morning, Sean,' I say, coming out of the bathroom, now dressed, my hair still wet.

'Unghh, morning,' he says, registering the unfamiliar surroundings.

I set about deconstructing the pillows and towels, dumping them unceremoniously on the floor, happy for a maid to deal with the mess.

'What is the weather like?' Sean mumbles, bubbling with spit.

'I haven't been outside yet. Probably the same as yesterday.'

Sean makes a disappointed grunt to acknowledge this as an unsatisfactory answer. We have a whole day to kill before we scatter Brigid's ashes. I realise now that it may have been a mistake to book for longer than two nights.

'Does the weather matter?' I ask, stepping into the bathroom with the ice bucket, mixing in Sean's special dermatologically tested soap. 'Do you have something planned that I haven't been told about?'

'No.'

'Then why are you worried?'

'I am used to knowing. I miss the radio.'

'How did you sleep?'

'Sore,' he says, allowing me to clean under his arm with the flannel.

'The sheets?'

'I do not know.'

'I thought we could do the Stations of the Cross – that's what all the guides recommend. There's a big hill I'd have to push you up, but I think we can manage.'

'Okay,' he says.

'You could sound more excited.'

'Tired.'

I have forgotten to bring any shaving foam, meaning that we will either need to buy some, or just let his beard grow out. Brigid wouldn't have put up with this. But Brigid's not around to interfere.

'Do you think you would ever want to grow your beard properly?'

'It is already too long.'

'But would you ever consider it?'

'Mum did not like me with a beard.'

'Of course.'

I inhale deeply before ripping the seals on Sean's pad. He lifts himself slightly to help me remove it in one motion, into the refuse bag I've got ready. He's hard again.

'Do I have a rash?' Sean says.

'A rash where?'

'My back,' he says, gesturing awkwardly with his head.

'I know where your back is, Sean. And no, there's nothing there.'

'Okay,' he says.

'Does it hurt if I press there?' I say, as Sean tenses up against my touch.

'Yes,' he says through a locked jaw.

I wait a moment before I stop pressing, then clean him in silence. By the time I'm securing his pad, he's no longer hard. I choose not to read anything into this.

'You said it was still warm,' Sean says as we leave the hotel.

'No, I said it was probably the same as yesterday and that I hadn't been outside yet.'

'It is cold.'

'Do you want me to go back up to get you a jacket?'

'Do not worry.'

'I'd rather go back up and get it for you now if you're going to be complaining.'

'I will be fine.'

'I'm going to remind you that you said that.'

'Have you got Mum with you?'

'The urn is upstairs.'

'Good,' Sean says. 'She will be safe there.'

Lourdes is a particularly inconvenient site for a miracle. Especially one that is supposed to benefit disabled people. Calling a town built on a hill 'wheelchair friendly' seems like a sick joke.

We've spent the morning exploring on foot, following the

river. The water flows quick and clear. We stop to watch children play along the lush, low banks, throwing stones and dipping their toes, wary of the cold.

I push Sean up to the town, past a seemingly endless parade of shops, all selling the same tacky religious merchandise, all of them full of eager customers, wearing bum bags and fleeces. Sean spots a Virgin Mary wall clock. I point out a Virgin Mary snow globe.

It's warm again. I take off my hoodie and stuff it in Sean's bag. His chair feels even heavier than usual. I suspect that in reassembling his chair, the hospitalier has over-tightened his wheels. Either that, or Sean has put on weight through grieving.

We head towards the Domain, the town's focal point; within the Domain is the Grotto, site of Bernadette's vision. At the entrance, a poorly translated sign informs us to treat the whole of the Domain as though it were a church. No smoking, no phone calls.

'No fun, eh?' I say to Sean, pointing at the sign, hoping for a smile.

He says nothing, so I take the opportunity to step away from him and enjoy a cigarette, standing right on the threshold of the sacred space.

The 4G in Lourdes has been very patchy; notifications and messages come through in bursts. Facebook alerts me that it's Chloe's birthday. I message her, typing with one finger while I smoke. I apologise for being a shitty friend, and promise to catch up when I'm back. I sign off the message: 'Your favourite bully, Janet.' I cast my eyes back to the gift shops, wondering whether to buy her a couple of the Virgin Mary embossed lighters. I think of jokes about miraculous tumours.

The entrance to the grotto is on a steep slope. I watch other people wheeling down chairs backwards.

'Ready?' I say to Sean, leaning to stretch my hamstrings.

'Yes,' he says softly.

I push him forward onto the slope, feeling the weight of him immediately. I lean back to counterbalance his chair, making little, shuffling, penitent steps down towards the Domain. Sean is very still, hands heavy in his lap.

'Sit back for me,' I say through my teeth. 'I can't deal with you slipping out your chair.'

'I will not,' Sean says, not adjusting himself at all, tapping at his seatbelt.

'Please just sit back.'

Sean adjusts himself with an awkward lean and shuffle.

'Thanks,' I say, jaw clenched, my palms sweaty, thighs burning.

By the foot of the slope, huge sweat patches are blooming under my arms. I shake out my hands and catch my breath, leaning forwards, into Sean's shoulder.

'Look,' Sean says, gesturing towards a man in camouflage holding a semi-automatic gun. He's pacing the base of the slope, inspecting bags, wearing a beret and sunglasses, occasionally pressing his finger to an earpiece, talking to himself.

'I guess they're still on high alert after all the attacks at the start of the year,' I say.

'Scary,' Sean says, pointing out two other officers in the distance, the distinct shape of guns in their hands.

'Bags, please,' says the guard as we approach, somehow knowing to speak English. I turn Sean's chair compliantly and unzip his backpack. As the man bends towards Sean's chair, for a moment, his gun points straight at me. I feel a needle of fear move through me, starting at the base of my spine and piercing upwards. It feels like skin shredding.

'Go,' the man says, satisfied, waving us through.

We follow a flow of people into the Domain, my pace set by the group in front of us. They are being led by an elderly man, who is speaking loudly in what sounds like German, an unopened yellow umbrella raised above his head.

I wipe Sean's chin and remind him to keep an eye open for an appropriate, semi-private place where we can return to scatter Brigid's ashes. He moves his head in acknowledgement, pulling a serious, pouty expression.

Ahead of us is a huge Byzantine-style church, with a gaudy, gilded façade, topped with a literal ornamental crown. Sean identifies it as the Rosary Basilica – Lourdes' main cathedral. The architecture is reminiscent of a Disney castle – all spires and tall windows. The building is an overcast grey. There's nothing about this space that seems warm or miraculous. There's certainly nothing I'd associate with healing.

There's a row of aqueduct-like arches leading out from either side of the church. As we follow the group under the closest arch, Sean twists his head and explains to me that they've been designed to symbolise arms, stretching around the central courtyard, welcoming and embracing the pilgrims.

The path leads us down another slope, back to the river-bank. From the side, the church appears to have been cut straight into the rock, emerging like an inevitability. The cliff face is overgrown with verdant greens – mosses and weeds and flowering bushes, seemingly unfazed by the onset of winter.

In the near distance, I can see the stream of people consolidating into a single file, partitioned by a barrier and long stretches of velvet rope.

'What are they queuing for?' I say, lowering my head to Sean's shoulder.

'The Grotto,' he says. 'We have to get in line.'

We join the queue and limp slowly forwards, until a teenage boy in a HOSPITALIER sash rushes up, gesturing to say that we're being fast-tracked to the front.

'*Pour l'infirme,*' he says, shepherding us to a ramp, up to an altar, set inside the cliff face. This is the Grotto – this is where Bernadette's vision appeared. We join a gap between two families. Ahead of us, people process, running their left hands over the cliff wall, which has developed a soft shine at shoulder height. In an alcove about six feet above us, there's a dirty-looking plaster cast of the Virgin Mary, illuminated by candlelight. Her expression seems sad.

I move Sean's chair as close as possible to the cliff face. He stretches up his left arm, bumping the curve of his wrist along the wall. As we move slowly forwards, his eyes are firmly fixed on the statue. I allow myself to reach over and touch the stone – it's colder than I expect, and I pull away.

Above us, a bell chimes from the Basilica, ringing out the tune of the 'Ave Maria'. This is followed by thirteen longer, firmer tolls. It is already one o'clock.

*

It's lunchtime and we're in a picnic area within the Domain, right by the riverbank. The sun seems to be directly above us.

I've moved Sean from his chair to an uncomfortable concrete bench. No one offered to help me. The bench is laid out with Sean's usual meal kit, and the packed lunch that the hotel has provided for us.

'This article says you're supposed to reapply sunscreen every couple of hours,' I say, sat opposite him, facing the river, reading from my phone. 'That can't be right.'

'I do not know,' Sean says, dribbling slightly as he chews.

'It says that you just sweat it off. Why hasn't anyone ever told me that? Why isn't that on the marketing material for sun cream? Surely it's in the company's interest to make you use more and keep reapplying it.'

'I do not know.'

'Apparently there are two different types of UV rays – there's the one type that gives you a tan, and another type that gives you cancer.'

Sean's attention is entirely focused on his spoon, suspended in mid-air, heaped with a glob of mash.

'I better put some more sun cream on you, then,' I say, standing to retrieve the travel-size bottle of lotion from his backpack.

'Do not bother,' Sean says through a triumphant mouthful.

'Are you saying you want cancer? Because Brigid would probably come and haunt me if I let you get skin cancer.'

'It is not even that sunny.'

'Have you ever been burned?'

'Yes.'

'And how did that happen?'

'Mum got us lost,' Sean says, angling his arm to approach the plate for another spoonful. 'We were lost in Cork. We were on holiday.'

'I didn't know you went on any holidays.'

'Just that one,' Sean says, readjusting his grip and stabbing at the plate.

'Well, I'm going to ignore you and put on the sun cream anyway,' I say, uncapping the bottle and lotioning up my hands.

'I said no,' Sean says, more forcefully, twisting away as I bend under the concrete table to access his bare legs.

'Help me out here.'

As I reach out to rub his leg, Sean's left knee jerks up, catching me on the underside of my jaw, tipping me backwards onto the gravel. I've bitten my tongue – my blood tastes sour, like rust and batteries and pain. People at the other tables turn to look, but no one moves. I stand up and dust myself down, waiting for an apology.

'Well?' I say, my tongue thick.

'I said no,' Sean says, looking guiltily at his plate.

'Are you serious?' I say, heavy on the sibilance, rubbing my jaw as it starts to throb.

'I did not mean to hurt you. I am not going to get cancer.'

'I hope you fucking do,' I say, sitting back down. I squeeze the lotion bottle and make a dramatic show of rubbing it into my own arms and face. I've used too much and I have to lift my top to wipe off the excess. For a moment, I catch Sean looking.

We sit without talking. I tenderly probe my jaw with one finger, and run my tongue over each tooth with medical precision, feeling out the hurt, testing for looseness. I scroll through articles on my phone, greasing my screen with the remnants of the sun cream. Sean makes his way through the mashed potato, not pausing to ask for water like he usually would.

'I do not want to speak about her,' Sean says after a while, his words much more clear than usual.

'About Brigid?'

'I do not want to speak about her today.'

'Okay,' I say, suddenly feeling stupid.

'But we should scatter her there,' he says, turning his body slightly, gesturing to the other side of the river, upstream, to a cluster of trees by the riverbank.

'That looks good to me,' I say, offering him water.

Once Sean's finished eating, I force down a dry sandwich and a hard-boiled egg. I throw away a ring pull can of tuna, promising myself that tomorrow, once the deed is done, I'll spend a few of the euros on a proper lunch. It is what she would have wanted.

We spend the rest of the afternoon exploring the Domain, counting eight churches in total. It's coming up for six and the sun is setting. My feet feel sore.

'Let's sit for a while,' I say. 'Before we tackle that slope again.'

We're directly across the river from the Grotto. I see a bat flit around the edge of my vision, darting over the fast-flowing water, paying no respect to the miracle. We watch floodlights come on around the Grotto, a Mass being prepared. Faintly, in the distance, I can hear a choir going through vocal warm-ups, sliding their voices up and down a scale in perfect harmony.

To the right of the Grotto, there are hundreds, maybe thousands, of trembling flames, each candle a prayer, one firm breath away from vanishing.

I shut my eyes and concentrate on the noise of the river. I think about a great flood. The banks bursting. The town dowsed in holy silt. The moneychangers and novelty stalls, all drowned, thrown out from the temple.

Bells strike for the hour and the sun disappears. There's a chill to the air again.

Mass is beginning in the Grotto. I watch as the priest makes the sign of the cross, his arms wide and open, welcoming us. I watch a small congregation raise lighted candles, blurring together into a single line of flame.

Suddenly, I feel very calm. The feeling eases through me, like a deep breath, lifting me, keeping me perfectly in place. The cold of the wind eases, and I'm bristling. Somehow, I feel different. Like a gear, shifting into place. The machinery of me running smoothly for the first time. There's a warmth I haven't felt before. My face is flushed and I'm close to crying.

I stare across the river and my eyes refocus, moving away from the quivering flame. I look to the river, the deep greens of the bank – everything is somehow sharper, in a brighter filter, blanched of weariness and mourning. The water flows at a constant speed. Everything seems impossibly beautiful, and pleased to finally reveal itself to me. It's as though the river is speaking to me, shyly admitting it had been there all along, with me, waiting for me.

There's a soft ringing in my ears – the hanging resonance of a switch flicked for the first time – the first time in many years.

'Can you hear that?' I whisper. Sean makes no sign of reply. 'I have to move out, Sean,' I say. 'I might have to leave London. Sean?'

I uncross my legs and ease up to my feet. Sean's face is red with tears. There's snot in his beard.

'She talked about how she wanted to die,' he says, sobbing. 'Every time she drank. She said it was her fault. She would drink, and say she deserved to suffer, that she must have sinned. He left, and she just blamed herself. She apologised to me, for making me this way. For letting this happen.'

I stand patiently, still joyously calm, allowing him to speak, my legs waking up. 'I didn't know she drank,' I lie.

'Sometimes,' he says. 'It was not easy for her.'

'She didn't kill herself,' I tell him, now bent to eye level. 'She was sick. There's nothing anyone could have done.'

'I ruined her life,' Sean says loudly, now drawing attention from passing pilgrims.

'I think it's time to go home,' I tell him, taking off his brakes, and wheeling him away from the river.

Sean continues sobbing as we leave the Domain, maintaining his pose, inclined forwards, his head bent like prayer.

At the top of the slope, the wind has turned, and I feel the chill. I feel the sudden desire to smoke. The cafés are all still open – tipsy pilgrims spilling out onto the road, Britpop tracks playing at full volume. Some raise their glasses, toasting Sean as we pass.

We eat dinner at the hotel. There's no menu, just the man from reception, presenting me with a plate of meat in dark gravy, a silver platter of overcooked runner beans and a palatable-looking ceramic dish of Dauphinoise potatoes.

'*Bon appétit,*' the man says, failing to smile.

Sean quietly feeds himself a bowl of white fish and orange mash, making no comment, but screwing up his face in displeasure.

We agree that it makes sense to have an early night and arrive at the Domain just as it opens, to ensure as much privacy as possible for the scattering.

'Are you really leaving London?' Sean says, as I settle him into bed, just after nine.

'I haven't decided yet. I might not have a choice.'

'You should live with me,' Sean says. 'We can find somewhere. My tenancy is only for a year.'

'I think you need to sleep.'

'Lots of carers do it.'

'Are you asking me, or telling me?'

'You should consider it,' Sean says, allowing me to wrap the cast around his wrist, securing the Velcro.

'I already have,' I say. 'But I need to think about it. I don't know if I could put up with your snoring.'

Sean snorts out a small smile – maybe his first of the trip.

'You didn't ruin her life,' I tell him. 'You're all that kept her going.'

'Thanks, Janet,' Sean says, his eyes now closed.

The bells ring for 5 a.m. We're outside the Domain, waiting for the gates to be unlocked. I'm smoking my second cigarette of the day, paying attention to the direction of my falling ash.

Inside, I brace Sean down the steep slope, my legs and feet aching from yesterday's full day of walking. We make our way past the Basilica and over the bridge, quickly to the spot that Sean has picked out. I force his chair off the path, onto the grass, down towards the cluster of trees by the riverbank.

I use my nail scissors to cut into the bubble wrap, tearing gently. The urn is emerald-coloured porcelain, ornamental, and lighter than I remember it feeling. There's a gilded, Latinate inscription around the side, but it may be Gaelic for all I know.

'Is this all of her?'

'I think they give you just a little.'

'What, are they saving the rest?'

'I do not know.'

'It's too small to put your hand in,' I tell him.

'Let me try,' Sean says.

'Take a look, genius,' I say, brandishing the urn at him. 'Your hand isn't going to fit in there.'

'Then you will have to do it,' he says, annoyed. 'Just shake it.'

'Do you want to say a prayer or something?'

'No – it is fine. Let us just get it done.'

'I don't know what way the wind is blowing,' I say. 'I don't want this to be like *The Big Lebowski*. I don't know if I can do this, Sean. I barely knew her.'

'You knew her well, and she loved you. We are here now. Just get it done. Please.'

The lid has a rubber seal, so I have to use my nails, then tug firmly to get it open.

'You ready?' I ask.

'Ready,' he says, watching me, leaning his body to the left.

With that, I face away from him, hold my breath, and turn the urn upside down at arm's length.

A sandbag-sized baggie falls out, and I nearly drop the urn in shock.

'You've got to be joking.'

The baggie has burst open upon hitting the floor. There's a fine grey dust blowing over the toes of my boots. I pick the baggie up by one corner in a surgical pinch. I have no idea how this made it through Customs.

'What now?' I ask.

'Just get rid of it.'

Baggie in hand, I take a few steps back, wind up, and make a disappointingly girly throw into the middle of the river. The baggie bobs for a moment on the surface, and then is quickly swept downstream. There's grey dust all over my right hand.

'That was basically littering,' I say, bending down to wipe my hand on the grass.

'Look,' Sean says, raising one arm to point across the river. An elderly couple in matching baseball caps are gesturing angrily at us.

'We should go,' Sean says.

'What do you want to do with this?' I say, offering Sean the urn.

'Stick it in my bag. We need to go.'

'You owe me for that,' I tell him, taking off the brakes and bracing against the slope of the bank.

At the hotel, I wash my hands three times, still feeling the grit of her under my fingernails. Our plan is to go back to sleep, get some lunch, then attend the afternoon Latin mass at the Basilica. Our flight is at ten in the morning, and Sean needs a minimum of eight hours sleep to be tolerable, so I'll need to pack everything this evening.

'Is there anything you want to do before we leave?' I ask, reassembling the pillow and towel balustrades.

'I am supposed to bring back holy water for my uncle,' Sean tells me, completely sincere.

'We don't have time for that. We can just give him some from the tap and it will be fine.'

'Please, Janet.'

'Why are you only telling me this now?'

'I forgot. I am sorry.'

I sleep on my front, my dirty hand tucked under my pillow. Drifting off, I picture Sean as a chef, seasoning a freshly painted canvas with his mother's ashes, one awkward, grieved pinch at a time.

I'm woken up by room service. I answer the door and politely tell the maid to let us rest, using my most aggressive fuck-off expression. It's one in the afternoon, meaning that by the time Sean's massaged and back in his chair, we'll have already missed the hotel lunch.

I feel myself ache with every movement, tender in all the places where Jordan likes to hold me.

We head back to a café that Sean had spotted yesterday. We sit outside, almost on the street. A backfiring car startles Sean, who scolds me when I laugh. The waiter brings us laminated menus printed in English. I order myself steak and frites, with a large glass of white wine.

Sean orders soup and bread. When it arrives, I put a napkin round his neck and one on his lap. I rip up the roll for him, allowing him to grab chunks with his claw, his whole hand dipping into the hot soup. He lifts each dripping, steaming clot of food towards his face, smiling hungrily. The soup drips down his arm and I tell myself not to care.

Once he's done with the roll, I get a straw from his bag and lift what's left of the bowl to his lips, allowing him to suck up the liquid.

My steak is a little overdone. I chew hard and feel the bruise in my jaw from Sean's knee.

After we've paid and Sean's been cleaned up, we head back to the Domain. I buy a small, Virgin Mary-shaped plastic figurine and fill it with holy water from a tap at the base of the Basilica wall. Yesterday evening, Jordan messaged me to say that half a litre of holy water from Lourdes sells online for £22.59, not including delivery.

I push Sean up a ramp to the Basilica, using an elderly couple as pacesetters. I even imitate their shuffle – one foot at a time, in perfect harmony with each other. I briefly imagine Jordan and me at their age, then drift to thinking about the wife tripping over and bringing the husband down painfully on top of her.

By the time we're inside the chapel, I'm audibly panting, my legs cramped and impossibly heavy. I imagine my face in divine Baroque suffering – a sheen of earned sweat that I refrain from wiping away.

The space is low-lit and cavernous, and far more empty than I anticipated.

'The restoration is bad,' says Sean, gesturing to an oil painting of Christ on the way to Calvary, hanging just above my head.

'How can you tell from there?' I say exhaustedly, only slightly exaggerating my fatigue.

'The gloss,' Sean says. 'They have painted straight over the original varnish. You are supposed to remove the varnish, then make the changes, then add another layer.'

'Since when are you an expert on restoration?' I say, barely holding myself upright as we move down the chapel, past the other Stations of the Cross.

'I watched a YouTube series.'

'Naturally – where all experts congregate.'

'There is this thing called craquelure,' Sean says with complete authority. 'It occurs naturally in all oil paintings. Usually around the edges, but it can be present anywhere. And restorers and forgers have to create fake craquelure to keep the paintings looking antique. It maintains the illusion of age. People prefer things when they are not perfect.'

'Of course that's the message you take away from it,' I say, now choosing to wipe my face.

'It is pretty easy to spot fake craquelure, if you are look-ing for it.'

'So how soon do the paintings start to age?'

'I am not sure,' Sean says. 'I guess immediately. But it depends on the atmosphere. That is why all the galleries are temperature controlled. To manage time and maintain illusion. I am sure that these paintings,' he says, gesturing to Station Thirteen, the Lamentation, 'are copies of a series which is much older than St Bernadette's miracle.'

'So if they're copies, why would they need restoring?' I say, trying to sound curious.

'Even copies are expensive. And you cannot temperature control a chapel in the same way as a gallery.'

'Please don't try to tell me that this place is short of money. The money's got to be going somewhere.'

'I do not know what you want me to tell you, Janet,' Sean says, examining the architecture without moving his head.

'You're such a fucking know-it-all,' I say, almost inaudibly.

'Do not swear here,' Sean says.

'Fuck you,' I say, affectionately, applying his brakes and sitting down on the front pew.

'Could you help me out the chair, please?' Sean asks, making no attempt at eye contact.

'I'm knackered. You're fine as you are,' I tell him, collapsing onto the bench, my legs giving way.

We sit for twenty minutes, watching middle-aged acolytes prepare the altar for Mass – lighting six-foot candles and the incense, testing the microphones. This pre-ritual is silent, their movements modest and sure.

'Did you know,' Sean says in his version of a whisper, breathy and spitty, slumped into himself, 'that no one was ever supposed to see the Parthenon Frieze?'

'The Elgin Marbles?' I whisper back, eyes forwards.

'Yes – British Museum. That one.'

'What made you think of that?'

'The height of the art here. It is the same in every gallery. Nothing is intended for close inspection at wheelchair height.'

'No shit,' I say, flinching on the swear word.

'But no one was ever supposed to see the Parthenon Frieze. It was twelve metres off the ground. It was art for the sake of art.'

'What point are you trying to make?' I say.

'No point. Just something to consider.'

The incense here is like nothing I've smelled before. There's an unpleasant acridity to the burn. It's a smell felt behind the eyeballs.

The Mass starts with organ music, Gregorian and totally out of place in this space. I listen to an invisible choir sing the Kyrie, trying to pick out individual voices among them.

The priest has a kind, rounded face. I close my eyes and my mind starts to drift. I think back to the river, to that heavenly sense of calm. I wonder whether the moment was real, whether those feelings were a product of exhaustion, or something else. Something bigger.

To the chime of a bell, the kindly priest raises the monstrance and moves it like a security camera, scanning the room once, then twice. The hall is wired up with a surround-sound speaker system – from the front row, I can hear the priest's real voice, and a crackling one ten feet above my head.

Sean's chin is in his neck, patchy with thick stubble. He's pulling a listening face, even though he speaks no Latin.

Further down the front row, a long-limbed man in a wheel-chair has been panicking loudly for most of the Mass. He appears to be deaf, dumb and blind. He is wailing for reasons known only to himself and his Lord, while a woman (almost certainly his mother), chastises him by tugging hard on his earlobe. The wails have become an ambient noise, in spite of the silence.

'Amen,' Sean says across two long syllables, his eyes closed, the rest of the congregation in chorus.

I think about the craquelure of the paintings on the walls. Lines made by time, following the path of least resistance. I visualise my brain. I think about how often my own thoughts follow a path of least resistance, how easily and readily they flow back to hurt.

The thought is broken as Sean's arm jerks violently into my side. His head is hung at a right angle, his lips already bubbling with frothed and gurgled noises. Without hesitation, I unbuckle him from the chair and drag him forwards, easing his twitching body onto my own, then down, heavily onto the floor.

The priest has stopped the service. The speakers above us play a static hum of whispered instructions. There's a babble of French around me, but no one is making any attempt to clear the chairs from behind us.

'Pass me a coat,' I announce to the crowd, holding Sean's head off the tiled floor. 'Un coat, un jumper,' I say, louder, playing charades with my free arm. The incense is somehow stronger down here. I feel dizzy. Organ music starts up – loud enough to drown out the commotion. The priest has made his way from the altar, and seems to be praying over Sean.

'Get out the way,' I snap at him, snatching a jumper from the proffering mother of the long-limbed man. She grants me a meek smile and backs away.

'The ambulance comes,' says one elderly man from above me.

'No ambulance,' I say instinctually, shouting over the organ music, attempting to shield Sean from the view of the crowd. 'He will be fine. He is epileptic.'

'She comes,' says the man, a shrug in his voice.

The fit is intensifying. Sean contorts like a fish on land, his body reacting to a thousand invisible assailants. His eyes are rolled back to the heavens, teeth bared and gnashing. Each frenetic breath seems stolen from the world.

My mouth is completely dry and the tile is hurting my knees. Like last time, I am lightheaded, willing the fit to stop, internally insisting that I've got everything under control.

'I am a nurse also,' says one bushy-haired lady, forcing her way to the front of Sean's audience. 'How can I help?'

'Keep them back,' I tell her, gesturing with a drool-soaked hand. 'He will be fine. He is fine.'

Turning my attention briefly away from Sean, I watch the lady and the acolytes usher the congregation to the back of the chapel, where the priest is now administering Communion.

I'm gently cradling his head on the mound of clothes. The jerks of Sean's neck make it seem like he is flinching against my touch.

'Why now?' I say to the body below me. 'What's wrong with you this time? You're supposed to come to this city to get healed. Only you could come here and convince everyone you're on the verge of death. You better hope I've remembered to pack one of those suppositories.'

Above the altar, a handsome, gilded version of the risen Christ hovers above a gaggle of awed saints, his arms open, palms raised. He looks down blankly on the contorting mess of Sean's body and his carer. This kneeling, aching woman, stupid enough to suffer alongside him.

As the fit abates, I settle Sean's unconscious head on the mound of clothes and rise stiffly to my feet. As I rise, the remaining members of the congregation break into a small applause. Some make the sign of the cross.

I hover at a slight distance from Sean's still, foetal body, wary of letting him throw up over my only pair of flats when he regains consciousness. I'm now shivering myself, soaked with sweat and cold without a jumper.

Minutes later, paramedics enter the chapel, all men in their fifties and sixties wearing orange high-vis vests. They pause to get their hands blessed by the priest, who then points them over to the crisis that is Sean's body.

'English, yes?' says the first man to arrive.

'Yes,' I say. 'It was a tonic-clonic seizure. He has cerebral palsy.'

'He is sick?' says the man.

'No – not sick, he is disabled. He is fine now. He needs to rest.'

The man nods in an attempt at comprehension, and without asking for permission, waves over his colleagues, who ghost past me, surround Sean and shift him onto a stretcher.

In moving Sean's leg, one of the men has disturbed his catheter bag, releasing a stream of urine onto the stretcher, which trickles down onto the chapel tile as they lift him off the ground and carry him towards the entrance.

I gather our stuff and wheel away Sean's chair, following the trail of urine out of the chapel and back into daylight.

I've been watching the monitors for twenty minutes now. The main screen is split into three lines, scrolling from left to right, each recording something essential, each colour-coded for a vital sign.

I'm sitting on my hands by his bed, my head level with his body. The room has the universal stale smell of hospital.

Sean sleeps in his usual position. The oxygen tube plugging

his nose hoops around his ears, then off to a switchboard of machinery.

It all seems a bit excessive. I had communicated the need for a suppository and the basics of his medical history. Sean regained consciousness just long enough to confirm to them that I was his carer – that I was here by choice.

I am trying to stay engaged – trying to think about how willingly the body is prepared to give up its secrets. How, under the right touch, Sean is just another cluster of ciphers.

Aside from an occasional beep, the monitors are silent. As I watch, I find myself thinking of waves. Of the ocean, beating against a sandbank. A shoreline stretching as far as my mind will allow. The beeps, the waves – constant and hypnotic. The ebb and flow of something ancient and primal.

The ward nurses do a handover every three hours. Aside from this, there is very little said. They will stand a foot from me, and talk as though I were part of the chair I've been confined to. Because Sean and I share no blood, it is a crime for me even to look at his charts. At least, I've convinced myself it would be.

I shift my weight and my hands come out numb.

So much of my recent life has been spent in these spaces, around medical professionals. I've decided that there's a big gulf between being a nurse and being a carer. It is the space between profession and vocation. I am in the void between a calling and a sentence. If nurses were art, they would be polished marble, the Grotto wall – their empathy smooth and perfect from being handled too often. Their lack of visible affection would never be labelled psychopathic. It is a serene, classical wisdom.

I think about ripping the cord from Sean's nose. I imagine the IV bags and poles toppling, alarms immediately sounding – the sensors that know when an artwork has been touched. A firm hand on my shoulder. Sean bolts upright, gasping for air.

'Rest,' says a passing nurse with a thick French accent. 'The café – F block. *Il ne ferme pas.*'

'Thanks. Uh, *merci*,' I say, pleased for permission to leave.

It's just after one in the morning and the hospital car park is still half full. I smoke, leaning against the hospital wall, feeling totally drained. I scroll through pictures from Chloe's birthday party on my phone and begin walking. She's wearing a pretty navy jumpsuit and looks happy. There's one picture of two handsome men kissing her on each cheek, her mouth wide in a fake expression of delighted surprise. I tap *like* on all the photos, finish my cigarette outside F Block, and ring a bell to be let in.

I can see the café through the glass. The barista looks up, makes eye contact with me, then looks back to his phone. I count to ten before I ring the bell again. He looks up, and makes a non-committal gesture, which I interpret as 'use the other entrance'.

Inside, I dig through my pockets for change and communicate that I want tea.

'English?' the barista says, somehow knowing.

'Yes – *Oui. Merci beaucoup.*'

The tea is scalding and bitter. I take it back outside and smoke my last cigarette, reading through all the birthday messages on Chloe's profile, all our old school friends, with their jobs and lives and husbands and children. I scroll, half expecting to see Florence's name, her fat, angled face.

On returning, I find Sean awake and propped up.

'That doesn't look comfortable,' I say, taking in the sight of him.

'Sore,' Sean says – his lips crusty and chapped.

'I'm not surprised. You've been asleep forever. I think they drugged you.'

'What happened?' he says, his voice swollen and thick.

'You had a full-blown fit during Mass. They brought you here. We have to stay for the night. We're probably going to miss the return flight.'

'You can go,' Sean says, his eyes closing.

'What, back to our lovely hotel? Yeah, because there's definitely going to be someone at reception to give me our key. No, I'm stuck here. I'm stuck here and I'm out of cigarettes, and I doubt I'm going to be able to buy any more in a hospital. So you're going to have to keep me company. You have to talk to me.'

'I am tired,' Sean says, his eyes still closed.

'Then you can pick what we speak about. I've only had priests and nurses to speak to.'

'Is there a priest here?' says Sean, suddenly animated.

'Calm down – there are loads of priests. There's a chapel on every floor.'

'Did they come to see me?'

'One did. He didn't seem too worried about you. He probably sees a lot of bodies like yours. Take a look around you.' I gesture to the rest of the wing, to the beds, filled with disabled men, leashed to machines.

'I think,' Sean says, some hesitation in his voice. 'I think I am ready to speak about her.'

'Brigid?' I say, sitting up, sliding my right leg under me.

'She liked to tell stories,' Sean says. 'She was a storyteller. She says – said – that it was the way she grew up. She said her home was always full of stories.'

'What kind of stories?' I say.

'Anything. Pirates. Wars. She told me stories about animals in our garden. She told me stories about herself – her time in the convents. But she would tell those stories without looking at you.'

'Maybe she thought stories were a good way of helping with your language,' I suggest. 'Maybe she thought that it was a way for you to spend time together without forcing you to speak.'

'It took me a long time to realise that she got some of the stories wrong. She changed them. Like *Little Red Riding Hood*. She told a version where the wolf was some strange Old Testament plague, sent by God. I do not know what I was supposed to learn from it. I remember being scared.'

'Did she read to you from the Bible?'

Sean takes a moment to think.

'I do not remember her ever reading directly from the Bible. She did not talk to me about God directly. We went to Mass together, but never discussed it afterwards.'

'How come?'

'I do not know. I think she worried that I might hate God. That I would hate God for making me this way.' He makes a small laughing movement and closes his eyes.

'Do you hate God?' I ask.

'That is not fair,' he says, now sniffing.

'I didn't mean to upset you,' I say, raising a tissue to help him blow his nose.

'God chose me to live,' he says. 'That is all I know.'

For a while, we sit in silence. I drift off to sleep and wake up with my head tilted against his mattress, my neck stiff. A nurse is standing on the other side of the bed, taking Sean's temperature and recording his vital signs. She smiles at me and I smile back, neither of us with anything to say.

Sean clears his throat. 'Ja-net?'

'Mhmm?'

'If I went to heaven, what kind of body do you think I would have?'

'Mmm?'

'Heaven,' Sean says breathily.

'What makes you think you'd get into heaven?'

'It is hard for me to imagine a different body.'

'A normal body wouldn't suit you,' I say.

'I am normal,' he says.

'Good night, Sean,' I say.

Sean is discharged just after six, after the doctor's first rounds. On the way out of the ward, the nurses stop to kiss him on each cheek and hang a rosary around his neck.

'*Dieu te bénisse,*' they say as one, waving as the lift doors close.

By the time our taxi gets back to the hotel, it's after eight, and we're guaranteed to have missed the flight. I take Sean to our room and change him, packing everything else away as I go. I'm weary and aching, but focused on the task at hand.

Once Sean is in his chair, I take a long, hot shower, scrubbing every inch of myself, using nearly a whole travel-sized bottle of shampoo. I turn up the pressure and feel the water beat against my neck and inside my thighs. I tell myself this is healing water.

I take the showerhead off the wall and move it between my legs, touching myself, leaning against the thin partition dividing me from Sean. I tell myself that this is the same water that flows outside, the same sacred water that sells for a premium on the internet. I tell myself I am being saved, that I am being cleansed.

I orgasm quietly, biting my lip, my legs quivering like a seizure. I pull on my clothes and dry my hair, stepping out of the bathroom, made new. Born again.

We arrive at the airport around lunchtime. I explain our situation to a bored-looking customer-service lady in a mixture of English and gesturing. She disappears for ten minutes to speak to her manager, then agrees to give us a hundred-euro discount on the replacement tickets, putting us on the next flight, which takes off in an hour.

'Thank you,' I say, struggling to seem grateful.

I push Sean through Customs, where he is forcefully patted down by the same guard who kept us waiting on arrival.

Once we're at the gate, I use the rest of our change in the vending machines. I haven't eaten anything since the steak from yesterday. I buy crisps and sweets and chewing gum and three bottles of water. As I walk back towards Sean with full arms, I spot a child across the lounge eyeing me enviously, tugging on his mother's arm and pointing.

'I have a question,' I say, poking Sean in his arm, waking him from a daze. 'Why did Brigid keep your dad's surname after they got divorced?'

'They were not divorced,' Sean says groggily.

'You're kidding?'

He moves his head in a no.

'But didn't he leave you, like over twenty years ago?' I say, hungrily scooping M&Ms into my mouth.

'Mum did not divorce him. She never signed any papers. She did not want to.'

'But that's totally crazy.'

'She took vows. The Church does not recognise civil divorce. She was married until one of them died.'

'Didn't someone try to convince her?'

'She was busy with me. And other things.'

'But he paid no money. He sent no child support.'

'She did not want any contact with him.'

My chest feels tight and my fists are tensed. I crunch hard on the M&Ms. I don't have the energy to be this angry. I feel like I want to kick something. I feel like I should be screaming.

'How can you be so at peace with this? Don't you hate him?'

'I do not think about it,' Sean says, adjusting himself with an awkward shuffle. 'It was her choice. Can I have some water, please?' he says, gesturing to the three bottles piled on the seat next to me.

'So you've just forgiven him? That's some fucking saintly level of forgiveness.'

'I did not say that,' Sean says, now reaching towards the water. 'I said I do not think about it.'

I pass him the bottle and get a straw from his bag, helping it into his mouth. His beard is now a thick fuzz, the acne buried deep below. He looks mature, somehow.

'But now she's dead, you don't have to keep his surname.

You could switch to hers. Or anything. You could rebrand yourself.'

Still drinking, Sean moves his shoulders in a shrug.

'I can't believe this. I can't believe you'd want anything to do with that man. I can't believe you'd want him associated with you.'

'He is my father,' Sean says, spitting away the straw.

'Who gives a shit?'

'My mum did. And he makes an effort. He follows me on Twitter. He has not forgotten me.'

I wipe down his mouth and shove the rest of the snacks into Sean's bag. I feel like there's a stone in my gut. I feel bloated with anger.

A boarding call goes out for priority passengers, meaning us.

'Was he at the funeral?' I say, standing and taking off his brakes.

'Yes.'

'Did you speak to him?' I say, joining a queue of other people in chairs.

'Yes.'

'Why didn't you tell me?'

'You did not ask.'

'What did he have to say for himself?'

'He said he was living in Spain, with his partner. He said she could not join him. He said he was very sorry about Mum, and that he would be there if I needed him.'

I laugh forcefully. The people ahead of us in the queue turn.

'He said that he wanted to get in touch, but knew that Mum would not ever allow it.'

'Jesus Christ,' I say. I reach into his bag and pull out the pill organiser. 'Just take these before we get on,' I say, popping the tablets into his mouth. 'I can't even deal with this conversation. This is fucking unbelievable.'

Sean swallows them dry with a grimace. 'Why do you care?' he says, now with a tone.

'Because it's not fair that he gets away with it. You're allowing him to get away with being a monster. What he did was unforgiveable.'

'We should go,' Sean says, pointing ahead of us to the beckoning flight attendant.

'Shit,' I say, shoving the pill organiser back into the backpack and pushing him forwards, onto the plane, back to England, to London, to home.

Chapter 5

It's been forty-eight hours since we got back. So far, I've only spoken to Jordan once, to say I'm safe but exhausted, promising that I'll message him soon. I still feel completely drained, but I'm slightly less sore. I've been putting off opening my laptop, wary of my inbox.

I start on Facebook. Chloe has linked me to the episode of *Panorama* on care homes she had mentioned.

I sit up in bed and watch as a serious-looking woman with a northern accent explains that, despite an eleven per cent growth in the UK's population of over sixty-fives, the number of care-home residents has remained stable, increasing by only 0.3 per cent. The woman says this is down to the lack of new government-funded homes being opened, and the lack of affordable private care. She says that the government has stripped back funding across the board, and that the most vulnerable people in society are increasingly dependent on charities and the good will of relatives.

The episode focuses on one private care home in Birmingham, previously rated as 'Good' by the Care Quality

Commission, where an undercover BBC reporter worked as a locum care assistant for six weeks, secretly filming the staff. Despite having no specialist training, the reporter is assigned to a man with severe dementia. She finds his bed with a loose guardrail, having just been told about the man's tendency to fall. She uses hidden cameras to catch the staff talking about him, mocking his smell, his anxiety. They mention that a bit of morphine would 'shut him up'. They mention that no one has visited him in six months.

There are interviews with horrified GPs and politicians, forced to watch the footage in full. Surveys and statistics are quoted, estimating that one in ten residents aren't fed adequately, and that one in three people in care live in fear of physical abuse or harm. There's a general consensus that while these may be isolated incidents, something must be done. I've never heard the term negligence used so often.

The show's climax is a two-minute clip of a care assistant beating a senile man round the back of the head as he refuses to eat, spitting out the food that she aggressively forces into his mouth.

I feel my heart seize up – despite her blurred-out face, I immediately recognise the person hitting the man. I recognise her movements, her accent, her broken English. I am absolutely certain it is the Bangladeshi lady I was paired with during my training.

I'm stood up, breathing heavily. I feel dizzy and faint. I feel like there's a hand around my neck, tight and rising – it feels like being caught, exposed.

It occurs to me that this is the reason we were always paired together. I feel sure that she must have learned this from me – that maybe there really is something within me, something toxic and awful, corrosive enough to leak out and spread.

I open the window and call Chloe, lighting up a cigarette, leaning outside. It's just after four in the afternoon and it's dark out already. Sirens flare in the distance. Chloe's number rings through to voicemail.

'Hi, this is Chloe, leave a message and I'll get right back to you.'

'It's Janet. I've just watched that thing you linked me and it's fucked me up. Call me back and I'll explain. I'm going to need to drink, so let me know where to meet you.'

I smoke right to the filter and pace the flat, moving in a circuit from the front door to the kitchen, doubling back through my room. Alex will complain about the smell, but he's leaving soon anyway. I am rotating my arms in wide circles, focusing on my breathing, waiting for the revelation that won't come. I tell myself that this will pass, that it doesn't mean anything. I tell myself I'm getting worked up over nothing, that I'm only responsible for my own actions. I tell myself that I'm not capable of that behaviour. I tell myself every lie I can.

I shadowbox the air, remembering Jordan's training. I stand in front of the bathroom mirror and throw jabs at my own face, ducking and dodging, breathing and crying, blinking hard, wiping the tears, moving through an upper cut, a cross, following through, throwing my weight forwards, sobbing now, filling the flat with my sound, the tightness in my neck spreading to my chest, my jaw.

Slumped on the bathroom floor, I hear Chloe calling back and I let it ring. I let it ring and ring and ring.

*

In the developed world, the life expectancy for someone with cerebral palsy is pretty much the same as a healthy, able-bodied adult. Being left-handed has more of an impact when you look at the numbers. What the numbers don't reflect is that people with cerebral palsy age about a decade faster – when Sean is thirty, he'll look forty.

Effectively, cerebral palsy is just a type of brain damage. It has the widest scope of impact of almost any condition. At the Paralympics, an athlete with cerebral palsy could compete in one of five cycling categories, one of eight track and field categories, and one of ten swimming categories. Some events are pretty much dedicated to athletes with cerebral palsy, like boccia and football.

If Sean were to compete, he'd be classified as CP2, meaning he's quadriplegic with a high degree of spasticity and likely some ataxia. He has no ambulation, but a relative amount of upper-body control. The line between CP2 and CP3 is mostly a matter of stiffness.

At Sean's check-up yesterday, the doctor told us that in spite of the bindings and in spite of the flights, this is the most control and flexibility Sean has had at any point in his adult life. It's all thanks to the daily therapy and massages. It's all thanks to me. She prescribed more hydrotherapy and a course of SSRIs, insisting that the latter was optional, and only if the depression got worse.

From the street to Sean's bed, there are five doors between me and his body. Five excuses to turn back. Five ways to leave him there, to allow him to regress, asleep in his own filth. Five decisions to be overlooked – made mechanical.

Sean's tenancy in the Mills Grand Estate is locked in for

another six months. He hasn't raised moving in together since our conversation in the hotel. Technically, all the hoists and slings and transfer boards we use are owned by the property. All the medical equipment Sean grew up using moved with Brigid to Ireland. If we were to move in together, we'd either have to bring it back over from Ireland, or buy it all from scratch.

It feels safe to limit my thoughts to all the practical reasons that could prevent us from living together. If I start indulging the idea seriously, the prospect becomes too tempting – too real. I am highly aware that living with Sean would bind me to him for the foreseeable future.

I'm stood outside the entrance to the Mills Grand Estate, smoking, on my phone, still programmed to expect to see her emails. But there's nothing. There will never be an email from her again.

This morning, Owen's article was published on the *Frieze* website. He's included two pictures – one monochrome shot of me crouched over Sean, holding the camera above his head, the other of Sean's empty chair, surrounded by lighting equipment. My name isn't mentioned in the interview.

The Twitter post sharing Sean's interview has fifteen retweets and twenty *likes*, including the regular *like* from his father. Sean seems to be following everyone who interacts with the post. He's changed his profile picture to Owen's image of us in the studio – the dimensions mean I'm mostly cropped out the frame.

Today will be our last studio session of the year. Most of the college has already broken up for Christmas, meaning we should have free choice over studio space and unlimited access to lighting.

Sean wants to create a piece dedicated to Brigid. He says that after this, maybe it's time to start doing something different, that the bindings have run their course. He says he doesn't care about whether they're commercially viable. He says that he'd prefer to be making the most of his college experience. He'd prefer to be experimenting and innovating.

'Are you happy with the article, then?' I call to him, now inside the flat, preparing the bathroom. 'With your answers?'

'I guess,' he says, propped up in bed, iPad in hand.

'What do you mean, you guess?'

'I think you were right. I think that I am not right for that format. I do not think I will really stand out. I do not understand why he needed to do the interview in person.'

'Have you spoken to him since?' I say, wheeling the hoist around to his bed.

'Not really. Only to send over my biography. He liked a few of my tweets.'

'I think that counts,' I say. 'Maybe the art world just has a short attention span. Maybe we need to market you more aggressively.'

'Maybe,' Sean says, entrusting me with his iPad, allowing me to pull off his T-shirt.

Sean's biography at the bottom of the article says he is Irish, raised in England. It mentions his condition and where he's studying. It mentions that he can be reached on Twitter.

I undress and shower him without saying too much, the radio turned up to drown out the silence. I think about my training in this room – how Brigid cut his hair without consulting him. The broad, confident whirr of the electric razor in her hand, the trust between them as he offered her his head and neck.

For the first time in weeks, Sean allows me to cut his fingernails.

'She would be very proud,' I say to Sean, roughly drying his hair.

'I know.'

'Have you sent your uncle the article?'

'Not yet.'

'Are you going to?'

'Not sure.'

'I'm sure your family would like to see it. I'm sure they'd be grateful for some good news.'

'Okay, Janet,' he says, snappy.

'Sorry,' I say, the word catching in my throat.

Sean leans forward and wings out his arms, freefalling on his shower seat. I towel him down, gentle over the bruising.

'Feel dry?' I say, removing my plastic shower apron and turning off the extractor.

'All good. Hungry.'

'I can offer you some delicious banana, some not so delicious purée, or a peanut-butter milkshake. All served with a side of pills.'

'Can I have a banana and peanut-butter milkshake?'

'Now we're talking,' I say, fastening the shower sling to his hoist and raising him in the air, wheeling him back across to the bed, his feet hanging loosely, dripping a trail behind us.

I massage Sean on his bed, classifying his body with my touch, easing him from CP2 to CP3, pressuring the stiffness into possibility. I work his legs in the air, moving through a bicycle of motion, extending him through himself, directing his pain through to me. I feel the sweat patches blossoming under my arms. I feel the rest of my life in his skin, ageing before its time.

Sean's phone is ringing.

'Suzanna's calling,' I say, answering and putting her on speakerphone.

'Hi, Suzanna,' Sean says, his legs back in the air, suspended in my hands.

'Hello, my darling Sean,' Suzanna says, her voice tinny and distant. 'I'm in Milan for the holidays – so sorry I can't be there with you, but I read your article. I think they've really got you. They've really captured something. It's very clever what they've done. You have such a strong voice. I have arranged for it to be sent around to everyone.'

'To everyone?' Sean says.

'It is going in the college bulletin. We will share you as much as we can. You're my star!'

'Okay,' Sean says, turning his head to the window.

'This is the start of something wonderful for you, Sean. Your work is going to touch so many people. Your mother would be so proud.'

'Thank you! Bye, Suzanna,' Sean says.

'Bye, Suzanna,' I say, hanging up.

Once he's dressed and still, I tidy up and make breakfast. While Sean drinks his milkshake, I read about a three-year-old girl from South Africa with eighty per cent burns. A barbecue explosion, supposedly. Forty-one pieces of skin were flown from around the world to patch her up. The article accuses her of being beautiful, then has the audacity to include images.

There's someone knocking at the door. In nine months of working with Sean, there's never been a knock at the door.

'Expecting someone?'

'No,' Sean says, unbothered.

'Hello?' I say through the door.

'It's Keith – I've got a delivery for Sean.'

I unlock the door and Keith hands me a long poster tube.

'We had to pay import tax on that for him. We'll add it to his bill.'

'Right, okay,' I say.

'It's from Canada,' Keith says, heading back down the hall. 'Fucking Canada. Merry Christmas, Jane,' he says.

'It's Janet,' Sean shouts from the dining table.

'Told you he's a fucking idiot,' I say, bringing the tube over.

'Yeah,' Sean says, finishing his breakfast. 'Is it from Ashley?'

'Of course it's from Ashley,' I say, turning the tube to show him her name on the return address. 'Who else is going to be sending you things from Canada?'

'I expected it to be framed.'

'That probably would have cost her hundreds in shipping costs. I don't think Ashley has hundreds to spare.'

'Could you open it, please?' Sean says, wiping his mouth on his forearm.

I carefully remove the tape around the top of the tube and uncork the plastic cap – there's a faint musk-like smell.

'I think it got a bit wet,' I say, sliding out a roll of thick canvas. 'Looks like it's just at the edges though.'

I pinch at the corners, shaking out the canvas, allowing it to unroll. It curls up a little at the bottom. I stand at a distance from Sean, the picture between us.

'Well?'

'You have got it the wrong way round,' he says, excitement in his voice.

'It's a grid,' I say, lowering my arms, peeking over the top of the picture. 'How can you even tell?'

'I recognise the piece,' he says, smiling. 'It is my favourite. She sent me my favourite.'

'My arms are getting tired, can I lay it on the floor?'

'Sure,' Sean says. 'I should call her – I should let her know it has arrived safely.'

'I think it will be like six in the morning for her. We can call her later. Just send a message for now.'

'Can you take a photo of it for me? For my Twitter?'

Sean is back up to speed with his tweeting, averaging three or four tweets a day, mostly sent in the evenings, after I've left. I feel like tweeting may be the only private thing in his life – the only activity I play no part in. He is yet to tweet anything about his mother's death.

'Why is this one your favourite?' I say, unlocking his iPad and opening the camera.

'No reason,' Sean says.

'But you always have a reason. You have a reason for everything when it comes to art.'

'I just think this one is very beautiful. I like what Rosalind Krauss says, about how the grid is hostile to narrative. How a grid turns its back on nature.'

I weigh the corners down with heavy art books from Sean's shelf and climb up onto a chair to get a better angle, to fit the whole piece in shot.

'Be careful,' Sean says.

'Are you going to send Ashley something back, then?'

'Photographs are different.'

'Right, I didn't think of that.'

Ashley's grid is composed of red and black lines. They are thick, dark spines, running from edge to edge. They start bold, but ghost out on the far side as the paint fades from her wheel. Looking closely, you can see the lines aren't perfectly straight. There's a slight angle to the movement. The definite impression of tyre print.

'Are you planning on going to Canada, then? To see her?'

'I could not do that,' Sean says, incredulous.

'Why not?' I say, climbing down, handing over the iPad. 'You're an international traveller now. The flight would only take a few hours longer than to France.'

'And where would I stay? Who would be there to help?'

'It's not like going to fucking Somalia or something, Sean. There are probably facilities available. If you really wanted to, we could make it happen. I could help make it happen. If you're going to be this big-shot famous artist you're going to have to get used to globetrotting. You can do anything you want, remember?'

'Thanks, Janet,' Sean says, looking at the picture on his iPad.

'You could even change that hairstyle. If you trust me to cut your hair, we can get you a nice Mohawk going.'

Sean laughs a splurting, warm sound, his body jerking like a fit. I feel my face arrange itself into a big smile.

'Where are you going to hang it, then? Once we've got it framed?'

'Um – I am not sure. What do you think?'

'You want my opinion?' I say, trying to mask my surprise.

'Yeah, what do you think?'

'I think above your bed. It's about time you had something other than a crucifix above your bed.'

'Yeah,' Sean says, smiling.

'This is your home now.'

'Yeah,' he says, looking away.

The college is almost empty. We're in the lobby, waiting for the lift. It's quiet enough to hear Christmas music playing from the café down the hall.

'Did you have any Christmas traditions?' I say to Sean, directing his attention to an upside-down Christmas tree that's been installed in the ceiling, suspended by its roots, which seem to be covered in gold leaf.

'Mass,' Sean says.

'Obviously Mass, but did Brigid do a turkey? Did you ever get any cool presents?'

'I do not want to talk about it,' Sean says.

As we leave the lift, strip lighting in the hall triggers on, annoyed to life by our movements. I can sense the overwhelming emptiness of the space, the creepiness of the half-formed art, abandoned for the holidays. I sense the strangeness of the task at hand. I wheel Sean forwards, feeling like the victim in a horror movie, a padded echo in my footsteps.

'Shall we put on the radio while we work today?' I say.

'No Christmas songs,' Sean says.

Our regular studio seems to be being used as storage space – filled with stacks of chairs. We enter the smaller one next door, the studio we used during our session with Owen.

There's a thin film of paint dust covering the whole floor. Sean's wheels make a track as we move inside.

'I'll have to sweep up.'

'Yup.'

'Or we could find a different one?'

'Here is fine.'

'Right.'

After ten minutes of cleaning, we're ready to go. I borrow a paint-splattered radio and lay out the mat.

'What's the plan?' I say, trying to sound enthusiastic.

'I want to do a photo of us,' Sean says, clear and precise, holding my gaze. 'I want a photo of us in a *pietà*. I want you to bind me with all the tape and cord we have left, and I want you to hold me in your arms.'

This is an intense level of eye contact, an intensity I would associate with interrogations, proposals.

'But, I'm just in my jeans. I don't have any make-up. I don't have anything—'

'That does not matter,' Sean interrupts. 'I will crop out your head from the frame. I just want to be held in the photo.'

'We'd have to set up a timer. I've never done that before.'

'I know how,' Sean says.

'Are you sure this is what you want? This is the piece you want to end on? You had so many other ideas.'

'I am sure.'

Out of the wheelchair, out of the straps, he's all limb and bone, no trace of progress, no evidence of improvement, still hunched into the shape of a victim. I set the radio to Classic FM. *The Planets Suite* plays softly as I set up the lights and empty our supplies into the corner.

'Ashley replied,' Sean says from the mat. 'She is glad I like it. She thinks above the bed is a good idea. She suggests a plain black frame.'

'That shouldn't be too tricky, then,' I say, untangling the red and black cords. 'We can get that sorted tomorrow. It'll probably be ready by Christmas. Have you decided when you're coming back after the holidays?'

'It is up to my uncle. He will have the van.'

'Right,' I say, my fingers straining into a particularly tricky knot.

'I have eighty new followers.'

'Amazing.'

I pull at the knot with my teeth, tasting the chemical twang of plastic.

'This person called me a spastic,' Sean says in a neutral tone.

'Well, that's Twitter, I guess.'

'Yeah,' Sean says.

I rub Vaseline over his feet, over his scars; I butter up his ankles and calves, his thighs, twitching under the surface of his skin, even now, still suspicious of my touch. The radio plays a string symphony by Mendelssohn.

I consider the possibility that I've spent more time touching Sean than any person will ever spend touching me. I consider the possibility that no one will ever know my body as intimately as I know Sean's.

I imagine Brigid's reaction to the article. I imagine her emailing everyone she ever knew, prouder than any mother ever was. I imagine her in the studio doorway, haunting us, both understanding and not. I imagine her praying for us in some distant place, praying that everything remains like this forever, just as she would have intended it.

I cross Sean's ankles and start with the hemp rope, matching the ends and finding the cow hitch. I place the join on the top of his foot, wrap round and pull through, splitting the gap, then doubling back, widening the band, then lifting and slipping the rest of the rope up and through the loop. Sean cranes his neck off the mat and watches my hands. I tug firmly through the loop and secure the knot.

'That okay?'

'Yeah. Now the tape.'

I start just above the ankle, taping him in one long roll, moving in a strict diagonal, up the length of his shins, all the way to the knee. His legs are a cocoon.

'We might run out,' I say, showing him what remains of the tape.

'That is okay. We will make it work. It does not have to be neat.'

I think back through all the pieces we've created. There must be nearly thirty by this point, not including the failures, all the positions he couldn't quite bear. I think back through all the pain I've caused, all the photographic evidence of that hurt. I imagine an archivist, stumbling across the pictures in a century's time, baffled and distressed by the obvious suffering, by the lack of context.

I lubricate Sean's body from the neck down, slicking his dark hair to his skin. Under the studio lights, he shines like a bodybuilder, oiled up for a show.

Sean instructs me to leave one of his arms free and bind the other behind him. I tape the end of the cord to his right palm, and pull his arm round, all the way behind his back, until his wrist touches the far-side of his hip, a place it could never ordinarily reach. I draw the length of the cord over his left shoulder and under his rib, tight like a seat belt, winding round him three times until his arm is fastened behind him, locked in place.

'Is this what you meant?'

'This is good. Just right,' he says, clearly uncomfortable.

I use the remaining tape to bind round his torso, covering the cord.

'Can you breathe okay?' I say, pulling round his chest, the harsh rip of the tape filling the space with violence.

'Fine,' Sean says, watching me work, something strange in his eyes, something desperate.

'Why a *pietà*?' I say.

'Because it is the end of the relationship. Because she suffered more than anyone and she never asked for any of it. She suffered and no one explained anything to her. She suffered with blind faith, and they took her son anyway. They took him and no one really fought it. It was a plan she had been cut out from. She knew nothing. Her role was finished long before.'

From the floor, Sean talks me through how to set up the timer. We finish with a black cloth round his eyes. He blindly instructs me to sit on my knees, to hold his head across my body, his free hand falling before us, reaching towards the camera, his bound legs hanging heavily over my own.

I set the timer for thirty seconds, which proves much too quick. We try a minute instead and get the shot, but apparently my back isn't straight enough. We take another seven exposures and I remain patient, going through the adjustments, straining my back as straight as it will go, trying my best to be compliant, to match his vision, to play the mother.

'You did it again,' Sean says, as I show him the camera, now slick with grease from where I've been holding him. 'I told you to lift me more.'

'I'm trying my best,' I say. 'It's a lot to remember.'

'It is not that hard. Just set it up and try again.'

'We only have time for a few more,' I say, checking a clock on the wall, staying calm.

'Well, you better get it right this time,' Sean says, spitting a little.

I put the camera back on the tripod, set up the timer, and rush back to him, lifting him across me, finding the right angle, pulling the right posture. The flash goes off before I'm quite ready and for a moment, I'm blind. Sean slips from my arms, falling forward heavily, his forehead smashing off the studio floor.

'Owwww,' he screams. 'You fucking idiot, Janet. Why are you such a fucking idiot?'

'I'm sorry,' I say, panicked, getting to my feet. 'The flash – it surprised me. You are so slippery. Are you okay?'

He pulls up his blindfold with his free hand, pressing the hurt.

'I am not okay,' he says. 'I want my mum.' And suddenly, he is crying, his face hard against the floor, snot bubbling from his nose.

'I want my mum,' he says in a long whine, louder. 'I want my mum.'

I'm stood over him, not sure what to do with my hands.

'Are you bleeding? Do you want me to unbind you?'

'I want my mum,' he wails, his left arm now grasping up at the air, clawing, flailing.

I can see a big red mark on his forehead, a bump swelling below the surface, but there's no blood.

'Sean,' I say, trying to sound calm. 'Sean, I need you to stay still so I can unbind you.'

I hear footsteps from down the hallway. 'Do you need some help in there?' says a man's voice.

'We are okay,' I say, rummaging desperately for the scissors.

'I want my mummy,' Sean sobs, his voice hoarse and breaking, barely even words.

'What in the name of hell is going on in here?' says a tall man in a cleaner's outfit, now stood in the doorway, eyeing me, brandishing scissors, my T-shirt covered in grease. 'Buddy, are you okay?' he says to Sean. 'Did this lady hurt you?'

'My mum,' Sean says, much more softly, hiccupping between sobs.

'He is saying he wants his mum,' I translate. 'She died recently. He is a student here.'

'I know who he is,' the cleaner says. 'Everyone knows who he is. But I don't know who you are.'

'I'm his personal assistant – his carer – every time he's here, it's with me.'

'Well, I don't remember ever seeing you before. Stay here. I'm going to get this boy some real help.'

'Sean, tell him,' I say, crouching by his body. 'Tell him who I am.'

But the man has gone, his footsteps rushing towards the

lift. In all his writhing and twisting, Sean's nappy has come loose. A stream of urine leaks from him, spreading over the mat, onto the floor.

'Oh fuck, Sean,' I say, standing back up. 'You've got to let me help you. Please stay still so I can get you unwrapped.'

I've just finished unbinding his legs when the cleaner returns, along with a police officer. They both clearly smell the piss, now puddling like evidence.

'Why don't you explain what's happened here,' the police officer says to me, stood at a distance.

'He slipped and fell,' I say, realising how suspicious the words sound. 'He's just very emotional because his mother's died recently.'

'Is there a medical emergency? Does he need an ambulance?'

'No, no – he just needs to calm down. I'll get him cleaned up and home.'

'And what's your relationship to this,' he pauses, 'this gentleman.'

'I've never seen her before,' the cleaner interrupts. 'I've never seen that lady once in my damn life.'

'I'm his carer,' I say, tears now apparent in my own voice. 'My name is Janet Lamb. I care for him. His name is Sean.'

'Sean,' says the police officer, taking off his jacket and slipping it under Sean's head. 'Sean, do you know this lady?'

He opens his eyes, red and pained. He looks at me.

'Yes,' he says.

'And does this lady care for you?'

'Yes.'

I wipe hot tears from my eyes. I feel my lip trembling.

'Do you want me to call anyone else for you?'

'No,' Sean says. 'Just Janet.'

'He says he just wants me.'

'I understood,' the police officer says, rising to his feet. 'I'll stick around in case you need me. I'll be waiting just outside.'

Once they're gone, I turn the radio off and cut his arm free, pulling his body away from the urine and sitting him upright, balanced against his wheelchair. Sean makes pained, whimpering sounds, gasping and hiccupping, doubled forward, arms above his head, as though he were braced for impact.

'We don't have a spare pad,' I explain.

'Okay,' he says from inside his arms. 'I am sorry, Janet. Let us go home, please. Please take me home.'

Once Sean's in his clothes and I've lifted him back into his chair, I return the police officer his jacket, thanking him. He wishes us a merry Christmas and walks away.

It takes another twenty minutes to pack our stuff away and wipe up the mess. Sean sits in silence, vestigial, curled into himself, holding a bottle of water, his breathing returning to his version of normal.

'She would be proud,' he says.

After his mother's funeral, Sean sat with his uncle and tried to be practical. They discussed what to do with her clothes (donate them to the Church), what to do with her jewellery (donate it to the Church), what to do with all her earthly possessions (donate them to the Church).

Sean made a list of everything he wanted to keep and everything he would need. Father John agreed to store his medical equipment in his parish basement until Sean finishes college. The rest of the stuff would need to come to London.

Father John is driving back to London today with a boot full of memories. Sean and I are clearing space for the boxes. We are freeing up drawers for the photo albums and his spare summer clothes. We are clearing display space for the knick-knacks that Sean built his life around, the possessions that witnessed him grow and hurt.

'Where do you want to put all these?' I say, holding up a sheaf of exhibition catalogues and flyers.

'I need to keep all of those.'

'You're going to have to give up something,' I say, dumping the papers in a pile on the floor. 'You can't clear out space without throwing some stuff away.'

'It is not as easy as that.'

'Do you think she cleared out much when she moved to Ireland?' I say, wiping a dust cloth over the newly emptied shelf.

'No – she kept everything. She gave us the tour on Skype, remember?'

'How can you possibly tell from just a Skype call?'

'I do not need to tell. I know what she did.'

Flats in the Mills Grand Estate are designed to enable access, mobility and independence. They are not designed for storage. In Sean's bedroom, there is a thin wardrobe and a single set of drawers. The living space doubles as a kitchen, offering enough room for a two-seat dining table and a single bookshelf, tucked behind the front door.

'I think that's the best we can do for now,' I say, dusting off my hands like a job well done. 'He's supposed to be here in twenty minutes. I'm going to pop out for a cigarette. By the time I'm back, I want you to pick out what you can bear to part with.'

'Okay,' Sean says, hands extended, waiting for me to pass him his iPad.

I grab my coat and brace for the cold. Outside, the sky is full and heavy with grey. I smoke and watch the traffic, guessing what will arrive, imagining the car of a holy man. I watch the lights change, the darting movement of people rushing home, heading back to loved ones. Native Londoners can be spotted by the way they cross roads.

Back inside, I open a window and light two candles to burn off the bright stink of his body. I find gum from my bag and tidy myself in front of the bathroom mirror, moving my hair into a trustworthy shape.

'The framers say that Ashley's piece is ready,' Sean says. 'They have emailed me.'

He turns the iPad proudly, holding up the good news.

'Great,' I say. 'We can pick it up on Monday.'

'Cool,' he says, negotiating the careful manoeuvre of turning the iPad back round.

'Did you decide what we're throwing away?'

'Not yet,' Sean says, his focus on the machine.

'Do you need me to decide for you? I'll happily throw all of this crap away.'

'You would not do that to me, Janet,' Sean says, smiling properly for the first time in a while.

And with that, there's a bell ringing.

'He is always early,' Sean says.

'Hello,' I say, into the intercom.

'Two guests for Sean Keily,' says the receptionist.

'Two?' I say, turning to Sean, the receptionist already beeping them through.

Sean shrugs and leans to put his iPad on the table, his freshly ironed shirt coming untucked in the process.

I open the door to two men. One balding, dog-collared, familiar, and behind him, the face I beat in my dreams.

'Janet,' Father John says, taking my hand and holding it in both of his like a blessing. 'It's good to see you again. May we come in?'

Without waiting for an answer, they move over the threshold and head towards Sean.

'Hello, son,' says the second man, bending at the waist, their heads level.

'What are you doing here?' Sean says.

'That's no way to greet your dad now, Sean,' says Father John, his hand on Sean's shoulder. 'Are you not pleased to see us? We've been driving all day.'

'Why is he here?' Sean says, looking to me.

'He asked why you're here,' I say, stood back from them, still by the door.

'I can understand my own son, thank you,' Peter says, pitching his voice low, so as not to alarm. 'I'm here, Sean, because I want to be part of your life. I've always wanted to be part of your life. And now there's nothing in our way.'

Sean turns to me, his mouth slack, his eyes wide.

'Where is my stuff?' he says.

'Your mother's things are down in the car,' Father John says, now familiar with Sean's speech. 'Aren't you glad to see us, though? Your dad's put himself in a lot of bother with his missus for even being here, you know?'

'Who?' Sean says, meek and confused.

'Ah, we'll get into all that,' Father John says. 'We've got time on our hands. Though we might bother you for a cup of tea first, before we get on with all the lifting and hefting. Remind me where can I put my hands on some mugs, Janet?'

I move automatically, compliantly opening the kitchen cupboards, offering sugar. I breathe through my nose and hold my hands in front of me, waiting for the crash, waiting for Sean to say something.

'I'm so grateful for you bringing Sean out to Lourdes for us, Janet.'

'It's fine,' I say. 'It was good for him. He liked it.'

'Hate it there myself,' Father John says, heavy handed with the mugs. 'Awful place really. Can't be dealing with it.'

I breathe and move away. The room has never seemed so full – this is not a space designed for hosting.

'So these are the pieces you're sharing on Twitter?' Peter says with an ugly laugh, flicking through an upright stack of prints as though they were vinyl albums. 'Is she the one who does this to you?' he says, pointing at me.

'Yes,' Sean says.

'You allow her to do this to you?'

He roughly pulls out the *Agnus Dei*, turning the canvas to Father John. 'Will you have a look at what they're doing here, John? And this is what's popular now?'

'Dear, oh dear,' Father John says, chuckling, pouring the kettle.

'And how much are you paying this college to put yourself through this?'

'I do not know,' Sean says.

'And how much is she being paid to do this to you?'

'Her name is Janet,' Sean says.

'Well then, Janet,' Peter says to me, moving towards me like a threat. 'How much is he paying you for all your help?'

'Brigid arranged—' I start, my back to the wall.

'No need for that name,' Peter says, turning on his heel. 'Let's not upset anyone now. It's still all very raw. Isn't it now, Sean?'

Sean meets his eyes and moves his head like a nod, mouth still wide and dumb.

'I think you can go for the day now, Janet,' Peter says. 'I'll make sure you're paid for your time.'

I'm stood two feet away, feeling the distance between us, sensing an ending that I'm not part of.

'Do I need to repeat myself?' Peter says slowly.

'I need to do his medication. His physiotherapy schedule is—'

'I'm sure we'll figure it out. We have the man himself to talk us through it.' He places his hands on Sean's shoulders, posed like a boxer and trainer.

'Sean?' I say, meeting his eyes, seeing the child inside him.

'I'm going to be around for a while,' Peter says, now squeezing him. 'It's all been arranged. We're going to get to know each other. Man to man.'

'Thanks for everything, Janet,' Father John says, taking my hand back into both of his, processing me towards the door. 'We'll be in touch if we need you.'

I grab my bag and coat and turn to face them, to Sean, pleading with my eyes, pleading for the life I don't want, pleading for the chance to do better, to be better.

I look at him and he looks at me and I'm not sure who is first to look away.

Outside, all light is gone and the rain has started to fall.

Before I moved to London, Alex lived with his friend Ralph. They'd been colleagues at Alex's first job in the City. They went on holidays together. Alex says their Vegas trip was the best week of his life – Alex cashed in a World Series of Poker Event, and Ralph got kicked out of The Mirage for dancing with a billionaire's wife. They'd tell stories and argue over the details, mutually calling out each other's bullshit, their exaggerations. There are over three hundred shared photos of Alex and Ralph together on Facebook. For a while, there was talk of them taking out a loan and starting up their own recruitment business. They even had a list of names.

At Alex's request, Ralph moved out so I could move in. Ralph found a place in Clapham, then got a different job, closer to his new home. It's been a while since we heard from him.

I'm sitting on the couch with a bowl of pasta, watching Alex pack. He's been up since nine, getting everything in order. It's unheard of for Alex to be up at nine on a Saturday.

I slept terribly and got up when I heard him hustling about. I've chosen not to mention anything about what happened yesterday, telling myself that I'm being considerate, that he could do without the added stress of knowing that he's abandoning his newly unemployed sister.

Alex looks focused and deliberate as he gently lifts a layer of clothes from his suitcase to jigsaw in his headphones.

'Won't you need those for the flight?'

'Shit,' he says, taking them back out. 'Thanks.'

'You've always been terrible at packing,' I say, licking tomato sauce off my fingers.

'Are you offering to help? Because I could really do with some help.'

'It's funnier to watch you struggle. That's all going to need ironing when you get there.'

'Isabel likes to iron.'

'Of course she does. Perfect, perfect Isabel. Perfect Isabel, offering you a way out of this hellhole. You make it sound like destiny.'

'Maybe it is,' Alex says, now sitting atop the suitcase, forcing round the zip.

'No one really likes ironing, Alex. You're just in the honeymoon period where you believe anything she says.'

'Long may it continue.'

'Did she ever even consider moving here?' I say, my mouth full of sauce and carbs.

'We spoke about it.'

'And?'

'And it wasn't the right choice for us.'

'Good to see you've already adopted the Royal We.'

'I said us. Not we. I don't think there's a Royal Us.'

'I'll google it,' I say, reaching for my phone. Still no messages from Sean.

'I wish you wouldn't eat tomato-sauce meals on the sofa, Janet,' Alex says, now emptying his section of the bookcase into one of many boxes.

'What does it matter? You're about to fuck off. I may even stop using plates.'

'You're right,' he pants, a little short of breath. 'Nothing matters once I leave. You can start shitting on the floor too.'

'Thanks for the suggestion,' I say, loading up my fork, stuffing my face.

'Do I need to be worried about you, Janet?' Alex asks, fetching another box.

'Nope,' I say, spitting out a tiny piece of pasta.

'I honestly thought you were starting to really settle here. Things seemed to be going okay for you. I don't want you to feel like I'm abandoning you, or something.'

'I'm not a child, Alex,' I say, straightening my back.

'Have you considered looking at getting back on the antidepressants?'

I chew and look away, angling my head so that my hair hides my face.

'You were right. There's nothing on Google about a Royal Us.'

'I know you don't like them, but they were helping for a while. I just thought it would be worth considering.'

I swallow firmly. 'Is it you thinking this, or is it Mum?'

'What difference does it make?'

'Fucking knew it,' I say, slamming the pasta bowl onto the coffee table, my fork rattling for emphasis.

'You're going to have to talk to them directly now,' Alex says, his arms full of books. 'I'm not going to be around to play messenger any more.'

'I have nothing to say to them,' I mumble, resisting the urge to pick the bowl back up, to finish my meal.

'It's not Mum's fault you got kicked out of art school, Janet. It wasn't Mum stealing supplies and putting them on eBay. Mum wouldn't have been so stupid. She wouldn't have got caught.'

'How long have you been saving this up?' I say. 'Is this your big dramatic exit?'

'No, this is your worried brother, reading the warning signs, trying to make sure you're not going to go into self-destruct mode again.'

'Do you just believe everything Mum says? She just hates that we're both gone, Alex. She hates it that we're here and she's not. She's stuck above that morgue, and she knows she's going to be stuck there until we're putting her body down there with the rest of them. She's only worried about herself and her legacy, because there's a chance that her pathetic little family business isn't going to survive another generation.'

'She cares about you, Janet. She's worried about you. She doesn't understand how care work is any less gruesome than undertaking.'

'None of you have any idea what I'm putting myself through every day,' I say, using my best soap-opera voice, now standing, my arms overacting the part. 'You have no idea how hard I'm working just to survive.'

'No one ever claimed that you're not working hard.'

'Well, you're implying that I'm on the verge of some fucking breakdown.'

'Are you?' Alex says, now turning to face me. 'Because when you keep talking about how you're a bad person, that's how it sounds. None of us understand why you decided to steal, but we've all forgiven you. It just seems like you haven't forgiven yourself.'

'I'm not having a breakdown,' I say, sounding very much like someone having a breakdown.

'What you need, Janet, is to grow up,' Alex says, kicking a box of books up against the wall and picking up his suitcase. 'It seems like you still need to find peace with what you did. You don't need to keep punishing yourself and thinking you're a bad person because of those mistakes. You're not proving anything by putting yourself through the care work and saying how much you hate it and how hard it is. You've got to be brave and grow up. Who are these supposedly good people you're measuring yourself against? Look at that gap between your ideas about the world and your experience of it.'

'Look at yourself!' I say, moving to block the doorway. 'With your little escapist fantasy. You've excused yourself from the parlour completely, and now you're running away to go live with some girl you barely know. Watching the same cartoons you've been watching since you were eight years old.'

'Again, you're projecting your own behaviours onto me,' Alex says, calmly putting on his coat. 'I'm not running from anything. I'm making a short-term sacrifice for my longer-term happiness – that's what being an adult is about.'

I pull a hair off his coat collar – one of mine, long and dark, curled at the tip.

'I thought your flight was at 7.30.'

'It is.'

'You're going to be so early.'

'I don't like rushing.'

Alex reaches in for a hug. I can't remember the last time he's hugged me. He smells of sweat and effort. He smells of home.

'When do I have to move out?'

'Our tenancy expires in February and I've covered the rest of the rent for you. You can extend it and get someone else to move in, if you want to stay.'

'Covering the rent doesn't seem like a very good way of encouraging me to be an adult,' I say, attempting a jokey tone.

'Being an adult is taking responsibility for how your choices impact others,' Alex says, pulling away, digging into his pocket.

'You're really doing this?'

'It's all booked and arranged,' he says, sliding the door key off his keyring, extending it towards me like a promise.

'Is this where I'm supposed to offer to come to the airport with you?'

'Enjoy your weekend,' he says. 'I know how hard you work.'

I grab Alex by the coat and pull him in for another hug, tipping him off balance, his suitcase moving with us.

'Ultimately,' he says, over my shoulder, one arm holding me, 'people are going to judge you on your actions, and based on your actions, you're no worse than anyone else. So get over this stupid fantasy about being "Janet the Monster". Stop caring about what everyone else thinks of you.'

'Any other wisdom?' I say, stepping out of his way.

He pauses. 'It's freezing, so don't get locked out. If you get locked out, you're fucked. Mum has the spare.'

I close the door behind him and return to my pasta, now cold and sad, stuck to the bowl.

Among all my friends at college, those who claimed to love me were among the first to fall away. They were the friends I lived with, the ones I got stoned with. They were the ones who supported my art, no matter how morbid, no matter how garish. They were the friends I always imagined I'd have – creative and vibrant and uniquely similar. They were the ones who encouraged me, who found it all hilarious until we were caught. They were the ones who were happy for me to take the blame. They said they'd stay in touch, no matter what. They said it was all bullshit anyway; that great art comes from the heart, not from college training.

They fell away. They left my messages on *read*. More recently, they posted pictures from their graduation ceremonies, their parents' arms around their shoulders – families of proud, wide smiles.

Alex has been gone for about an hour. It's silent in the flat. Just the padding of the old man above us – above me – and the drip of the bathroom sink. I open up Alex's box of Christmas decorations. It smells of musk and sandalwood. I pull out a tangle of tinsel and fairy lights, knotted together like a hangover. I put on the radio and spool the lights onto the floor in a long cord. I can picture the cord wrapped around Sean – one large, deformed decoration, contorted into the shape of a star.

I have been mentally rehearsing all the things I should have said at Sean's flat, to those men. I imagine myself looming over a diminutive Peter, pointing him in place, telling him about boundaries and respect and the value of great art. I imagine small, compliant noises coming from his ugly mouth, his ugly smoker's teeth. I imagine him agreeing to know Sean on Sean's terms. I imagine lecturing him about his mistakes, chastising him for the arrogance of his assumptions. I imagine saying my piece on how Sean should never even begin to consider forgiving him. Imagining his submissive expression, I feel proud of myself for honouring Brigid's memory – the woman who provided me with my second chance.

Instead, I think about how I followed orders and slipped away. I feel ashamed.

At the bottom of the decorations box, there's a kitschy angel intended for the top of a Christmas tree, some puckered baubles and a dusty wreath. I balance the angel on a candlestick and place it on the coffee table. It tilts at an acute angle.

I hang the fairy lights around the living-room walls with Sellotape, ending just above Alex's empty spot on the couch. I drape the tinsel around the television and above the window. I turn on the lights and stand back by the front door to survey my work. A few of the bulbs remain dark, but the rest cycle through a rainbow of camp light. I look upon my kingdom and feel ready to weep.

I slump down onto the couch and check my phone. Sean hasn't posted anything to Twitter since I left him. I'm sure that some of the papers I signed after Brigid died make me liable in some way for him. If Sean gets hurt or dies, it's my name on the emergency contact sheet. The Mills Grand Estate probably don't have anything on file at all about Peter. They may not even know he's there.

I've come to the decision that it will be necessary for me to return to the Mills Grand Estate. I will have to go back today, without notice. I will go back in order to sort out the paperwork, and establish a clear and proper handover. If a fight or an argument is necessary, then so be it. I am ready for it. If I've already lost my job, then there's nothing they can do to me anyway. There's nothing they can prove about the money.

I feel ashamed and I want to fix things. I want to make sure Sean is safe.

I haul myself off the couch and turn off the radio. I dress for a confrontation – chunky boots and slim-fit jeans, a slash-neck black top. I pull on my coat and head out to catch the bus.

I take a seat towards the back of the top deck and mentally will the other passengers away. I spread my legs like a cocky teenager and put on an imposing expression. I need this time to get in the zone. I need this time to prepare what I will say, to Sean and to those men, the pair of them. I feel the weight of an apology in my mouth like a round, smooth stone.

The bus slowly progresses through Islington, towards the West End. In the rush to head out, I've failed to charge my phone – only fifteen per cent battery remaining. I may have left the fairy lights on.

I've got more important things to think about than a house fire. I decide to conserve my phone battery, looking out the window at the city, at the smudged glow of wet neon, the pavements filled with Christmas shoppers and tourists. After nine months of work, I know the rhythm and flow of this bus route, but I've rarely taken the time to look out of the window.

Despite all this time in the city, London still feels unknowable to me. It feels impossibly vast and strange – a lifetime's work. London feels like a language that you would need to learn young – where only the native can ever truly master full fluency. London feels less like a city, and more like a hiding place – a hiding place for people, for money, for every type of imposter. London is a shapeshifting mess; a place where reinventing yourself is a coping mechanism, a means for survival.

I look skyward and watch the delicate aerial ballet of construction works, the graceful rise of huge steel beams, suspended impossibly in the air, the sway of the cold wind testing the engineering. Down below, huge excavated pits of land, destined for air-conditioned, modern living, hopelessly out of reach.

The seats in front of me fill up with other passengers. The bus heaters are on full-blast and there's a strong, stale smell – brewed sweat and spilled tea.

A woman walks up the stairs, laden with bags. She has a markedly familiar face. As she approaches, taking the seat next to me, I do a very unsubtle double take. She meets my eye with a defensive expression. I feel almost certain this woman is Beatrice – this is Jordan's wife. I turn away and try to stifle a sudden urge to cough. I pull up my collar, tuck into myself and clear my throat with a sound more like gagging. The woman hugs her shopping and subtly angles her body away from me, looking down at her phone, held just so I can't see the screen.

Despite the hours I spent researching and stalking Beatrice, I can't be sure it's her. My mental image of Beatrice is horribly neutral and mask like, devoid of animating features – in all those photos, she is almost aggressively plain and professional.

There are only three stops before I need to get off for the Mills Grand Estate. In this moment, there is a version of Janet Lamb that forgets about Sean – this version remains on the bus until it is possible to be certain. This version of me is prepared to follow the woman from a safe distance, back to her home. This version of Janet is looking for evidence – every suspicion needs to be confirmed.

This is all a matter of priorities – responsibility versus fantasy. Shame versus curiosity. Sean versus Jordan. Janet versus Janet. I adjust myself and stare at the woman in the reflection of the bus window. In the indistinct blur, I look at her sharp, unlovable jaw, at her slightly damp hair. I can see she is wearing earrings. I can't imagine Jordan ever buying jewellery as a present. The only presents Jordan has bought me are a yoga mat, trainers and a shitty advent calendar.

The bus turns a sharp corner towards Cambridge Circus and the woman leans into me, our bodies pressed together for a moment. This is my stop and I need to let her go.

'Excuse me,' I say, standing to shuffle past. I take a glimpse at her phone and see she is looking at BBC Weather. This feels significant.

Off the bus, I rush under a doorway to light up a cigarette, then walk through the light drizzle towards Mills Grand Estate. If for some reason they are not at home, my plan is to wait in the flat. I decide to avoid the staff, in case they are under Peter's instructions. It seems unlikely that Sean would have revealed anything intimate or significant to the likes of Keith. It seems impossible that he could trust anyone other than me.

I am practising my speech to Father John as I turn onto Sean's street. I take the edge of the kerb, avoiding the umbrellas, the flow and bump of bags and bodies. I look up to Sean's window. There's a light on. But as I move to cross the road, I see them. I see Sean and Peter under the entrance awning, side by side, father and son. They are smoking together. Peter leans over his son, a cigarette dangling from his lips as he helps Sean take a drag. Peter is wearing just a T-shirt against the winter chill. Sean is wrapped up in his coat, smoke and warm air rising from him with each laugh.

They haven't spotted me. I shuffle between bodies, away from the edge of the pavement. I position myself behind a bus stop. I watch a slightly distorted version of them through the Perspex – behind this screen, the scene feels almost filmic. There's a clichéd warmth to their interactions. I watch Sean laugh and smile, taking long drags against his father's fingers. I watch Peter light up his own cigarette, seemingly impervious to the cold. With a cigarette in each hand, he gesticulates with wide, excited gestures, performing a story for his son, sometimes stepping out from the awning, into the rain. Sean keeps his gaze, looking up at him, entranced.

I remain in my voyeuristic spot as the bus stop empties once and twice, until Sean finishes his cigarette and Peter wheels him back through the automatic doors, back inside, to a life without me.

I give up on my plans for confrontation. My speeches have all but vanished from my mind. I walk back to the main road and catch the next bus home, draining the battery on my phone so it dies just as I have my keys in the front door. The Sellotape has come loose. The fairy lights are on and blinking, decorating the floor.

Jordan has agreed to leave his friends at the pub to spend the evening with me. On the phone, he sounded at least three pints in.

Despite his size, Jordan is a lightweight drinker. His first taste of alcohol was on his stag do, just six weeks after his injury. For years, he'd been the designated driver. He'd tried every virgin cocktail, heard every variation of the associated teasing. Jordan was always aware that he needed to be awake at 6 a.m. for training. He knew that in order to be elite, you need to make sacrifices.

In Jordan and Beatrice's wedding photos, he's still using a crutch. The deposit had been paid, and at that point, the doctors were estimating that he had an eighty per cent chance of making a full recovery.

'I don't see why I had to come here,' he says at the door, pinching off his gloves and stuffing them aggressively into his jacket, moving straight past me, squeezing past the piles of boxes.

'Nice to see you too,' I say as he heads to the bathroom, violating Alex's no-shoes policy.

I've made an effort for him. Since getting home, I've reattached the fairy lights, shaved, and changed my bed sheets. I'm wearing the low-cut V-neck jumper from our first date, the one he threatened to tear off me, only two drinks into the evening.

I've piled up most of Alex's remaining boxes in our entranceway. The flat almost looks normal. Jordan whistles as he pees, scatty and tuneless.

'Did you get robbed?' Jordan says, coming out of the bathroom sans coat, wiping his hands on his jeans, scanning the empty shelves.

'They're all in the boxes, dummy,' I say. 'Alex left today. Remember? I told you about it last week.'

'You said he was probably going to change his mind. You said that there was no way he'd go through with it.'

'Well, even I can't be right all the time,' I say, moving over to him, latching myself to his waist, pressing all of me against him. His jumper has the stale smell of a smoking area. 'Thank you for coming over.'

Jordan leans across me, plucking a tennis ball from the top of an open box.

'I'm pretty tired, Janet. We can do it if you want, but you'll need to do most of the work.'

'You always know just what to say,' I say, detaching from him. 'Take your shoes off, please.'

Jordan rolls his eyes and pulls off his shoes, balancing perfectly. He throws them underhand, one at a time towards the door.

'Happy?'

'Would you be happy if I treated your home like that?'

'I need a drink,' Jordan says, slightly too loud, headed to the kitchen, throwing the tennis ball from hand to hand.

I've decided not to mention my possible interaction with the woman on the bus. Jordan has been consistently hesitant about revealing anything beyond the essential details of his marriage. He told me upfront about being married. He told me that she had left in order to 'explore her sexuality'. He told me that they'd discussed a divorce, that he'd agreed to store her stuff until further notice, but that she was gone and that it was over. On that first night at Jordan's place, he showed me his ring. He told me about how they'd picked it together, how she picked out wording for the engraving, how he had needed to go to a doctor to help him get it off.

'So how long are you going to stay here?' Jordan says.

'Alex paid the flat off until February, then the contract is over and it's my decision whether to renew.'

'Is this the part where I'm supposed to jump in and invite you to live with me?' he says, opening the fridge, staring.

'I can't afford to live with you,' I say, waiting for him to disagree.

'You definitely can't afford to live with me. I can barely afford to live with me.'

'And I think I may be unemployed.'

'What?' he says, a little dazed.

'I said I think I may be unemployed.'

'Are you serious?' Jordan says, a bottle of white wine in one hand, the tennis ball in the other. 'Has he run out of money already?'

'His dad turned up yesterday. They told me to go home. I haven't heard from them since.'

'Did you try calling him – the man? You know, the man?'

'Sean.'

'Yeah, Sean.'

'I'm not calling him,' I say, scoffing. 'I was going to go see him today, but it didn't work out.'

'Whatever,' Jordan says, pouring two glasses. 'His money was going to run out eventually. There's no way he was going to be able to afford to keep you.'

'To keep me? I'm not his pet, Jordan.'

'Well, isn't he just paying you out of that legal settlement?'

'It's not just the settlement. I think he gets some benefits,' I say, taking my glass. 'I know the college offered him a bursary.'

'That's not the point,' Jordan says, moving to the sofa, resting his feet on one of Alex's boxes. He throws the tennis ball against the ceiling, making a dull thud. 'The point is that the money couldn't last forever. He has no potential for income.'

'Two of our pieces sold at that show you wouldn't come to.'

'For how much?'

'He under-priced them, I think.'

'Unless he's selling them for ten grand a pop, he's got no future. I'm sure we can search for some statistics. The statistics will probably say that only like one in a million artists makes a living from it. Making money from art is like winning the lottery.'

'And since when were you such an expert?'

'You don't need to be an expert, Janet. Just do some basic math. Who do you think paid for his mother's funeral? Who do you think paid for those flights to France?'

'I get it. And I do feel worried for him. I feel guilty and worried. I'm not sure why his dad would come back into his life just like that. I think he just wants Sean's money.'

'So what?' Jordan says, swigging down his first glass, reaching for the bottle.

'So I feel like I should be doing something.'

'Since when do you care? You've spent months complaining about him, about how much you dislike the job. This is your chance to do something else.'

'I've never said I disliked him. Just what's required of me in order to do the job properly. And it's not as easy as that,' I say, thumbing the lipstick around the rim of my glass. 'It's not so easy to just walk away.'

'Of course it is,' he says, frustrated, now squeezing the tennis ball like a stress toy. 'You just want to make it complicated. You always want to make everything so dramatic. You want to make my marriage into a big deal. You want to make some dumb email into a big deal. None of it matters, Janet.'

'Maybe it matters to me – did you consider that? Does it ever occur to you to consider me?'

'It's painfully obvious what you're doing, Janet. You're completely transparent. I'm sure your brother saw it too.'

'I really don't need this today, Jordan,' I say, my eyes closed.

'You're trying to live vicariously through him. You've found a way to return to art school, and you're trying to live like a student again. You're trying to live out this fantasy that you could still be a famous artist.'

'If you're going to be like this, I think you should go,' I say, taking the glass out his hand.

'The truth is,' he says, now standing, his tone changing, throwing the tennis ball wildly away, across the room. 'You never had the talent. Deep down, you know that. You never had enough talent, and you weren't prepared to put in the work.'

'Get the *fuck* out my flat, Jordan,' I say, shrill.

'Whatever,' he says, lurching to the bathroom, retrieving his coat. 'Thanks for the shit wine.'

I watch him stumble into his shoes, leant up against Alex's boxes, his balance betraying him, conceding to the drink.

I open the door and dodge his body as he passes me. I watch him climb the stairs, his weight on the handrail. I watch him climb and I count the steps, counting down his chances to turn back and apologise.

I count him to the street, and after a moment, there's only the wind.

*

It's nearly midday and I'm hungover in bed. I finished the wine on my own. I'm sat up in bed on my laptop. The heating is on full blast, and there's no one around to criticise. Alex has messaged on Facebook to say that he's arrived in New York safely, and that he's arranged for our parents to collect the boxes later today. He says that I don't have to be here, but that they'd both like to see me. Especially if I'm not going home for Christmas. Alex has changed his profile picture to a selfie of him and Isabel kissing in the JFK Arrivals hall. He looks happy.

I know I should eat, but I'm not sure I can bring myself to leave bed for what's on offer. I know there's a frozen curry in the freezer and a can of tomato soup in the cupboard, but both seem too pathetic to consider. Both seem like admitting defeat.

According to the weather forecast, it's due to snow.

I read about a newly discovered organ, hiding in plain sight. The article says the mesentry had previously been thought of as distinct, unexceptional fragments of the digestive system, when in fact, they were a single, continuous organ. The discovery is likely to significantly improve scientific understanding of abdominal diseases, and should ultimately lead to new and better treatments.

A notification flashes up from my inbox – it's an email from Sean. He has written to ask me to come over, saying that he needs my help urgently, that it has to be now.

I get out of bed, pull on clothes and leave immediately, texting to say that I'm on my way.

'What's happened?' I say, stepping into Sean's flat, breathless from the rush, trying to sound calm. I put my bag down in the corner, in the usual spot. 'Where's Peter?'

'He is not here,' Sean says, his chair in the middle of the room. 'He is speaking with his partner. He went back to his hotel to use his computer.'

Sean looks blanched and scruffy, his face masked by two days' worth of beard. I can tell his T-shirt is riding up his back, and that his jeans haven't been done up properly. These are the details I couldn't possibly have picked up on from across the road.

'I need help,' Sean says. 'Everything is wrong.'

'What did he do? Has he hurt you?'

'No, he would not hurt me. We went to the framer's. We went to get Ashley's piece. The framer said it was more tricky than he expected. He said that it was done and ready, but that it would be another forty pounds. Dad said he was a scam artist and told him to fuck off. He said that he could keep the work and hang himself. There was a lot of shouting.'

'So, hold on. The big crisis is that you want me to go pick up Ashley's art?'

'No – yes – I mean, I want the piece, but Dad said Ashley's work was shit anyway. What if they throw it away?'

'And what are you hoping for me to say?' I growl, Jordan's words from last night running through my mind. 'Am I supposed to be saying, yes master? Am I supposed to be excited to be your errand girl? Am I supposed to be applauding you for coming to this big fucking epiphany that your dad is a massive dick? I'm not being paid for this any more, Sean. I'm only here because I was worried that he had hurt you. You made it sound like you were in danger. This is not my understanding of urgent.'

I feel the hangover prickle back into my head. The ache throbs at the front of my brain.

'I do not know how to fix this. He keeps saying how much trouble he is putting himself in with his partner for being here and I do not know what to do. I do not want to destroy his relationship. He has suggested going back to Spain with him. He says that it would be easier for everyone if I dropped out and we all lived in Spain. I do not like it, Janet. He is serious. I do not want to leave here. I want things to be normal again.'

'What the fuck does normal have to do with you, Sean? Since when was any of this normal?' I make a dramatic gesture to the room, my heart starting like an engine. 'Why are you telling me and not him? Why is he not here for this conversation?'

'Because I am scared and I need you. I need your help.'

'You missed your chance to say that. This was what you were supposed to say on Friday.'

'I know,' Sean says, desperate. 'I know.'

'This is what you were supposed to say from the moment he stuck his nose in. Your mother would be so fucking annoyed. She would never forgive you for speaking to him, for allowing him back in your life.'

'So, will you help me?' he says, meek and pleading.

'I have no idea what you expected from this!' My voice is unattractively shrill. 'How am I supposed to help here? Do you think I'm going to fight to keep working for you?'

'I thought you liked working with me. You just said you were worried about me.'

'Don't try to twist my words.' I feel the hangover beating through my brain. I feel angry and hot and sweaty. 'There's nothing special about you, Sean. About any of this. There are another thousand people in London, desperate for care workers. Am I supposed to drop everything in my life and just wait around until your dickhead father disappears again? Am I supposed to guard the door and not let him in? Am I supposed to tell him to fuck off on your behalf?'

'I thought,' starts Sean, panicking, his breath short and fast.

'No, you fucking didn't. You didn't think at all. You've fantasised and that's different. You've built this little fantasy where I devote the rest of my life to being your carer, fighting your battles. Or worse yet, the footnote in your biography. The biography of Sean Keily – great disabled genius.'

'I thought you cared about me,' Sean says, each word clipped with a gasp.

'I was paid to care about you, Sean. I cared *for* you – got it?'

'But how will I—' he says, now welling up.

'How you will anything is not my problem any more. I don't care what happens to your art. I don't care about your fucking degree. I don't give a fuck. Is that clear?'

I'm breathing heavily. I feel the words hanging between us and a part of me means them. Sean is no longer looking at me. He's sunk forward into himself, shuddered sobs wracking through him.

'I am not your mother, Sean. I am not your girlfriend. I am not one of your little internet art buddies or some sycophant journalist. I need you to understand that you are just a job. You mean nothing to me.'

'But you said—' he says, barely forming the words.

My heart is pounding and my head is pounding and my legs feel heavy. This feels different from adrenaline and more complex than anger. I'm stood at arm's length from him, waiting for his sobbing to subside. I will not allow myself to feel guilty in this moment. Sean's still husked forward, hands now up by his face, the curves of his wrists pressed hard to his forehead, as though to staunch a wound.

'It is not true,' he says, even more sloppily than usual.

'What did you just say?' I ask, running my tongue over the sharp of my teeth.

'I said it is not true!' He bolts upright, almost shouting, a sluice of spit careering from his mouth.

'So what is true, Sean? Enlighten me.'

'You do care about me. I know you do.'

'You literally know nothing about me. You know that I turn up, I work and I leave. You never ask me anything.'

'I know who you are. I see the real Janet.'

'Oh my God,' I say, laughing in a particularly false way. 'You are fucking deluded. You have no idea what goes on in my head. If you had any idea, there's no way you'd defend me. There's no way you'd want to be anywhere near me.'

'You are a good person, Janet.'

I cover my ears in an exaggerated way. 'I can't deal with this,' I say.

'You are a good person. Mum trusted you. She saw how good you were straight away.'

'I've been stealing from you for nearly a year,' I say. 'From the first day I started.'

'You are good,' Sean says, sobbing heavily. 'You love me.'

'Shut up,' I say, stepping towards him, sizing up.

'Admit it,' he says. 'You love me.'

My open palm snaps forward and connects just around

his cheek and ear – I feel my whole body follow through the swing, driving me off balance, swung on one foot in a clumsy pirouette. My arm jerks away as though I've touched fire. Sean's chair rolls backwards slightly, his body lurching over one side with the weight of the hit.

Backing away, I can feel the tension in my muscles releasing, my body exhaling, the sting in my hand, the thumping beat of blood in my ears and my face fully flushed, every part of me primed for fight or flight. Sean's ear is a scarlet red.

'You hit me,' he says, moving upright, one hand raised to his cheek.

I can't manage a reply. My heart is in my throat. I feel outside of myself – a witness to the moment, one I've mentally rehearsed for nearly a year. My hand hangs heavily by my side, a quivering deadweight. My skin feels tight, stung with his surface.

'You hit me,' Sean says again, more firmly, expecting a response.

'I don't love you,' I say, meeting his hurt eyes, my lip quivering.

'Why?' he says. 'Why have you hit me?'

'I'm going to go now,' I say, turning away to find my bag.

'No – you cannot go – Janet, do not go.' Sean leans forward in his chair, one arm extended out towards me, the other still pressed to his face. 'Please do not go like this.'

'I didn't mean to hurt you,' I say. 'I'm sorry – I can't help you.'

'Please do not go,' he repeats, his voice high and desperate, stretching to reach the brakes on his chair.

I'm out the room and out the door. I'm down the hall, pressing the lift button and ignoring his voice, the pained panicked voice, calling my name. I know I'll never be back here again.

In the lift, I text Jordan to say I'm coming over. He replies, *Okay*.

At the door, I launch into Jordan. I kiss and continue as he tries to break away. With my lips, I move him backwards down the corridor, stumbling.

'The door isn't closed,' he says, pressed to my mouth.

'Let them come,' I say.

In the bedroom, I guide his hands through stripping me. I feel my top rip a little as he drags it over my arm. I'm still sweaty and stinky and disgusting.

'So you've decided to forgive me,' he says, more statement than question.

'Yes. Sure. Get these off.'

Jordan kicks off his trousers and pants and socks and moves to his bedside drawer, where he keeps the condoms.

'Don't use that,' I say.

'Really?'

'Just come here. Hurry up.'

'I think we should use it.'

'Whatever. Just come here.'

We fall to the bed together. He makes a low growl and moves on top, the weight of him against me, damp and warm.

'I thought you'd never speak to me again,' he says.

My feet hang back over the edge of the bed, kicking up like a reflex with each shift of his weight. He bites at my neck, my collarbone.

'I want to try something,' I say, straight into his ear. 'I want you to hit me. I want you to hit me and tell me I'm bad. I want you to tell me I'm a bad person.'

'I'm really not into that,' Jordan says, continuing to nibble.

'Don't think about it. Just try it for me. Hit me here,' I say, presenting my cheek. 'Hit me as hard as you like.'

Jordan sits up, looking at me scared. 'This is weird, Janet. You're being weird.'

'Please, Jordan – please just do this for me. If you care about me, you'll do this for me.'

For a moment, it looks like he's considering it. I see his right arm flex a little, sure of itself, sure of his power.

'I've got to go close the door,' Jordan says, climbing off me, his dick still hard.

It's cold in the flat. Alex's boxes are gone. On the fridge, there's a note.

Sausage rolls and salad inside.
Call any time.
Love Mum x

I open my inbox and find the email – it's after seven already. I dial the number, not expecting an answer, hoping for voicemail.

'Melissa Ye.'

'Hi, Doctor Ye. My name is Janet Lamb.' I hesitate, waiting for her to interrupt. 'Sorry, I just wasn't sure if you'd answer. My name is Janet Lamb. I received an email in November from one of your patients. A lady called Florence. The email said I could get in touch with you.'

'Janet,' she says, cold and neutral. I visualise her typing my name into a database, the system flashing up with a bold red warning sign. 'Janet, I remember, yes. Janet, I am no longer working with Florence. She has completed her course of therapy.'

'Okay,' I say. 'That's good. I'm glad. But I have some questions. I wanted to ask you—'

'Yes, I understand. Miss Janet, I am pleased to advise that Florence has now completed her therapy. She is recovered. She is at peace.'

'But,' I start.

'You may book your own appointment if that is your need. You have my details, yes? I suggest booking an appointment and we can start to deal with these issues, yes? There is a waiting list but your time will come soon. Very soon, yes?'

'I was hoping—'

'Thank you for calling, Miss Janet. Contact my office on Monday for the appointment. Thank you for your interest. Have a nice day.'

Outside, it's snowing.

I put on the radio and reach under my bed, to the shoebox. I hold it out, at arm's length, and turn it upside down, spilling the notes over my duvet, over the floor. I watch the notes fall and try to feel something.

I try telling myself that this is a turning point. I try telling myself that I'm free and that anything is possible.

I sit on the floor and start counting the money into piles of hundreds.

I tell myself that meaningful work is harder to find than

ever before, and that even seemingly meaningful work is just damage limitation in a world past saving.

I tell myself that ultimately, there's no real difference between an office job and care work. I tell myself that care work just requires a stronger stomach and stronger arms.

I try telling myself that there's no upper limit on the cruelty I'm capable of, that there's no threshold to selfishness. I try telling myself that no matter what you do, you will always disappoint someone. You will always let someone down, and it's the people closest to you who you'll hurt the most.

I try telling myself that despite all this and more, there is forgiveness and there is sacrifice if you seek it, if you know where to look. I tell myself that there are parts of us hiding in plain sight, and that in those parts, we may find a cure, a way to be saved.

I tell myself that money is just another measure of the pain you're prepared to put yourself through, and that this is my final count.

I listen to the Christmas songs play and know that I am alone and everything matters and nothing matters. I tell myself that I am alone with over two thousand pounds in cash and that Christmas is a time to spend.

Epilogue

For years, I refused to learn. I'd been destined for London from the age of fourteen. In London, I wouldn't need to drive. To teenage Janet, the pressure of extra, unwanted exams seemed almost abusive. I felt certain that driving would be a gateway to a myriad of unwanted, very adult responsibilities. Overnight, I would become the family's designated driver. I would become the chauffeur. I would be called home on weekends to cover for our staff. I would be another step closer to replacing my mother. To becoming my mother.

It's almost midnight, and I'm driving alone for the first time. The parlour's Mercedes is proving much easier to handle than my instructor's Volvo. Even with the windows slightly down, there's a distinct, familiar smell of leather. This is the smell of home.

As it turns out, I'm a confident driver. My instructor says I'm a natural; among the best she's ever seen. I've chosen to believe her.

For tonight, I've left the radio off. All my attention is on the road. I can feel my heart against the seatbelt. I can sense the whole car, just through the steering wheel. The weight and the power. My body feels like an extension of the machine. All my movements feel very deliberate. There's heft and strength to every adjustment.

I'm on my way to Heathrow to collect Alex and Isabel. They're scheduled to land any minute now. In my peripheral vision, I can see the airport in the distance, the sky strobing with light. Usually, Dad would be the one to pick them up, but my parents have to be up at six to prepare for a midday service. I was volunteered by default. Mum insisted that at least one of us should be there to give them a proper welcome.

This will be Isabel's first visit to the UK, and Alex's first time home since he left for New York – over two years ago now. My parents volunteered their own room and bed, but Alex has opted for a hotel. Sharing one bathroom between five people is simply not practical, particularly given that Isabel is five months pregnant.

Away from London, driving is essential. Everything worth leaving the parlour for is at least thirty minutes away. Travelling to my therapist takes nearly an hour – sometimes more, depending on the traffic. When Dad drops me off, he waits in the car for the whole session, and insists he doesn't mind.

I know that this novelty will wear off. Soon enough, driving will be just another part of my job at the parlour. Dad has stressed that he will need to train me separately to drive the processions. Supposedly, maintaining a slow and steady pace is trickier than you might imagine. It takes more than confidence to hold up traffic.

I turn onto the motorway and merge into the queue for Terminal 2. The road ahead and above me is a clutter of signage: blinking amber and green, every alert competing for my attention. For a moment, two moments, my eyes linger on a sign written in both English and Chinese. I snap back and bite my cheek, refocusing.

Inching forwards, I realise that I haven't been on a plane since returning from Lourdes. My longest break in the last eighteen months has been three days. I haven't had a conversation with Alex lasting longer than five minutes in two years.

It's nearly 1 a.m. The airport is bustling with life and artificial light. I take stock of the excellent wheelchair access, the commendable selection of disabled toilets.

Everyone else in Arrivals seems to have come better prepared. They're equipped with food and water and heartwarming homemade signs.

WELCOME HOME, MUMMY

HAPPY BIRTHDAY, OLIVE

CONGRATULATIONS!!!

I position myself close to the taxi drivers. All of them are men. They share a common expression, hung somewhere between catatonically bored and slightly inebriated.

I recognise Isabel first. She's shorter than I expected, a pretty face, tracksuit bottoms and a plain white T-shirt, stretched over a rounding middle. She moves forwards, belly first, suitcase in tow. I make a small waving gesture until Alex spots me. My hand continues to wave as I walk round the barriers to meet them.

'I am so pleased to finally meet you!' Isabel says, pulling me into her body. 'Thank you for coming to pick us up. We're really grateful. Aren't we, Alex?'

'Thanks, Janet,' Alex says, gently shepherding us towards the wall, out of the gangway of bodies. 'I can't wait to entrust the life of my girlfriend and unborn child to a learner driver.'

'I missed you too, Alex,' I say, relieving myself from Isabel's arms. 'Congratulations again to both of you.'

Alex looks tired and thinner than I remember him. I'm not sure whether we're supposed to hug.

'Do you know where the hotel is?' Alex says.

'I have my phone. I'm sure we can figure it out. Oh, by the way, Dad says that you can borrow his spare phone if you—'

'We'll be fine,' Alex says, wincing as he rolls his shoulders, elaborately stiff. 'All phones are region-free these days. Let's just get going. I'm wrecked.'

'Do you want me to take one of your suitcases or something?'

'You're such a sweetie,' Isabel says, allowing me to take her bag. 'There are presents in there for you. Alex told me all about what you like.'

'Did he now?' I say, turning to Alex.

'He's very good with gifts,' Isabel says.

'Did you know he used to buy me videogames for every birthday, so he could play them?'

'Not now, Janet, please.'

'For my fifteenth birthday, he bought me *Resident Evil 4* on GameCube, knowing I would never play it.'

'Can we just get going, please?'

Downstairs, in the car park, I make a sobering discovery. I have no idea where I've parked. Upon arrival, I failed to make a mental note of the car's position in the lot. As we wander round, scouting, I apologise half a dozen times. Alex is scowling. Isabel insists that it's all very funny, that she doesn't mind at all.

We split off into teams, Alex and Isabel, me and the bags. Inevitably, Alex spots the car first, and beckons me with a sharp whistle. He loads the suitcases into the boot and clutches his neck.

'You've become a good whistler,' I tell him, fastening my seatbelt.

'You've become a useless sister,' Alex says. Isabel laughs uncomfortably.

At the exit, I pay £11.30 for the parking. On my current wage at the parlour, it will take me over an hour to earn this back.

The motorway is gloriously empty. I glide between lanes, speeding past behemoth delivery vehicles, slipping between dawdling taxis. At this pace, it will only take us fifteen minutes to get to the hotel, but Isabel seems to have fallen asleep already, her head lolled heavily against Alex's shoulder, mouth slack, her perfect teeth just visible in the rear-view mirror.

'I can't believe Dad is trusting you with the car,' Alex whispers, adopting the hushed tone we've been raised on.

'Mum wanted someone to meet you,' I say, matching his voice.

'She's just using you as reconnaissance. She's going to grill you in the morning.'

'They're letting me sleep in.'

'Oh, how generous of them. Does Dad still bring you tea in the morning?'

'I have a lock on the door now.'

'That's a big victory,' Alex says, genuinely impressed. 'How did you get Mum to agree to that?'

'She's not that terrible any more,' I say. 'You always make it sound awful. It's really not that bad.'

'Jesus, listen to you. I never thought I'd hear you defending them. Are they letting you bring men home?'

'Well, she's not changed that much.'

'What about the guy you were seeing? The gymnast.'

'I haven't spoken to him since I left London. Facebook makes it look like he got back with his wife.'

'Sounds about right,' Alex says.

'My friend Chloe saw his profile on Tinder though. So who knows?'

'And who cares.'

'You're the one who asked.'

'And do you ever hear from Sean?' Alex says. 'The man you worked with?'

'He's doing well,' I say, eyes on the road. 'From what I've seen.'

'That's nice,' Alex says. 'I'm glad. It sounded like he was really talented.'

'There's actually an exhibition coming up. It's his graduation show on Thursday. There's an open invite, if you'd both like to come.'

'I think Mum has our whole schedule planned.'

'We'd love to come!' Isabel says, her voice bright and wide-awake, sweetly American.

'Oh – great. I'll get you the details.'

'Super,' Isabel says.

'Super,' Alex says, imitating, partly affectionate.

'Are you joining us for dinner tomorrow night, Janet?' Isabel says. 'I think your mom is taking us to an Italian place.'

'No, sorry, I have to work.'

'At the parlour?'

'No, I do some other work. Evening work.'

At the hotel, Alex proudly refuses my help with the bags. I wait until they've headed inside, then drive away, back in the direction of home.

I turn on the radio. It's the weather report. I think of Sean.

The art we made together, the series of bindings, Sean has called them *The Vestiges*. Twenty-six works in total. He has a website now – it's black and has text in Helvetica. Very professional. Available in both English and Russian.

Each piece in the series is available to view in super high definition. You can zoom all the way in: on my knots, on his skin, the meeting places between us.

At the bottom of the homepage, there are links to every piece written about Sean over the last two years, descending chronologically, all the way down to that first interview in *Frieze*.

I can tell that the copy on the website has not been written by Sean. At least, not by the Sean I knew. He would not write in third person. He would not make repeated references to his disabilities, to his 'struggle'. He would certainly never use the word 'triumph'. I feel grimly aware that these are concessions Sean has made for the sake of his art. He has almost certainly been advised to play upon his limitations, to promote a Hollywood-style disabled narrative about over-coming. These are the compromises Sean will have to make throughout his career, until he has accrued enough power to reclaim his own voice.

Until last week, I have had no direct contact with Sean since leaving. Since running away. Over the last two years, everything I've learned about his recent success has come to me through the internet.

Doctor Ye thinks it is significant that Sean never chose to block me on social media. She thinks it is significant that last week I received a Facebook notification from Sean, inviting me to his graduation show, to be held at the Lethaby Gallery this Thursday evening.

It's clear to me that Sean has sent out the invitation to his whole contact list. But according to Doctor Ye, the invitation was very deliberate, and Sean wants me at the show. Doctor Ye thinks the show is an excellent opportunity for resolution. She thinks I will never be fully at peace until I apologise directly to Sean.

According to Doctor Ye, a lot of what seems obvious to me should be treated with suspicion. 'Obvious' thoughts tend to be among the least healthy and most destructive. The purpose of our Cognitive Behavioural Therapy sessions is to recognise these unhealthy and regressive patterns of thought – the illusion of the obvious. CBT has equipped me with the means to make choices about my thoughts. These choices should then inform my behaviours. Doctor Ye has repeatedly emphasised that this takes a lot of hard work. CBT is resistance. It is labour. Reconditioning my brain will be a lifelong project. Doctor Ye says that if I'm prepared to commit the time and energy required, it is possible to work through anything.

I've spent the last two years following Sean's successes on Facebook and Twitter, careful to avoid accidentally hitting *like*. Through these channels, I know that he has remained in London, at Central Saint Martins.

After I left, Peter only called me twice from two different numbers: once to ask about renewing a prescription, and once to check the address for Sean's hydrotherapy sessions. I've relived these brief conversations endlessly, both in and out of therapy, picking apart Peter's words for deeper meaning. Doctor Ye agrees with me that it seems unlikely that Sean has told anyone what happened. What I did.

I still have their numbers saved into my phone: Sean's and both of Peter's. Peter's English WhatsApp profile picture is an image of himself and Sean, the Thames in the distance. They're smiling. His Spanish number has a selfie of Peter kissing a tanned woman wearing sunglasses on the cheek. She has a very serious expression.

I know that last year, one of our bindings was accepted into the Summer Exhibition at the Royal Academy. I know that *The Vestiges* was awarded runner-up for Central St Martin's prestigious NOVA Award, a prize rewarding 'truly original creative thinking, risk-taking and innovation'.

I know that the anonymous buyer of Sean's work from the Christmas Show at the Lethaby Gallery was Dimitri Surkov, the father of Katya, one of Sean's moderately talented classmates. According to Forbes, Surkov is supposedly one of the most successful oil traders in the City. I've read Surkov described as both incredibly ruthless and incredibly generous in the same article.

Surkov is a patron to three galleries across Europe. He has over forty thousand Twitter followers of his own, and retweets nearly everything that Sean shares.

From what I can tell, Sean now works exclusively in photographic portraiture, and produces all of his work unaided.

There is far more written in Russian about Surkov than in English. When put through Google Translate, one article outlined the 'stable' of talent that Surkov sponsors. He supposedly sees himself as a classical benefactor, financially supporting a new, multinational generation of geniuses, including Katya, whose work usually receives the most column inches.

Among the many articles about Sean, I am yet to come across a single mention of my own name.

I haven't totally abandoned the idea of writing Sean's biography. Surkov seems like a perfect character: a second father figure with suspicious intentions and potential criminal links.

According to Doctor Ye, a lot of my thought processes are still shaped by the context of Sean – the context of his body. I pay attention to how accessible certain buildings are. I mention the importance of ramps to anyone who will listen. I judge people who buy cheaper, less nutritionally balanced baby foods. Apparently, this level of fixation is more commonly seen in bereaved parents and spurned lovers. It is common among the guilty.

It's 5.30 and the sun is gone. This evening's class is being held at Bedford College. I've spent the whole day in the morgue and I've ridden my bike through rush-hour traffic to arrive on time. I'm tired and I feel very unattractive.

I'm here because I don't have a patron. This work is helping to pay for both my driving lessons and my new degree. I'm studying History of Art through the Open University. I'm currently eighteen months and six modules into the course. Doctor Ye says the course has been good for me. Studying is a healthy way to direct my 'excess energies'.

I tell Doctor Ye that the degree is keeping me sane. It is my excuse for limiting my work in the parlour to three days a week. It is my excuse for returning to London as regularly as possible – gallery visits are an essential part of the course.

In the English-speaking world, art history is a relatively young and bastard discipline, borrowing heavily from literature and philosophy to make up for the lack of its own canon. Western art history is currently in a moody, teenage phase, constantly forced to defend itself. This awkwardness is perhaps most evident when exploring art history's fascination with that most burdensome and nuisance subject: the body.

There has been an abundance of art history written on the concept of the body, and more specifically, 'the nude'. A lot of this literature is written in a defensive tone, starting with the need to justify the nude, typically setting it in contrast to 'the naked'. Most critics are in consensus that the body presents the most available, varied and endlessly fascinating subject imaginable. From the Lascaux cave paintings, through to the abominations of the Chapman brothers, the body is inescapable and essential.

The acclaimed art historian Kenneth Clark famously argues that successful nudes lean away from accurate representation, and towards impossible, ideal forms. The nude is a meeting place for mathematical and imagined ideals. Clark suggests the nude is a vehicle for reconciling our contradictory desires for both a priori order and intense sensation. The nude is both subject and object, God and mortal.

This is my first time modelling at Bedford College. I lock my bike and text the instructor to let her know I've arrived. In my experience, it's near impossible to navigate an unfamiliar college. Often, these sessions are held deep in the building, in a repurposed classroom: tables pushed up to the walls, chairs stacked in corners.

The instructor arrives phone in hand, waving timidly from across the car park. She escorts me inside, up two flights of stairs, outlining the three poses she'd like me to take, apologising for the mess and the lack of facilities for me to change. As we enter, there are already a few people in the room, smiling politely as they register the role I'm set to play in their evening.

For every other session, I've been provided with a folding screen or an annexed room. You'd have thought this would be the bare minimum. Without a screen, I'm unsure of the etiquette. Usually, I change into my robe and appear only when called upon, at the final moment, when the class is set to start, once the instructor has outlined the goals and aims and theme for the evening.

Perhaps this is the difference between naked and nude. Perhaps the nude is supposed to appear like magic – an unknowable mystery, the body under the robe, hidden behind the screen, revealed like a triumph. Perhaps being naked is stumbling out of jeans in front of a room full of strangers – strangers pretending not to look, despite having paid for permission to do so.

Since leaving London, I've lost nearly all the muscle tone I'd gained through care work. The morgue requires sporadic lifting and occasional brute force, but it doesn't compare to the full-body workout that accompanies the maintenance of a person. Away from Sean, I've softened.

I stand in the corner of the room and pull a silk robe from my drawstring bag, slipping it on over my clothes, shuffling out of my jeans and underwear with as little movement as possible. I undo my bra and slip my arms through the straps under my jumper, removing both in one fluid motion. I wrap the robe tightly around myself and hold the bundle of clothes to my chest, standing with my back to the class. With nowhere to hang the clothes, I place them on the floor in the corner, assuring myself that they'll be safe.

People continue to trickle in for the next ten minutes. They leave their phones in a bowl by the door and each claims an easel. Some have brought their own palettes and brushes. The class makes small talk, pretending to ignore me. I stand in the corner, naked under my robe, busying myself with my phone.

Just after six, the instructor welcomes the class and intro-duces me. I resist my instinct to curtsey, and instead, I turn around, smiling confidently in acknowledgement. Today, the instructor is asking the class to focus on my hands and feet. It occurs to me that this particular theme makes my nudity rather redundant, but so be it. Each pose will last an hour. First of all, I'm to sit on a cushioned chair with crossed legs, my left hand on my thigh, my right hand slung across my body, gently gripping my left shoulder.

I remove my robe and take position in the middle of the room. Though this is a relatively undemanding pose, I know that I cannot afford to be complacent. Upon first starting out as a life model, I couldn't have imagined how physically demanding the work really is. Remaining still for up to three hours, even in the most natural poses, requires an almost Zen level of focus. For these sessions, I enter my head and become my body.

I try my best to zone out the audience, but even now, after what must be a few hundred hours of practice, I struggle. I sense the variety of their gazes. There are the late adolescent boys, thrown by the unmitigated permission to stare at the female form. Then there are the crotchety boomers who tut each time I shake out a cramp, or adjust my hair. I enjoy their shared industrious expressions, the shifts of focus between me and their canvases, their thumbs extended for scale, one-eye closed. I imagine them taking aim at my body, with protruding tongues and furrowed brows.

After classes, I collect the sketches they leave behind. Once I'm dressed and they're gone, I gather up these versions of me – their approximations of my body in chalk and charcoal. For them, I am practice. I am part of their training. My body is an education – I am the classical female form.

For every abandoned sketch, another version of me is taken home. The artists are perfectly within their rights to do so. These are evening classes – outside of their core curriculum, attended by both hobbyists and actual students. My body is provided at a premium, from six to nine o'clock, once per fortnight, in changing locations. I am paid a fixed rate for the three-hour session. My compensation does not change depending on the number of participants.

In these sessions, I've learned a lot about my own body – my tics and limits. I've become aware of my instinct to rub my forefinger and thumb while focusing. I'm newly conscious of how often I bite my lip. These are instincts that must be overcome – sublimated in the interest of fine art.

The hand gripping my shoulder is already a little sweaty. In these classes, it is challenging to predict where I will feel the discomfort first. Pain seems to emanate from extensions and from angles. In each session, I am newly conscious of the weight of my body.

The class are free to excuse themselves at any time: to fetch their phones from the courtesy bowl at the door, to use the toilet, to break for coffee. They work at their own pace. They work, while I endure. I can only take a break between poses.

I charge just below market rate, ensuring I get regular work. I'm listed on the official-sounding 'Register for Artists' Models', complete with my full name and a short biography. When I was getting started, I had to submit my old Criminal Records check. I auditioned in a group, and made up a brief history of previous experience, referencing my skill with knots and binding. My biography states I'm a student, 5'5, slim and fit, with moderate flexibility. I'm available for life, portrait, body casting and body painting, but only on weekends and evenings.

I'd like to think I'm good at this job, but it's tough to gauge. There's no option to leave reviews on my model profile. I've never had any proper feedback on my work, and I don't have a proper frame of reference for comparison. I'm aware that if I really wanted feedback, I could just ask. But I choose not to. I choose not to engage with them directly. I stay until they are all gone.

Sometimes, after the class, men try to chat to me. I have learned to be polite but firm – this is practically a survival technique. I make it clear that I have no interest, but often it doesn't stop them. Some men choose not to care. They think they've paid for the right to my time. They think this line of work implies something about my character.

After a day or two, I will forget the faces of everyone here. They will remember me, of course, but I will choose to forget them all. I will forget these people who are attempting to know me intimately – to capture my essence. I will make eye contact with them on the street, at red lights, in supermarket queues – I will look them in the eye, and they will never know more than my body.

I imagine futures for the versions of me taken home. I see myself rolled up, tucked under a bed; folded and filed, hidden like a secret. I imagine the would-be artists revising me away from the instructor's influence, fixing me into more perfect versions – their imagined ideals leaching into my body. I visualise my stretch marks being smudged away; my pubic hair being waxed into shadow.

The instructor announces to the class that we will be starting the second pose in five minutes' time. I will be moving into the foetal position. I will need to lie on my side, on a cloth-covered table. A makeshift altar for my sacrifice.

The instructor approaches and softly tells me that I can relax, that she will prepare the table.

I release my arm from my shoulder and curl forwards, suddenly lightheaded. With my head between my knees, I breathe. I can smell myself, heavy with effort. I stare at the floor until the floor begins to blur. I will stay like this until it is time. I will stay like this until the room stops spinning, until the floor becomes clear and the world makes sense. I will breathe until my body makes peace with my mind. If necessary, I will keep them waiting. I will be ready soon enough.

It's Thursday and the sun is setting. The sky is an anxious grey. Above me, a police helicopter is circling, beating ambient noise through the air. Alex and Isabel are late – ten minutes and counting. We've arranged to convene at the bottom of Caledonian Road at six, so we can walk across to the gallery together.

From my position on the street corner, I can see in four directions. I can see them not coming from every angle. I imagine myself as a statue – a Richard Serra installation – still among the flow of rush-hour bodies, flooding home en masse. People move around me, parting like a stream.

We had travelled as a group this morning, in order to give Isabel a full day in the capital. She had been feeling sick, but insisted on making the most of her time in our country. On the train to London, Isabel quizzed us on the towns we were passing through, astounded to realise how little we knew of our immediate surroundings.

For the rest of the journey, I read the most recent medical newsletter in my inbox. It had been months since I had last opened one of these emails. I could never bring myself to unsubscribe. For two years, they've been piling up. Avoided, like guilt.

The main article in the newsletter was about the appendix. For the majority of medical history, the appendix has been described as vestigial. Darwin equated the appendix to wisdom teeth – both left as trace evidence of our primate ancestry, evolved to aid the digestion of plant cellulose.

For centuries, the appendix was treated as a medical nuisance. But according to a new set of peer-reviewed studies, the appendix acts as an important reserve for probiotic bacteria. Those without an appendix are up to four times more likely to suffer from irritations to the intestine.

I left Alex and Isabel at Paddington, more than happy to use my degree as an excuse to avoid joining their shopping expedition. I have spent my day at the National Gallery, wandering between epochs, trying to engage, drifting back to the familiar.

To maintain focus, I challenged myself to select the single piece I'd save in a fire. I imposed practical limits on my hypothetical question: I would have to be able to carry the artwork while moving at pace. This arbitrary rule meant I was limited to paintings – around a quarter of the paintings on show.

I settled on a Vermeer – *A Young Woman Standing at a Virginal*. Because of his relatively concise body of works, nearly every Vermeer feels like a treasure. In the piece, a finely dressed woman stands at the titular instrument, her back bathed in sunlight, her face cast in shadow, turned obliquely towards the viewer, fingers hovering silently above unseen keys. *Young Woman* is classic Vermeer: through a simple, domestic composition, Vermeer draws out an honest and slightly awkward humanity, suspended in unheard music. This humanity is infinitely more memorable than the intended demonstration of wealth.

I spent my lunchtime in the gallery café, nursing a pot of tea and a cheese sandwich. On my phone, I read a *Guardian* article from 2011, saying that of the 2,300 works in the permanent National Gallery collection, only eleven pieces are attributed to women.

I light a cigarette and watch the helicopter move reluctantly in the direction of Euston, towards the darkening horizon. I'm getting a little chilly. I'm wearing a smart black dress and three-quarter-sleeve blazer. I intend to blend in. I don't intend to linger, once the goal has been met.

In yesterday's session with Doctor Ye, we developed a plan for this evening. We discussed a goal. We discussed best-case scenarios and worst-case scenarios. We discussed coping mechanisms and breathing exercises. We discussed a drinking limit. We discussed an exit strategy.

In all our planning, we did not account for the message I have just received from Alex on WhatsApp, confirming what I suspected: *Isabel throwing up. Got to get her back. Sorry.*

The show opened at six. From experience, I know that most people will only show up gone eight. Our plan was to have a drink as a group beforehand. But if I head over now, I should be able to get some privacy. I may be able to catch him one-on-one.

I finish my cigarette and begin moving upstream, through the rush of oncoming bodies, flowing towards King's Cross, towards the exit strategy. I practise my breathing exercises and lock my sights on a point in the distance. I move confidently, ignoring the fact that my arms are shaking; a mixture of adrenaline, fear and wind-chill.

Around the corner, I can see the near edges of the gallery. I can see the water feature in the forecourt – the fluorescent jets of water, spurting into the air, yet another obstruction to be navigated around. I can see a cluster of people stood outside, coming into focus. I can see a wheelchair among them.

My shoulders are stiff from the shaking. My teeth have started to chatter. I swallow my breath and the air won't come. Closer now, I spot a yellow and green motorcycle behind the group – it's an ambulance bike – a paramedic first responder.

In the wheelchair, a woman. I immediately recognise her as Ashley, Sean's friend from Canada. The phocomelia seems to affect all four of her limbs, and at least one ear. She's holding a cigarette in a tightly bunched fist.

'Excuse me,' I say, chattering the words into a harsh staccato. 'Is your name Ashley?'

'Come round this side,' she says, gesturing with her head and cigarette, her voice bright and Canadian. 'I can hear you better this side.'

'Is your name Ashley?' I repeat, squatting to chair height.

'Do you know Sean?' she says, eyes widening. 'Are you Janet Lamb?'

'Yes,' I say, holding the edge of Ashley's chair. 'How did you know?'

'Well, shit,' Ashley says, warm and bright. 'Sean only knows about three women. I know all about Janet Lamb. I know everything you did for him.'

'Is he inside?'

'He's had a fit. Overexcited, according to his dad. I think they're still in there. Someone called an ambulance.'

'Right,' I say, attempting a smile. 'Of course they did.'

'Seems like Peter is glad of the help. He's letting them get on with it. He's trying to keep people calm. A few people freaked out, but I think he's hoping that Sean can still enjoy the rest of the night.'

My thighs are already burning and the fumes from Ashley's cigarette are making me dizzy. 'Did you come to London just for this?'

'I came for him,' Ashley says. 'Same as you. It was time.'

'Yeah – time.'

'It's great to meet you, Janet. Go on now – let him know you're here. And stick around, eh?'

'Great to meet you too,' I say, rising to my feet, a little lightheaded as I step away.

Of the twenty-six pieces in *The Vestiges*, there's only one I don't recognise. As ordered on Sean's website, it is the last work in the series. The piece is a front-lit photograph of Sean, fully nude on a sterile, white surface. He is curled into a foetal position, his back to the camera. To the right of his head, a pile of our equipment. Tape and cord and zip-ties and rope, inelegantly messed together.

Inside the Lethaby Gallery, I see a paramedic stooping over that same body, that same pose. The paramedic has her hands on her hips. She can't be more than twenty years old. Behind her, I can see his empty chair and the small fluttering kick of Sean's feet, the perfect, unsullied soles of his dress shoes. I spot a suited Peter, leaning against the wall a few feet away, keeping his distance, chatting casually to concerned onlookers. I overhear him mention that there's nothing to be worried about, that this is to be expected. He's had a smart haircut and lost some weight. I am reminded of the resemblance between them.

Moving closer, I can see that Sean has grown a neat beard. He's wearing a dress shirt, buttoned up to the collar. His arms are locked to his sides, tight and twitching.

'How long so far?' I say to the paramedic, removing my blazer.

'Step back, please,' she says, unconvincingly. 'It's under control.'

I hitch my dress and get to my knees, folding and sliding my blazer under his head.

'Has it been more or less than fifteen minutes?'

'Are you with him? Are you a doctor?'

'I'm his – friend,' I say, unbuttoning Sean's collar, sliding him further away from the wall. 'He's having a grand mal. Has it been more or less than fifteen minutes?'

'Hello, Janet,' comes Peter's voice from above me.

'It's been about twenty,' the paramedic says, now stepping back.

'He told me about how good you were at this,' Peter says. I look up – he's smiling warmly. 'He said you always knew what to do. I reckon I could learn a thing or two from you.'

'Do you have his suppositories?' I say to Peter, calm and clear.

'We have some in the car,' he says, friendly as I've ever heard him. 'I'll go get them for you.'

'I'll take it from here,' I say to the paramedic, pressing my hand to Sean's cheek, warm with drool.

On my knees, my head bowed, I watch Sean choke on the air. I watch the fizzle and crack of his limbs, the taut stress of his neck, the blue and grey of his skin. I watch and wait – I wait for healing.

Around us, a small crowd has gathered, cameras drawn, arms extended. They whisper, but none among them attempts to engage. They stand respectfully, bearing witness, witness to the performance.

As the fit abates, Sean's body falls heavy and still. After a few moments, he gasps, coughing, desperate for air, his body twisting upwards, into me. His eyes open, finding focus.

'Ja-net.'

So much depends on enduring. So much depends on blind faith – the faith that healing is always possible. That given time, healing will come.

'You came,' Sean says, groggy and still.

'Of course,' I say, holding him, knowing him. 'Of course I came. I wouldn't miss this for anything. I can't believe you're wearing a shirt.'

'For her,' Sean says, his eyes drifting back closed, his body at peace.

Acknowledgements

Thanks to University of Manchester's Centre for New Writing 2012/2013 cohort and professors, who helped me shape a direction for the narrative, by recognising the heart of the story before I did.

Thanks to my early readers: Isabel Rogers, Abby Jones, Michael Seidlinger and Frances Dinger.

Huge thanks to my brilliant agent, Zoe Ross, who helped me realise my dreams and bring the best out of Janet.

Thanks to everyone at Dialogue and the extended Little, Brown family, with particular thanks to my champion and personal hero, Sharmaine Lovegrove.

Bringing a book from manuscript to what you are
reading is a team effort.

Dialogue Books would like to thank everyone at
Little, Brown who helped to publish *The Art of the Body*
in the UK.

Editorial
Sharmaine Lovegrove
Sophia Schoepfer
Thalia Proctor

Marketing
Emily Moran
Hermione Ireland
Hillary Tisman

Contracts
Stephanie Cockburn

Design
Helen Bergh
Charlotte Stroomer

Sales
Andrew Cattanach
Viki Cheung
Ben Goddard
Rachael Hum
Hannah Methuen

Production
Narges Nojoumi
Nick Ross
Mike Young

Copy Editor
Luke Brown

Publicity
Millie Seaward

Proof Reader
Jon Appleton